# Chop Down

By

Floyd J Williams

## Prologue

*June 30th Three o'clock in the morning.*

"Damn this boy's heavy," Blake groaned, pulling the body out of the Ford Expedition. It was wrapped in a dark blue blanket.

"Well he's big son," said Sam, Blake's dad, stepping out of the SUV. Blood stained his hands and his shirt. "He's gotta weigh a good two hundred and something." Pulling out a Malboro cigarette, he lit it with an American Flagged zippo. "Some bitch was eating good, all that money. Now his part of the pie's gonna be ours."

Blake dropped the body, giving his back relief. The street light rested on Blake, the body and the numerous black asphalt hills.

"Just leave him there," Sam said looking back at the highway. "Nobody should see it for a while."

Blake pulled the blanket off the body. A thin sheen of blood on the plastic covering gleamed. A single blood drop the ground before the body of Erving "Chop" Belle did. Part one of Operation Chop Down was complete.

## Chapter 1

*Eleven o'clock a.m.*

Mr. Collins started his daily walk from his house on Highway 17 to Black's Tire Service. Usually he'd be up at five and out the door at five thirty with Apollo, his loyal chow in tow. He'd been out of town at a relative's for a week and got back a couple hours ago. After a good walk and quick chat with the guys at the shop there would be a fitful sleep, Mr. Collins and Apollo.

With Independence Day nearing, the highway's traffic thickened. Heat radiating from the cars, Highway 17 asphalt and the Brunswick County sun made for an intense alliance. Apollo, usually a patrolman of the ditch and the woods, tried to break his leash running into traffic.

"No!" Mr. Collins hollered, yanking Apollo back when something squirmed under his foot. The head of the thing hit his bare leg. Looking down, he and the blacksnake met eyes. Mr. Collins had what's called a bum ticker. Letting go of the leash, he took long soft steps backwards. His heart tried to leap from his chest, straw hat flying from his head. The snake scurried into the ditch, slowly Mr. Collins' fear passed. Catching his breath with one hand on his knee and another on his heart, screeching tires and a car horn brought his attention to the highway. Apollo barely missed a SUV and an old Honda Civic, lowered to six inches from the road, before galloping into Long's Asphalt Plant. Mr. Collins picked up his hat and waited for a chance to cross the highway.

*Billy, the Father.*

Ms. Mabel Gore had been a deputy sheriff in Brunswick County for twenty-one years. Nine years ago she got shot outside of the Top Hat, a small black nightclub in the woods of Shallotte. Her responsibilities have been mostly clerical since, sometimes she'd dispatch. An hour ago she got a call about a body found in the defunct Long's Asphalt Plant on the Highway 17. The body had just been identified. Mabel took a box of tissues from her desk and the phone from her purse to the bathroom.

Silver Hill Grill, the seafood takeout place on Mt. Pisgah in Supply, was almost done with Billy Belle's lunch order. One flounder fillet, scallops and shrimp, all fried. He could've waited two days for his order. Sitting at a picnic table out front under a pine tree, he let his mind roam. Everything in his life, to him, was a luxury. The pleasure in cooking and scrubbing floors at his son's restaurant day in and day out with a smile and a good word for everyone who entered Chop's Diner made Billy a sometimes annoying ball of optimism and spirituality. Giddiness enveloped him when he entered his own home, watched on his own T.V and used his own bathroom. What would he do if the lady passing out the seafood in the pick-up window gave him a container with nothing but cold meatloaf patties like the ones he ate in prison? He shook his head smiled. He ate his last meatloaf patty seven months ago.

"Billy Belle!" the lady called from the window. Billy stood and strolled his 6'2" slim muscular frame to the window. *Cold meatloaf patty* he thought with a smile.

Billy opened the container to make sure it was right, paid the girl and walked off. On his way to the truck his phone rang.

"Hello."

"Billy?" Mabel said between snivels.

"Who this?"

"This is Deputy Sheriff- it's Mabel Billy." Mabel looked around the empty bathroom. The entire Brunswick County government complex was a circus after hearing the news.

"Who!"

"It's Mabel," she said wiping away tears, "Mabel from the young adult choir."

"Oh snap, hey Mabel, how you doing?"

Mabel sniveled and took a deep breath. "Fine Billy, fine." She took her head from the wall, straightened her back and wiped her face,

"How'd you get my number?" Billy asked, trying not to sound suspicious.

"Carol."

"Oh," Billy said at the mention of his lady friend, Mabel's cousin. "What's up?"

"Billy... I got some bad news."

Drivers turning onto Mt. Pisgah saw their lives flash before their eyes. Billy barreled toward the highway. The engine in his Chevy S-10 whined as he accelerated. Mabel couldn't tell him to stay away because he crushed his cell phone at Silver Hill Grill; it lay in the dirt Silver Hill Grill driveway beside the flounder scallops and shrimp. His big rough hands shook as he gripped the steering wheel.

"Mistake" he murmured and murmured. Ignoring the stop sign he entered Highway 17. He Chevy S-10 fishtailed through the grassy median. "They made a mistake."

He turned into Long Circle where the Long Asphalt Plant was located. It belonged to Ike Long, the second biggest drug dealer Brunswick County had ever seen. Sometime around the year 2000, the quality and general upkeep of the Long Asphalt Company hit a steep decline. Billy heard on the prison yard that Ike was making so much dope money with Erving "Chop" Belle, Billy's son, that Ike let the asphalt business go. The truth was that Ike acquired the asphalt plant from its former owner to resolve a debt. Ike never had the time to give the asphalt plant the attention it needed. Public and private contractors had been using the defunct asphalt plant as an unofficial dumping site for unused asphalt.

Billy barely beat the urge to plow through the sheriff deputy cars clogging Long Circle. He parked in the middle of the road and hopped out. Coroners, state troopers, and news reporters added to the commotion. The sun razed the top of Billy's bald head. Glares from all the windshields, folks bumping into him, Billy wanted to fight.

"Will you hurry the hell up!" Fran Williams screamed to her cameraman. "We need the first shot of the body for breaking news. Get your ass in gear, the station's waiting!"

Billy followed Fran and the cameraman around the news van, cop cars and under the yellow tape.

"I'm ready to film the body for Channel 6." The cameraman said to a deputy standing inside the tape.

"Hold on," said the deputy, walking away. He turned around and said "Stay here", stopping the cameraman in his tracks. Billy kept walking.

The scene was set up for presentation. Deputies were discussing where they would stand when the camera starts rolling. The sheriff was on his way. A couple Shallotte officers yacked it up in the sun with state troopers. Their uniforms had more spruce than necessary, a lot of medals and brass; this was breaking news. Billy saw the sneakers.

They were Air Jordans, tricked out in a number of bright colors, ugliest pair of shoes Billy ever seen. His son wore them yesterday to the restaurant, said his girlfriend Misty bought them off the computer. A white sheet covered him from head to ankle. It further angered Billy that the sun could shine so bright on a day like this.

One of three deputies standing over Erving "Chop" Belle made a joke and the other two doubled over in laughter. Billy didn't catch the joke but took it to be about his son, he could feel it. Terry Long, a short chubby freckle faced deputy with a Mountain Dew bottle holding his tobacco spit, saw Billy first. He composed himself and shushed the other two deputies.

"Mister Belle," he said behind a pair of Ray Bans and a bottom lip full of dip, "I'm real sorry for your loss."

Billy looked down at his son. He could remember dreams that felt realer than this. A snicker from one the deputies brought Billy's head back up.

"What's so funny?" he snarled, muscles formed from twenty years of hard time twitched under his blue Chop's Diner uniform.

The deputy responsible looked to Terry. Terry shook his head and slowly mouthed the word no.

"Nothing sir," the deputy said. "Just speaking with my colleagues that um," he looked to Billy's son "Chop here was known to have a lot of money. Yet his fashion sense was down there with my eight year old daughter and a parrot!"

Terry was the only one that could hold his chuckles. The other two were sweating and laughing.

"Hold on get back!" the deputy screamed as Billy hopped over his son.

Billy got both hands around the comedian deputy's neck and slammed him an asphalt hill. The comedian's head smacked the asphalt, causing a gash. Blood and soot ruined the crew cut he received only a half an hour ago. Terry tried to pull

Billy away as the other deputy punched and kicked him in the head and back, Billy didn't feel it. All he felt was the deputy's windpipe. He had the power to smash it like a bug. He decided the joy he'd have killing this kid would be short lived, more grief than it was worth. Terry was gone when Billy stood. The deputy comedian fell to the ground, a foot from Chop, gasping for air. Billy turned to Terry to see the darts from Terry's Taser found his chest. The voltage rendered Billy's body limp. He laid on his stomach and shook from the taser attack looking at his dead son a few feet away. The deputy comedian still hadn't caught his breath. Terry stood over the twitching, sweaty Billy with the man who shot Erving "Chop" Belle forty times. Sam Helms, the Sheriff of Brunswick County.

*Thirty minutes later.*

"How's he doing?" asked the Sheriff, taking long strides as he sipped a half frozen bottled water.

"Acting like an inbred pit-bull, that's how he's doing," The deputy comedian said, forced to put some effort in keeping up with the sheriff.

"Well whaddya expect, his youngest boy got shot to hell." The sheriff wiped drips of sweat from the lenses of his shades.

"I don't care if his mama was the one under that sheet. I'll put my clip in his ass if he even thinks about grabbing me like that again." The deputy comedian rubbed his neck and pulled out his taser as he and the sheriff approached the car.

Billy sat in handcuffs sitting in the back of a cop car. His knees were skinned through his khaki pants from being dragged over rocks and asphalt. His limbs began to move as he wished. A deep ache pulsed in his chest where he was tased. He unsure about what was and what wasn't. Was this a dream? Was Chop really dead? Where is Chop? Billy really didn't know. He felt a wave of relief from the confusion. One look out of the right side window drove reality home like a nail through lumber. Coroners carried the body with those ugly sneakers to their van. The sight tied Billy's heart and stomach together and ripped them out. With his chin on his chest, he cried. He didn't stop when the door opened.

"Mister William Belle," the deputy comedian announced. "Despite my own desire to lock your ass up for assaulting a police officer, I'm gonna take the sheriff's advice and let it go this one time."

The delicate nature of the comedian's windpipe entered Billy's mind. Just a little more pressure and he'd be in that coroner's van too. Billy stopped crying and shook his head. *A second life sentence for a freak accident* Billy thought. The deputy comedian put his taser between Billy's eyes.

"Now the sheriff's got something to say to you. You try something and I promise I won't let off this juice till you're shittin' blood."

The deputy stepped aside. The sheriff took his shades from his face in and placed them in his shirt pocket. He squatted in front of Billy.

"Billy Belle!" He greeted with a grin and squinty eyes. "Hey man, I'm sorry for all this. Ain't make no since how your boy ended up like that, it's truly terrible." Billy didn't respond. The deputy comedian said he'd let the assault go but Billy was still cuffed. He'd stop worrying once he got back to his truck. "But even so," Sam continued, "choking a police officer is the last thing a man, especially one on parole for murder would want to do, I'd hope."

Billy turned away from the sheriff, rolled his eyes.

"Hey!" snapped the comedian. "The sheriff is talking to you! I swear you're doing everything right for a-"

"Simmer down B.J," the sheriff said as he stood, "and let him go."

The comedian grudgingly put the taser away and pulled out his handcuff keys.

"Well," he said to Billy "what you waitin' for? Get out."

Billy put his feet on the ground and stood.

"Turn around."

Billy obeyed as the comedian yanked the chain between the handcuffs. He got directly in Billy's ear.

"You're an animal and I know how to handle animals. You'd better domesticate yourself quickly or I'll put you down."

Billy looked to the sheriff. The deputy comedian seemed to amuse him. Finally out of the handcuffs, Billy rubbed his wrists. The sheriff and deputy comedian walked away.

"Y'all know who did it?" Billy asked.

The sheriff stopped in his tracks, he turned slowly.

"Well," he said looking to the deputy comedian and back at Billy with the same grin, "I shouldn't say this but, he didn't die here, he was left here."

Billy's knees were losing their will to stand. He sat back down in the cop car. Who would kill his son and dump him like garbage by the highway? He looked up at the Long Asphalt sign.

"Now Billy, I know your boy and that boy of Ike's had a lot of differences. I don't know if leaving him here was a message or what. Whatever you find out you tell me, got it?" Billy was somewhere else. His mind showed him his son as a six year old boy, smiling and needing his dad as much as air. Billy felt like jumping out his skin. "Let me get to the bottom of this, you hear me Billy? Let me handle it!"

## Chapter 2

*Pound, the Brother.*

"Pound!" Kiana shouted, trying in vain to shake him awake. "Pound, wake the hell up!"

Julius "Pound" Belle exceeded his expectations last night. The lady he went to Anytime's to meet was late. He stayed at the bar with the club's owner Tremaine drinking and smoking the night away. Then shots rang out.

People hit the floor and crawled over each other for the exits. Pound calmly stepped his hulking 6'3" frame over people on the way to the door. The shooting spilled into the grassy parking lot. Young men and women ducked behind cars, jumped in the ditch by the road and got behind trees as they shot at each other, a dispute over nothing. North Carolina dope dealer versus South Carolina dope dealers. Women screamed though the gunplay exited some of them. To know someone could die over them passed for a validation. Other patrons screamed and ran as being chased by Godzilla. Pound strutted casually to his car. Everybody knew who he was, especially the knuckleheads shooting. If a bullet were to graze a thread of shirt, that shooter, his neighborhood and whole world would undergo an exhibition of raw hurt. He'd demonstrated so much in the last past five years that to see him smile in the club made it more festive and enjoyable for all.

When he reached his car, a baby blue '73 Impala, the lady he came to see was sitting on the hood with a friend just as fine. He tossed his keys to the one he knew. The other one followed them in a Yukon. It took fifteen minutes to reach the Radisson Condominium in North Myrtle Beach from the Anytime's nightclub in Little River, South Carolina. Ten stories up, he enjoyed more gin, more drugs and both the girls. Kiana, his pregnant girlfriend and mother of one, found him in the driveway at one o'clock in the evening slumped over the steering wheel, snoring and reeking of everything he indulged in.

"Pound!" Kiana shouted, slapping him across the head.

He came to. His vision cleared only enough to recognize Kiana.

"Kiki quit playing," he slurred forcefully. He turned toward the passenger seat and fell back asleep on the steering wheel.

For a moment Pound was back in the condo. The girl's names were Dalia and Carmen. Dalia, a 5'8" dark skinned stallion with long jet black curly hair and an unusually long tongue. Carmen, the 5'4" honey brown skinned doll with hazel eyes and auburn hair teased blond on the top, the sides and back were cut to a brush fade. While the girls popped their ecstasy, they all snorted Pound's cocaine. For hours they enjoyed a chemical fueled trance. They went past checkout time. Dalia charged another day to her Visa while Pound helped himself to her. When he left Dalia was asleep on the foot of the bed with her face buried in the floor. Carmen was curled up on the bed, body riddled with hickeys, rug burns and body fluids.

Pound didn't hear his door open.

"Ahh!" he screamed as he tried to escape the water with squirms and twists.

"Don't you holler now!" Kiana squeezed the sprayer on the hose as hard as she could. "You think I'm a keep playing with you then keep thinking. You know I gotta take Mama to the doctor and you gotta take J to get fireworks so get up!"

Pound was awake and sober and angry. Like a bull taunted with red, he charged at Kiana. Kiana dropped the hose and attempted to juke Pound. Not much of a strategy for a lady who's seven months pregnant. Pound wrapped her up and lifted her from her feet and pressed her face on the hot vinyl siding of their doublewide home.

"What the hell is your problem!" he barked. Kiana's feet were a half foot from the ground.

"The *baby,*" she whimpered. He let her down.

"Tell yourself that!" Pound took a handful of his shoulder length dreadlocks and wrung them out. He pointed his index finger into Kiana's forehead. "My interior better not be fucked up. And what the fuck you want anyway!"

Kiana, the most beautiful girl Pound had ever seen, Dalia and Carmen be damned. Even before the pregnancy her brown skinned glowed and her smile arrested. She made the most unsophisticated men straighten up in her presence, especially Pound once upon a time.

"Why you got to be out all time? Why I gotta find you passed out in the car? What about J seeing you like this? Smelling like weed and alcohol." She took a step closer to Pound and took a sniff. "You don't even try to cover your tracks. I guess its fuck what I feel huh."

Pound walked to the car. He took a lighter and the half of a blunt from the astray. He closed the door, leaned on the car and lit up.

"Go 'head with that bullshit cause you know I ain't trying to hear it."

Kiana crossed her arms and gave Pound the angry face that would terrified little Jared. Pound chuckled.

"Come here," he said walking to her.

"No," she said rolling her neck.

Pulling off his polo shirt and tossing it on the grass, Pound put his arms around Kiana. He tried to kiss her, she turned her face.

"Why you acting like that?"

"You stink," she said. "Now clean up cause you gotta take J to South Carolina for the fireworks. And some new clothes won't hurt him." Pound took a pull of the blunt, blew it away from Kiana.

"What you want from South Carolina?" he asked with smile.

"Get J some fireworks and clothes," Kiana tried her best to sound authoritative. "Damn it's hot out here. What do you want to eat tonight? "

"Mama!" Jared called. After jumping from the front porch, the four year old raced around the house to his parents. Never stopped running, just slammed into his mama's legs.

"Boy what's wrong with you?" Kiana asked. Jared looked up at Kiana and then Pound.

"Unca Chop," he said, watching Pound and holding his mom. "Did he die?"

*EJ, the Lawyer, the Best Friend.*

It was her lunch hour. Dion Johnson, the principal of Cedar Grove Middle School, lived five minutes from her job. She and her new husband Eric Johnson Jr took full advantage of the convenience. Lunch was leftovers and they barely ever got to it. After an intense thirty minute love session, Dion went into kitchen to prepare a couple plates. She turned on the TV sitting on the counter. Chicken, butter beans, rice and cornbread. The first plate was only half prepared when she heard it.

"EJ," she mumbled, then said, then called, then screamed. "EJ!" When she wasn't screaming she was holding her mouth.

"What! What is it!" EJ hollered from the bedroom, tying his tie in the mirror. His cell phone and house phone rang, he didn't answer them. He was late for a meeting. "Girl, what the hell you want? And why are you letting the phone ring?"

EJ stormed down the hallway to the kitchen. Dion, shivering, her heart shaped face tracked in tears, pointed a greasy spatula at the television.

*TV- "Again, this morning's Breaking News. A Highway 17 resident discovered the body of thirty one year old Erving "Chop" Belle. He was reportedly shot a "great number of times" in his chest, arms, legs and lower extremities. His body was found at the years defunct Long Asphalt Plant in Supply on Highway 17."*

"No," EJ said under his breath and then aloud. He put his face right in front of the small T.V.

The asphalt plant was electric. County deputies, state troopers, officers from Shallotte, Holden Beach, Ocean Isle Beach, Calabash and Southport were present.

*TV-"You may remember two months ago Ervin "Chop" Belle was acquitted of a number of charges involving the death of a West Brunswick High School basketball star. A fourteen year old West Brunswick High School student died from using "especially toxic" drugs believed to be sold at West Brunswick High by students working for Belle."*

"EJ." EJ turned around. Dion held the house phone for him.

"Hello," he greeted sullenly. It was Chop's grandmother Marie. Her blood curdling screams sent EJ to his knees and into a sea of tears.

*Misty, the Fiancé.*

"Is this everything?" asked Misty sarcastically to the nurse dispensing the pills in the paper cup.

"Mr. Cartwright needs all of these," the nurse said. "Make sure he swallows every one of these in front of you okay?" Misty pulled her strawberry blond hair back and put it in a ponytail.

"Mr. Cartwright is the worst perv in this place," she said, counting the hours left on her shift at Spring Care Rest Home. After work, Chop always made her take a bubble bath to scrub the old folks smell off.

"Hurry up and come back. There're some bedpans that need to be emptied." Misty sighed and marched with the pills to the common area.

Everybody stared into the TV, no chess, checkers, nobody was asleep.

*T.V-"Sheriff Helms says he has persons of interest but no suspects in the murder of Erving "Chop" Belle. If anyone has any info on this crime, please call 910-"*

The pills fell to the floor.

"Misty," the nurse called from the desk as Misty raced by her, her eyes bulged and mouth hanging, "what's wrong? Did you give Mr. Cartwright those pills?" Misty ran out the front doors into the parking lot.

She reached the car only to realize she left her keys in her pocketbook. The pocketbook was in the lounge. She headed back inside, screaming to the top of her lungs. She fell to her knees on the sidewalk clutching her stomach. The head nurse lead a half dozen nurses out the front door to Misty. They called 911 because they couldn't stop Misty's screams.

## Chapter 3

*Diana the Mother and Housewife*

Diana, a housewife of sixty-three. Since the day she moved into her two-story waterfront house on the Intracoastal Waterway in Southport, it was home. Her husband was supposed to stay in and help prepare the house for Independence Day but his job needed him. That was alright, she could handle everything until he got back. The neighbors were already radiating patriotic glory. Diana's house *would* be the main event on her street.

After a breakfast of grapefruit and leftover fried chicken she started cleaning the house. After the house, the wraparound patio deck would be next, then the yard. She filled the gas tanks yesterday for the lawnmower. Yard work kept her blood pumping. Her husband, for the third time in their thirty-six year marriage, took the initiative two weeks ago and cut the grass. He managed to mow down a dogwood tree and a couple of azaleas; it was almost the end of him.

She turned the radio on and the Rush Limbaugh show blared throughout the house. Diana wished Rush would stop the talk show business and run for office. He was in the middle of a rant on Islamic radicalism when the hourly news update came on.

*Radio-"It's 2:00pm on Rush Radio. In local news; Brunswick's most infamous figure found dead."*

Diana heard his name while sprinkling carpet freshener on the living room rug,

*Radio-"A Highway 17 resident discovered the body of thirty-one year old Erving "Chop" Belle. He was reportedly shot a "great number of times" in his chest, arms, legs and lower extremities. His body was found at the years defunct Long Asphalt Plant in Supply on Highway 17."*

Diana put her hand over her heart. She sat down on her husband's couch and grabbed the remote control. All the news channels were covering it. She thought to call her daughter Misty but thought better of it. She flipped back and forth between news channels. Erving "Chop" Belle, dead, murdered, gone, not alive anymore, over and done with. Diana's eyes got moist.

"Thank you Jesus," She uttered, looking to the ceiling with her hands clasped in front of her. There weren't any pictures of the body but the police identified him. That was good enough.

The Lord was the captain of Diana's ship. She did her best to plant religious seeds in her children. Misty's seed, in Diana's opinion, grew sideways. Jesus did love everybody but that didn't mean she had to love some hoodlum named Chop. It wasn't so much that he was black, in time Diana would've learned to accept that. He was a black drug dealer, a gangster, a predator, every fear Diana imagined made into flesh. A devil who had Diana's only daughter's heart. They'd been together since high school, it wasn't an off and on thing either. Diana knew it was some good in everybody because that half an iota swimming around in Chop shined bright when it came to Misty, no denying that.

Waves of anger enveloped Diana the few times she was in Chop's presence. Her husband, of all people, allowed his relationship with Misty, making Diana feel all alone. Anger eroded to resentment and finally to reluctant tolerance. When

Chop was arrested for that big high school drug ring business Diana's anger returned tenfold. After a year of pleading with Misty to break it off with Chop before the trial started, Misty announced as boldly as she could, over the phone, that she actually proposed to Chop in the middle of his publicized filth of a life and he accepted. Diana felt God's presence in Chop reaping his last harvest before he married Misty in September. Diana would be spared further grief and humiliation. All of her girlfriend's daughters married doctors, realtors and construction company owners but Misty...

Diana stepped outside on the patio and parked it on one of her new red, white and blue Red Oak rocking chairs. Figured she'd call her girlfriends over for crab legs and dish about the good news. Those hens had Hemi motors in their throats. Other people's business came a hair after breathing. They'd see to it Diana's Fourth of July party would be one to remember.

It was ninety-eight degrees, could be one hundred degrees in an hour. The birds were chirping. People had their boats trotting up and down the waterway while kids zipped by on water-skis. Everything was pleasant, people were happy, life was good.

The house looked like a hurricane hit it. The couch and sofas were flipped over. The TV along with the mirrors on the living room wall were shattered. Pound flipped the refrigerator. Jared screamed with his arms around Kiana's leg.

"Pound please!" She cried.

""Them muthafuckas!" was all Pound could holler.

"Please baby calm down," Kiana pleaded standing in the living room by the hallway.

Pound, standing in the kitchen, stomped over to Kiana. Jared took off out the front door.

"Them muthafuckas killed my brother!" he screamed in Kiana's face. She nodded quickly as she cried.

"I know baby, I know."

Pound balled his fists and squared his body as if he's was going to box Kiana.

"You know? What the fuck you know!" Pound poked his index finger into Kiana's temple. "What the fuck you know I don't know, huh? Say something!" Kiana slowly shook her head.

"I don't know what's going on baby, I don't know." The strong feeling to pee subsided as she turned to the front door. Jared sat Indian style in the middle of the front yard. His fear of Pound was immense. Pound never touched him but Jared witnessed Pound abuse Kiana. Watching mother tell him through tears and busted lips that it was okay conflicted with every fiber in his being shouting the contrary. He'd run through the woods behind or up the street and Kiana would have to call neighbors to find him. He stopped speaking and had become unresponsive in school. Kiana walked out onto the porch to get him.

Vehicles pulled in to the rocky driveway. In five minutes the driveway was full, cars and motorcycles lined the road in front of the house and across the street.

"J!" Kiana called, standing on the porch. "Come back up here!" Jared sat with his back turned to Kiana and watched the cars roll up.

Syncere, a tall black hustler from Shallotte, got out of his Escalade that he parked behind Pound's Impala.

"What's up Kiana?" he greeted. "Where Pound at?"

Kiana turned back to the house. Pound was gone. When she turned back to Syncere, Pound stood in front of him holding an AR-15 trained on his face. Syncere knew something like this could happen. On the way over he planned on talking real slow while keeping his hands in front of him.

"What the fuck is you doing here nigga?" Pound growled. Syncere put his hands in the air.

"Man, I just come to say first, I'm sorry about Chop. And I ain't had shit to do with it, nothing."

People, all hustlers from different neighborhoods in Brunswick County's south end, got out of their vehicles.

"Me too," said Lavelle from Johnson Town standing beside his Lexus. "It wasn't me and it wasn't none of my niggas."

"Yo Pound!" called James from Seashore straddling a black and gold Hiyabusa, "I'm paying my respects too."

"Yo Chop was my nigga!" Anthony from Supply sat on the hood of his Cadillac XTS with tears in his eyes.

All the doors were opened on most of the cars. Folks talked over each other expressing their condolences to Pound. Some were crying and holding each other, some were drunk holding near empty fifth bottles of liquor. Andre Long's name kept popping up. Has anybody seen him? Where has he been? What about Ike? But Andre ain't no killer, is he? Shot Chop up like *that*? But why? Who helped him? That nigga didn't do that shit. Yes he did and his punk ass daddy helped him.

"Hey!" Pound barked, the AR-15 by his side. "Y'all get the fuck on man!" Everybody kept talking. Music started playing and marijuana scented the air.

Pound shot twenty rounds in the air causing folks to fall to the ground. A simple negotiation of his machine gun and he could have mowed down a dozen of those idiots. Some motorcycles fell on top of their owners. He was done speaking. Walking around the back of the house, he hit himself upside the head over and over. "Think nigga think." Cars engines came to life and tires squealed down the street.

"J, get up here!" Kiana said. Jared stood and ran to the porch.

## Chapter 4

*The Ike Long Story . Cedar Grove Godfather. Chop Belle Mentor.*

Ike Long quit drinking three years ago. He used to need liquor to sleep and liquor to start the day. Depression was eating him alive. Unable to bear the toll it took on his body, Ike did something about it. He went to church to a revival meeting.

Prayer meetings are night worship services Cedar Grove Missionary Baptist

Church holds every night during the work week. The congregation participates more in revivals than in Sunday service with a sharing of testimonies. During the time allotted for testimony a person will stand and tell the church about how God has blessed them, how they need prayer dealing with an issue, inform the church of something they need to be aware of involving the community or simply to thank the Lord. Ike heard the snickers and sucking of teeth when he sat down. When Ike Long stood he was greeted with scowls and poked lips. He told the church about hit bouts with alcoholism. He feared if he didn't get help soon, the bottle would be the end of him. After sharing his problem Ike asked for prayer. Members of the congregation, some related to Ike, all aware of the plague he'd been on the community, voiced their long held grievances.

"My son's been hooked on that poison you been selling for twenty years," An old lady on the usher board spoke through tears. "He can't take care of his self, he can't get a job and can't stay out of prison." She left her post and stood at the end of Ike's pew. "You got the nerve to stand up in here asking for prayer?"

Folks in the church often sang of praising Jesus and defeating the devil. The congregation envisioned Jesus Christ as a brown haired blue eyed caucasian or a bronzed skinned brown eyed black man with permed lack hair to his shoulders. When a fair majority of the Cedar Grove Missionary Baptist Church congregation envisioned the devil they an image of Ike Long filled their mind. He was blamed with bringing hard drugs to the community. Folk felt that if he were ever go to jail, which he never had, the drug problem would go away and nobody would fill the void. Maybe God could bring him so low that he'd see the error of his ways and somehow cut out the cancer that he helped bring to Cedar Grove. The chances of that happening seemed slimmer with every day and every jailed or addicted family member. Then there was Erving "Chop" Belle. Ike made a monster out of a reasonably bright young man at least that was the public's opinion.

Ike knew the congregation well, the dark secrets he learned from users and hustlers that belonged to their families, the calls to the cops they thought were anonymous but were reported back to him for drug money, the dirty looks in the super market. His struggle wasn't just the alcohol. The community's problems were growing. Even Ike had to point the finger at himself, his grip was slipping in Cedar Grove. And he was losing Chop.

Small differences ended in month long fallouts. Ike and Chop's relationship had become too volatile. Chop had designs to be number one, no longer Ike's number one boy. People seemed to excuse Chop's actions, some more heinous than Ike ever imagined, while they talked about Ike like a dog. After stopping the affair with Chop's mother Angela, Ike moved to Ocean Isle Beach. There was no reason for Ike to continue living in Cedar Grove where the hustlers seemed to appear from nowhere. Chop had folks from age twelve to sixty-two, black gangsters, white female daycare employees, residential contractors, truck drivers, landscapers, mechanics, army veterans, even retirees selling everything for a profit. Ike's only hustle was heroine. Chop dealt heroine, coke, crack, ecstasy, crystal meth, a number of prescription drugs, codeine, marijuana and guns. A lot of folks were making money with Chop. The writing was on the wall. Chop was the man in Cedar Grove and a lot of hoods beyond Cedar Grove, Ike was in the way. The drinking escalated.

The story in his home was worse. His wife Flora suffered for years under her husband's mood swings and constant worry of her son Andre. Her declining health kept her a regular at the hospital and doctor's office. Flora had three nervous breakdowns in five years on top of developing diabetes. She had to deal with it alone while coping with guilt from turning her back on some of her closest friends and relatives. Nobody in the county was a spoiled as Flora when Ike Long courted. The jewelry, clothes and excitement that came with being Ike's girl turned her ears deaf to reason, logic and whatever else her family and friends were shouting at her. She used to be stunning, a trophy wife if there ever was one. The worry and drinking made her look far beyond her years when she and Ike separated. She moved to Conway, South Carolina.

Andre Long was his mother's child, sensitive, spineless and by Ike's own admission worthless. It was bad enough that Ike wished Chop was his son. Andre wanted to be under Chop like a woman and it infuriated Ike. When Chop got too ambitious, Ike began diluting the product he sold Chop while giving his son the best shit in South Brunswick. Ike taught Chop everything he knew about drugs except to find a dependable supplier. Ike would be the only supplier he'd want Chop to have and if it wasn't him then it was the penitentiary.

The money brought a little backbone to Andre, he started smelling his own shit. Ike and Andre parted ways with Chop. The money remained good but the feeling of camaraderie was gone. They missed Chop. His presence was magnetic, he was a motivator. While Ike drowned his sorrows, Andre used a number of drugs to cope, some in front of his mother.

That big house on the beach wasn't a comfort to Ike's conscience. His existence, to him, was proof there was a hell before death. If redemption was within reach he wanted to have it. Cedar Grove's boogieman was alone and afraid.

A man sitting on the back pew during the revival stood. "My wife's been using your junk for two years. I won't let her see her kids and I won't let her in the house. She sat on the steps at my back door and told me how she'd been selling herself to you to get high and-" The man, mid-thirties, lost his voice for a second before he continued. "She said as much as she loves me and her children she wasn't coming back. Said she was content with stealing and waiting on you to have her for some drugs. I can't pray for you Ike Long."

The testimonies went on and on. The more they continued the more tragic they became. Ike felt a foot tall, he needed a drink.

Reverend Fredrick Greene, a 6'4" three hundred twenty pound shepherd, stood. He left the pulpit and stood in front of the altar.

"I have a testimony," he said. The congregation leaned forward. Ike began to sit. "Un uh Brother Long, stand please." Ike looked around the church and wondered what the hell he was thinking attending revival. "I've heard so many testimonies as a pastor. Some right here, some in private. I'm not saying no names but Ike, you've been the subject of *many* private testimonies. I got a good word for ya but I gotta talk plain too." He walked up the isle to Ike's pew. His voice was strong, it carried and filled the quiet church. "This has been your church your whole life. You will always be welcome here Ike. I want to see you here praising our Lord. But as the pastor of Cedar Grove Missionary Baptist Church, the shepherd of *this* flock, I got to tell you this." The reverend stepped into Ike's pew. He squeezed by members of the congregation while Ike wished he could disappear. Reverend Greene grabbed Ike's shoulders. "We feel blessed but some of us are hurting. We've all done wrong Ike but before we make good we got to own up. I want you to know that nobody's too far gone to receive salvation. I know you came here tonight because you're sick of feeling God's absence! I know you came here because you want to be forgiven, *need* to be forgiven! You want the folks in here see that Ike ain't no monster! Ike ain't no demon, ha! Ike ain't hell bound, ha! Ike is heaven bound, ha! Ike is sick of the same old thing, ha! Ike is ready for God, ha! Ike is ready to show this community who he really is, ha! A child of God, ha! A child of God, ha! A child of God!"

Ike was on the floor shaking and crying. He hollered like he was in flames. When somebody caught the holy ghost, folks usually sang and praised the Lord. Some would clap their hands and stomp their feet while the ushers fanned the person filled with the spirit. As Ike whaled, folks turned in their seats or got up and walked to his pew. They silently watched the man they feared and hated experience a force greater than himself. The ushers fanned him until he calmed down after the reverend motioned for them to. They pulled Ike up and he sat on the pew, his shoulders drooped like a child on timeout. He told the congregation he was sorry, he was so sorry. After service, folks shook Ike's hand and hugged his neck. He got in his car and called Andre, told him to take the remaining drugs for himself. Andre laughed after hearing about his dad's transformation but respected his wishes. But Ike wasn't done.

He threw away all of the liquor bottles in the house. The women he'd been taking care of found themselves cut off. He found Sheila, a nice church lady from Calabash, NC and continued to do right by her for three years. She made sure Ike never veered off the path despite his heavy withdrawals from refusing to drink. Soon his body and spirit improved. He had no worries, except Chop.

Andre and Chop had been shooting at each other at clubs and creeping with each other's women. Ike knew Chop to be a killer, just like his brother. When someone from out of town posed a threat to Ike and he couldn't set them up for the police, Chop and for a brief moment Pound would get rid of them.

Andre was an addict of the fast life. It took Ike sixty years to turn his life around, he wasn't sure his son had sixty years to wake up. Andre had to be protected. Once Chop beat Andre within an inch of his life at a cook-out at some girl's house. Andre's so-called friends stood by and watched. While he was operated on the following day Ike entered Chop's restaurant, Chop's Diner and put a .38 revolver on the bridge of his nose. Patrons screamed and hit the floor. Chop sucked his teeth and put the most conceited smirk on his face.

"I don't care who did what between you and Dre. If you touch him again I'm gonna kill you." Those were the last words Ike spoke to Chop.

Two weeks ago Chop pistol whipped Andre outside of a club. Once again Andre's head was lumped, missing teeth and suffering severe headaches, his ego was on life support. Andre wanted Chop dead, swore he didn't care if he went to jail. Ike told Andre he'd handle it.

Sitting on the couch in his living room, Ike argued with his son standing in front of the TV.

"I don't give a fuck what you say!" Ike said. "You're going to your mama in Conway and that's it."

"For what! I didn't kill nobody. Why I gotta run for, huh?" Andre still whistled involuntarily. He'd seen the orthodontist, he was scheduled to receive a whole mouth of artificial teeth.

"It ain't about what you did and didn't do. They think you did it and you can die just for that!" Ike lit a More cigarette and watched the ocean waves through the many windows of his home while Andre marched back and forth.

"They?" Andre asked. "By they you mean Pound don't you. Ain't nobody scared of Pound." Ike, 5'8" two hundred pounds, shot to his feet.

"Fuck being scared boy! You can be fearless and dead!"

"I ain't running from no-"

"Shut up, just shut the fuck up!" Ike held his hand out. "Give me your keys so I can put your car up. You take mine and get to your mother right now."

Andre grudgingly gave his dad his keys. Shelia, Ike's woman, walked in. She was in the back packing her and Ike's things. They were headed somewhere too.

"It's for the best Dre." She said "We need to lay low just for a little while."

"Bitch, who asked you?"

Ike punched Andre as hard as he could in the jaw, his sweet sensitive jowl. Andre eyes grew wild as his knees folded. Ike stood over him and pointed his finger.

"Get your dumb ass down to your mama's, right now!"

## Chapter 5

The news spread like wildfire. Every neighborhood, store, street, even all the beaches found it impossible to speak of anything else. Facebook and Twitter users expressed sadness and disbelief. The six o'clock news reported the story again. The hip-hop radio stations in Wilmington and Myrtle Beach gave a shout out to Chop's family and Cedar Grove.

Billy pulled into his mother in-law Marie Lance's driveway. Forty years ago, Billy visited this small red brick house for the first time. He was a Malboro man then, two o'clock in the evening and a whole pack was gone. The Lance family was too religious for Billy, judgmental too. Billy was from Warsaw, NC. He never knew his dad and his mom wasn't in the church like that. That's why he fell for Angela, she everything Billy felt he didn't deserve. To his relief things worked out and he married Angela.

Billy parked near the mailbox and walked around cars belonging to Marie's children and grandchildren. Marie's cries reached Billy before he got to the door. When he knocked a conversation started behind the door. After three minutes Marie's oldest son Nathaniel opened the door wide enough to show Billy one eye and a nose.

"We having visitors tomorrow," he said and closed then closed the door. Walking to the truck Billy called Misty but she never answered. He called Pound. Pound couldn't talk through the sobs. When he did talk all he said was "Somebody gotta die!" Billy tried to talk but Pound cussed him and hung up.

"Oh my God Billy." Carol said rubbing alcohol on Billy's knees from being dragged over rocks and asphalt. She couldn't hold her tears either. "Chop was such a sweet boy. He was just getting his stuff together."

"I know baby." Billy said. He stared at the ceiling.

They got ready for bed but couldn't sleep, couldn't watch TV. Seeing smiles and happiness was off putting and cruel. Billy was feeling like the comedian officer did, choked for air, answers and understanding. Carol, the manager and head waitress at Chop's Diner, tried caressing him to sleep.

"Baby, I'll handle the diner. You need to be with the family."

*July 1st*

At eight o'clock the next morning, Marie's yard was packed with cars. Cars lined the road on the both sides. Billy parked at Chop's house Marie's and walked back. It was eighty degrees already. The gnats, mosquitoes and sand flies were on attack.

"Billy!" someone called as he entered the yard. It was Deputy Mabel Gore.

"Hey now!" Billy greeted as she approached wearing her deputy uniform and carrying a cake with both hands.

"Here," She said handing Billy the cake. "I got to get back to work." She started back to the car then stopped. "I heard what happened yesterday. Ain't nobody say to go up to that asphalt plant. You have to be careful Billy. Them boys want you and your other son to be caught doing something, *anything*. Don't give'em a reason to hurt you."

Billy nodded and headed to the house.

"Billy." She called. Billy stopped. "Tell Marie and them I said hey and I'm praying for'em. Chop was a good boy. He really was good Billy."

There was barely enough room to move in Marie's house. Old folks sat and smiled at the small children. Adults stood within ten inches of each other discussing things worlds away from Chop. The voices sounded like a mass choir of hushed tones as Billy made his way to the kitchen.

"Billy, boy where have you been?" Marie, a short slim brown saint, wore an apron over her t-shirt, blue jeans and sneakers. For a woman in her late seventies she moved around the kitchen like a cat. "I got twenty pounds of whiting at the pier waiting on ya. I got Peach cobbler baking and I'm about to start on this banana pudding. Go get the fish and when you come back head'em, gut'em, scale'em and fry'em out back." Marie checked the peach cobbler in the oven. "Go on now."

Billy started to the front door.

"Billy." Marie called. He turned around. Marie hugged him tight and smiled.

"We're gonna get through this baby. You and I have to see about everybody else." Billy nodded and walked away.

In the hallway hung pictures of Jesus at the Last Supper, Martin Luther King Jr, President Obama and various graduation pictures of Lance children. The last family portrait Billy ever took with Angela and the boys hung in the middle of the hallway. Angela's smile could soften the coldest heart. She was a vision, a true comfort. Billy had trouble understanding his mind state when he separated from her, had something to do with nagging and arguing. He wasn't ready for marriage but he wasn't letting Angela go. He began to tolerate in-law intrusions into to his and Angela's business less and less. Angela never told her family to let she and her husband handle their marriage and Billy felt betrayed. He'd leave the house for days at a time and eventually started to cheat. Billy still loved Angela, never stopped. Even when Billy went to prison Angela never divorced him. She visited him, kissed him, wrote him and sent him what precious little money she had. Breast cancer took her before Billy could get out. That's when he lost Pound.

"Billy?" Billy turned to his left.

"Harriett how you doing." Harriett, smiling so hard her eyes closed behind those thick glasses. She wrapped her short plump body around Billy.

"Oh Billy," she said as they hugged. "I'm praying for you. We all hurting but God's gonna see us through."

"I know," Billy said smiling.

"Bet you do." Nathaniel, Harriett's husband and Angela's older brother gave Billy the same look he'd been giving Billy since the early seventies, the look of disapproval. He looked at the Belle portrait, two down. He hung his head.

"Hey Nate," Billy held his hand out for Nathaniel. Nathaniel look at it, eventually he took it.

"You know," Nate said looking at the portrait and shaking Billy's hand, "I told Angela years ago not to have nothing to do with you."

"Nate!" Harriet chided. Billy snatched his hand back, the smell of gin finally reached him.

"I told her but she didn't wanna listen. Now look at what's going on."

Billy looked to Harriett. She shook her head. Billy made his way around Nathaniel for the front door.

"She married you right outta high school and threw her damn life away. Goddamn you Billy!"

Angela and Nathaniel were close, best friends. Marie told Billy that Nathaniel took her death especially hard.

"Billy I'm sorry," Harriett pleaded. "Nate's just broken up over Chop's passing." Nate's outburst got attention from folks on the other side of the house in the living room. Brunswick County's only black assistant district attorney was giving a show. People packed in and around the hallway. "A lot of people loved him because he was a really good boy."

"Please!" Nathaniel spat.

"Nathaniel!" Harriett jerked his arm.

"No no no Harriett," Billy said, "you gotta let Nate speak his mind. He must have something to say."

Nathaniel, six feet overweight and balding, stared Billy up and down.

"I don't give a damn about no muscles Billy. This is my people's house not yours, I'll fuck you up in here!"

"Nate!" Harriett tried to pull his arm again. "Come on. You said you wasn't gonna do this." Nathaniel shook her off.

"Now look, I'm sorry about Erving. He was good at heart but let's not get carried away." The old folks, children and parents standing around got quiet. He turned to Harriett. "Now woman I gotta say this." He turned back to Billy. "First you go upside my sister's head then you go to prison for killing somebody over another woman!"

"Nathaniel!" Nathaniel put his hand in Harriett's face.

"Then Angie gets sick and dies while Julius follows you to prison. At the funeral, you show up at the funeral in chains, looking a goddamn mess! Erving, 'scuse me "Chop", gets to selling that shit up and down the road like he's a king and this community is his kingdom to rape and piss on as he pleases! Got that white girl living in my sister's house."

"Nate!" Everybody turned to the end of the hall to Marie. "Bring your ass in this kitchen."

Marie went back to the kitchen. Nathaniel headed to the kitchen. At the end of the hall he turned around.

"Billy Belle, you put a black cloud over this Lance family. We didn't ask for it nor did we appreciate it. If you'd have left my sister alone like I said she'd probably be alive and happy. Now she's gone. Ain't leave the world nothing but two demons and –"

The punch to the gut caught Nathaniel in mid-sentence. Billy tried break his spine through his stomach. The wind escaped Nathaniel's body instantly, he backed into the wall and slid down slowly. Billy wound up another uppercut then he thought of Harriett and Marie. And the fact that Nathaniel is an assistant district attorney. Parents pulled their children close. Folks bunched together giving Billy all the space. They understood him to be a little unstable, understandable for a man who spent so much time locked up.

Nathaniel Hill was a puzzle. He was misguided. As a state attorney Nathaniel begged every to throw the book at every black kid, especially the offenders from his community. The things he said in court over the years about the offenders he grew up with were unforgivable. Obviously, he didn't want to be an assistant attorney forever. Whoever decided his professional future wouldn't be able to hold any "hook ups" against him.

Billy stormed out of the front door. He stomped the ground all the way to his truck in Chop's driveway, less than a hundred yards away on left side of Marie's house.

"Hey Billy." Billy was pulling keys out of his pocket.

"Misty?" Her usually healthy face seemed stressed beyond reason. The bags around her ocean blue eyes almost reached her nostrils. Her strawberry blond hair was all over the place. Her nurse uniform looked slept in. Poor girl looked as if she'd fall right over. "Come here sweetie."

Misty buried her face into Billy's chest. She screamed louder than she did the day before. Her body shook as Billy held her. She screamed Chop's name, screamed for him to come back, begged him. Nobody loved Chop more than Misty, not even Marie. Chop was her world and now the world was in the morgue. She always got a kick from how she dreamt of Chop only to wake up to him by her side. She used to visit Billy in prison with Chop and go by herself when Chop couldn't make it. That's how she and Billy got close.

"Where the hell were you yesterday?" she asked without pulling her face from Billy's chest.

"Aww sweetie I uh...I was in my truck smoking cigarettes and uh...just couldn't do nothing for nobody yesterday." Misty finally looked up at him.

"I couldn't either," She hugged Billy tighter.

"I know sweetie. Marie's got me working today though. Got me running already." He looked up at his former house. He remembered when he built the red brick house, slightly bigger than Marie's. The whole community helped. "I think it'd be best if you go down to the house and help her. She's going a hundred miles to keep sane." Misty shrugged her shoulders, never let Billy go. "I think it'll be good for you too."

"Probably so," she said, finally letting him go. "I guess I should take a shower too huh."

Chapter 6

*Please excuse my attitude*

*Sorry if I'm being rude*

*But I have something to say to you*

*Hoping you won't lose your cool*

*I want to take you out to play with me*

*You can spend the day with me*

*And we'll go out and see the sights*

*Yep, it's going down tonight*

Pound usually let something tougher rattle his trunk but what could be tougher than Scarface? Maybe it was because he resembled the rapper that he liked him so much. When Pound first heard the Geto Boys the music hit him like high voltage. The rhythm, energy and attitude spoke to Pound in such a way that he could listen to 'Face sing to a woman while he cruised Brunswick's south end at night looking for someone to kill.

Ike and Andre Long killed Chop, Pound reasoned. Who else? Chop told Pound about the incident between he and Ike at Chop's diner. Neither Pound or Chop thought Ike Long would carry out his threat after Chop beat up Andre for a second time. He probably hired someone to do it. Ike hired Chop and Pound to kill and dispose of more than a half dozen people. Ike wouldn't do it himself but he would have it done. Pound was prepared to scour the earth.

Turning onto Highway 17 Pound thought about the fools who visited him earlier to profess their innocence, funny. Pound was exactly who he wanted to be to them, a menace they feared and whom they gave undivided respect. If he was guilty of killing the brother of someone like himself he'd kill that someone before killing his brother, or he'd probably disappear like Ike and Andre. Dumping Chop at the asphalt plant was crazy. Why not dump away from their property or bury him? The weed and cocaine helped Pound push away any doubts about Ike and Andre being responsible for Chop's murder. Still, Pound tried not to blame himself.

When Chop beat up Andre in front of a crowd Pound laughed. When Chop got

Andre's girlfriend to have sex with him, he passed her to Pound. When Andre came to Pound asking for help settling the beef with him and Chop, Pound laughed at him. Chop continued to terrorize Andre. Everyone has a breaking point, even those who seem like pushovers.

The lights at Ike's Ocean Isle Beach home were off earlier and all the cars were gone. Pound called his homeboys for information about Andre's girlfriends. He visited three. They expressed their condolences, said Andre wasn't answering his phone all day. It was 10 o'clock at night. Treasure, Pound's sister in love, told him to check out Frieda, Andre's ex. She was at the Kangaroo.

The Kangaroo was the Supply gas station on highway 17, it was also a truck stop. Truckers could get a Subway sandwich, some pussy and drugs at the Kangaroo. Pound put the Impala up and rented a pickup truck from a neighborhood crack customer. Frieda was heading to the gas station entrance when he pulled up.

"Frieda!" he called. She immediately turned around.

Frieda was a beauty queen, turned experimenter, turned abuser, turned crack zombie. She used to look like Vanessa Williams from the 80s. Hands down was one of the finest girls ever in Supply. Now, standing in front of the icebox, the 5'3" rail thin nappy headed creature resembling a shaved cat fixed her huge eyes on the F-150 headlights.

"Frieda, get the fuck over here!"

She crossed her arms and sashayed over to the truck. She squinted to see who it was.

"Pound, what's up my nigga!"

"Get in," he said. Frieda put her hand on hip and sucked her teeth.

"For what?" she asked rolling her neck.

Pound didn't take much nonsense. Usually he wouldn't acknowledge someone like Frieda.

"I gotta talk to you." Frieda sighed and looked off to the highway. "I got twenty dollars for you.

"Shit, I just made fifty."

"Bitch, get the fuck in this truck!" Frieda tip toed around the front of the F-150. Pound unlocked the door and they burned rubber out of the parking lot.

As he cruised 211 north, his eyes found their way back to Frieda. She wore a sagging dingy wife beater tucked in her blue jeans. The parts of her bra poking out were caked in dirt. Her stench was an unholy mixture of must, funk and halitosis. Pound put down the windows and accelerated.

"So," he said, "You talked to Andre lately?"

"Hell no," Frieda said while her eyes darted around the truck while wondering why she settled for twenty dollars.

"You bullshitting me Frieda?"

"Nigga what the fuck is up!" she snapped "You want this pussy or what? Turn off somewhere or let me the fuck out."

Pound almost bit a hole in his lip as he pulled out five twenty dollar bills and dropped it in her lap. Her sharp shoulders bounced with approval.

"Like I was saying, you and Andre was tight once, right?"

"Yeah we were together for a minute. Andre used to be sweet. I used to leave Mama and them for weeks to kick it with Andre and his people." Frieda talked as she counted and recounted her money.

"Where did y'all kick it at?" Pound kept his eyes on the road, ears like nets in a stream.

"At they crib in Ocean Isle. Ms. Sheila used to cook Thanksgiving like dinners all the time." Frieda left her current world for the warm and pleasant past. "Oh man, I remember when Andre wanted to get away from his daddy and we'd go to Myrtle Beach."

"Where?"

"I just said to Myrtle Beach."

"Bitch, where in Myrtle Beach did y'all used to go?"

"Oh, it's right on the beach just past Red Lobster. I forgot the name but they got a parking lot like twenty stories up sitting behind the condo. Andre's condo is on the seventeenth floor."

Pound lit a blunt and slowed down some.

"So what else y'all do?"

"Shit...if we wasn't fucking and shopping we was getting high." She finally put the money in her pocket.

"What you mean rocks?" Pound was surprised to feel a little concern about his little brother's ex-best friend using crack.

"We used to smoke woos. I let that fool convince me we wasn't smoking no crack cause we was smoking it with weed." Frieda crossed her arms and watched the trees go by.

"He was doing that shit before he started fucking with you?" Frieda uncrossed her arms and turned to Pound. Frieda huffed and puffed.

"Let me tell you something Pound! That punk bitch Dre turnt *me* out! I didn't even drink before we got together. You niggas think y'all know every goddamn thing but don't know shit. Let me the fuck out!"

The F-150 screeched to a halt. In one motion Pound pulled silver a Desert Eagle from under his seat while grabbing Frieda's neck and slamming her head on the outside of his right knee.

"I know you ain't shit but a busted crack ho," he said trying to press a hole in her head with the barrel. His fingernails dug into Frieda's neck. Every jerk and strain broke her skin. She focused on staying still and quiet. "But I know you ain't as stupid as you talking. If I ask you something else and you get fly with me I'm a stretch your stanking ass out right here in these woods. Now when the fuck did y'all start blowing them woos?"

"It was after we got together," she said like she was testifying for a jury on the stand. Her eyes squeezed shut, a single tear tracked down her cheek. "His uncle had him doing it, Uncle Early. It used to be just them but then Andre made me do it. Now look at me. I can't let this stuff go."

Pound put his gun back under the seat. He threw Frieda against the passenger door. Frieda rested her head on the window and sobbed quietly.

"Where do Uncle Early stay?" Pound put the blunt down in the ashtray.

"In Phoenix," Frieda said slowly and clearly, holding back a hiccup. "We started going up there before we broke up. Early stopped smoking woos. He smoked straight crack out of stems and soda cans. Andre stayed smoking woos and I started smoking like Uncle Early."

"Where exactly in Phoenix does he stay?" Pound made a three point turn in the street.

Frieda gave him directions to Uncle Early's. Pound dropped her off at Treasure's in Supply. He relit his blunt and hit the Highway 17 north headed to Leland.

## Chapter 7

*July 2nd "Uncle" Early Long*

"I don't want to Early," Cassandra whined, sitting on the floor on her knees, lips pouted and her arms crossed. "I ain't no lesbo and plus Heather's my cousin."

She was a high school senior, Andre Long's little cousin's girlfriend. Behind his cousin's back Andre began seeing Cassandra. He started by giving her money and clothes. Within a month of their secret relationship, Andre introduced Cassandra to woos. By the end of the next month Cassandra let her cousin Heather, a high school sophomore, come along with her and Andre. By the end of the next month both Cassandra and Heather were Andre's toys. If he wasn't playing with them he let his friends play with them. Uncle Early began picking them up personally.

"Listen little girl," he said sitting at the foot of his king size bed. A grey polo shirt hugged his obese frame. One eye leaned to the side. A white doorag covered his massive head and sat above the folds of his razor bumped neck. He wore no pants, underwear or shoes. Food sex and crack were Uncle Early's only recreation. "You're gonna eat your cousin right now or you ain't getting no more dope." He reloaded his stem with a piece of crack that rivaled the top of his thumb in size.

Cassandra's mom called her constantly since she and Heather left their summer jobs at an ice cream shop on Sunset Beach with Uncle Early. Since her mom called the police one time, every now and then Cassandra would text her mom and say she was okay and would be home soon. Soon usually meant the following morning. She and Heather had been gone for two days, forty-eight hours in one room. The thick stench of crack and unbathed oversexed bodies hung on and around everything. It didn't bother anybody. Uncle Early took a hit of the stem. His eyes tried to jump out of his head, standing in front of Cassandra, his gut covering his privates.

"Well," He said holding the stem out for her. Cassandra moved to Heather and Heather spread her legs.

Stopping at the light on the highway, Hawk pulled a small grey pouch from his jeans pocket. He kept the nail on his right pinky finger long so he wouldn't need anything to scoop small amounts of cocaine. Three healthy nailfuls, a hell of a nasal drain and the damn light still hadn't turned green yet.

Pound vaguely remembered Uncle Early. Always joking, nice clothes, jewelry, black Beamer on 22s. A real fat motherfucker. It was soon after Pound's release from prison five years ago. His mother Angela was seeing Ike, Uncle Early's brother. Early was at the house when Pound and Ike got into a shouting match over Ike's disrespect of Angela. He and Ike almost came to blows that day. Pound went nuts because his mother told him not to give Ike any grief, even for his rudeness. If Early and Ike were to have jumped Pound, he didn't know if Angela would fight for him or just stand there.

The light turned green, Pound took off.

"I wonder if he gonna tell me something," Pound said to himself. "Fat some bitch is probably sleep."

Turning onto Lanvale, Pound mashed the gas, turning down the music and turning on his radar detector, he raced to Phoenix. Crossing the train tracks he slowed down and turned on the high beams.

"Indian River loop on the left."

There were five houses in Indian River Loop.

"First one on the right, it's brown." Frieda said before getting out of the truck thirty minutes ago.

Pound cruised through the circle. Every house was two stories, manicured lawn, the opposite of the rest of Phoenix. No lights were on in the loop except one on the side at Uncle Early's house. Andre's Range Rover, black with black rims, sat in the driveway. It was already midnight. Pound left the Indian River Loop. He parked the truck on the side of the road adjacent to Uncle Early's house. The woods were thick. Pound the cut engine. When his feet hit the ground he pulled the seat up. His black football gloves sat on a TDI Vector Machine sub machine gun. Pound bought it at a gun show in Greensboro North Carolina. The ugly all black gun shot a thousand .45 caliber per minute. Pound shot a hundred fifty round clips out of the gun at the makeshift gun range he built behind Marie's house in the woods. Pound could shoot it with one hand and the barrel wouldn't climb. Pound left the mask but put on a black stretch cap to hold his dreadlocks.

Sitting on the floor with her back against the dresser, Cassandra watched Uncle Early screw her fifteen year old cousin while sucking crack from a stem. Uncle Early and Heather had her believe they smoked all the crack away from her. Cassandra attacked Uncle Early, punching and biting him. Heather, high and naked, laughed as she sat Indian style hugging a pillow on the bed. Then Uncle Early slammed Cassandra to the floor. She rolled like she'd been thrown from a car, Heather stopped laughing and hopped up off the bed.

"Goddamn it Early!" She screamed, checking the bruises on her older cousin's shoulder and forehead." Why you always picking on her?"

"Cause she ain't you," he said, rubbing himself and licking his lips.

Heather marched to the night stand, pulled out a small sandwich bag of crack and tossed it to Cassandra. Cassandra snatched the bag from the floor and immediately grabbed the stem.

"Come here big boy," Heather said sliding back down onto the bed. Uncle Early, sweating from wrestling with Cassandra, cracked a smile.

Pound heard a body hit the floor. There was a girl screaming at somebody. He raced up the steps on the front porch. The neighborhood was still asleep. Pound kicked in the door and darkness greeted him as he crossed the threshold. Stepping further into the house he kept his right hand on the wall. Everybody seemed to be in that one room, the light came from the bottom of the door.

"Shit!" Pound said putting his free arm over his face. "They in there getting as shit," he whispered to himself. Bed squeaks and female moans wafted from under the door. Pound took his fist and hit himself on the side of his head. He did it again and again while hopping up and down until he felt he was ready. He started to kick the door in but tried the doorknob, it was unlocked. His eyes were dragged against their will to the bed.

Uncle Early's obese backside faced Pound, moving up and down with sustained effort. Two little white feet were poking out on his hips. The smell almost knocked Pound out of the room. The girl on the floor to his right was smoking. Pound walked up behind Uncle Early and kicked him square in the ass.

"Oww!" Uncle Early screeched, he pulled out of Heather, "Bitch I'm gonna-"

He turned around. The tall negro with the futuristic gun gave him pause and retarded his anger. Pound's, mouth screwed eyes bulged and stuck on Uncle Early's, Uncle Early took him to be a Leland drug dealer who just learned he was set up years ago for a fall and had returned. Unless somebody got parole that was impossible. "Hey man, whatever you see gone and take it brother. It's all yours my man." He sat on the foot of the bed with his hands up and his head down. Heather stayed on her back with her legs open. Cassandra had stopped smoking only to reload the stem. Pound took a step back from the bed, snatched Cassandra's stem and threw it against the wall. Cassandra, with her mouth hanging open, sat motionless.

"Where Andre at?" Pound asked, the Vector .45 by his side.

"I don't know bruh," Uncle Early said with a shrug. "I ain't seen him all day." Pound brought the shotgun up.

"You ain't seen him all day but his truck is in your driveway. Stop playin'Early" Uncle Early lifted his head. *Angela's oldest boy*, he thought.

"Hey man, I said I don't know where the fuck he at! Now get the fuck out my house fore' I call the police!"

Cassandra was dazed. Heather, still on the bed, watched the ceiling. Pound gave Early a half nod then put the Vector .45 to uncle Early's forehead. Uncle sucked his teeth and turned up his bottom lip studying the gun when the blast came. Hellish claps of thunder seized eight ear drums. Uncle Early's head disintegrated in five seconds. The Vector .45 opened the top of Uncle Early like an orange from his neck to his stomach as he was blown back an inch off the bed. His body twirled and gushed blood and organs. His remaining top half landed on Heather. The dopamine coursing through her brain rescinded like microscopic turtles in their shells. Sizzling shreds of his polo shirt exposed vaporized man breasts. Blood and flesh chunks rushed out of him and engulfed Heather. Pound watched her as it took her brain a minute to register what had just happened.

"No, no no no no," she said shaking. She kicked her feet and swung her arms with panic fueled energy as she screamed. Being also lurched into sobriety, Cassandra's senses became disturbingly improved. She seemed be to standing over Early, the stench of his death filling her lungs. She wanted to run away, wanted to fly. She grabbed her cell phone from the dresser.

"Put that fucking phone down!" he demanded, training the Vector on the top of Cassandra's head. She dropped her cell phone and he grabbed Heather's foot and dragged her from under Uncle Early to the floor. Blood, grey matter, skull fragments and clumps of bloody wavy haired scalp splashed over the bed, headboard and wall.

Heather, sitting by Pound's feet and in a panic, desperately tried to wipe Uncle Early's blood and brain fragments from her body. She only smeared most of it on her. The room was spinning and her ears were ringing.

Cassandra rushed to her and wrapped her arms around her. "I'm so sorry hon," she cried, Heather kept rubbing her arms.

Pound ran down the hallway and back to the front door. One house in the middle of the cul-de-sac had a light on, then the one beside it. Pound ran back in the house.

"Get the fuck up now," he growled pointing the Vector at the girls. Heather had thrown up when he left. Cassandra searched the floor for drugs. "Get up!" Pound shouted.

Cassandra shot to her feet. She pulled Heather up. Heather looked as if she was going to blow another load. Pound turned the lights on in the hallway.

"Can she put some clothes on please? She's stark naked man." Cassandra said helping Heather out of the room.

"I can leave both of you here dead or you can drag her out of here right now. Hurry the fuck up!"

Cassandra picked up the pace. Heather seemed to find better footing once they stepped into the yard. Pound stood on the porch watching for neighbors.

"Follow that wood line out to the main road. There's a truck on the left. Both of y'all lay down in the back."

They scurried out to the road.

"Hey there!" called a man from the house in the middle of cul-de-sac fifty yards away. "Y'all alright?"

The girls kept going. Heather was running along with Cassandra to the road. They hopped on the back of the truck.

Pound, stepped out of the house and pointed the Vector the direction of the man. It wasn't until Pound shot his remaining twenty rounds into the man's work van that he turned and ran. He turned and ran like an action hero running from a building set to explode.

"Cassie," Heather cried, laying one the bed of the F-150. "that dude's gonna kill us ain't he!" Cassandra put her arms around her.

"He ain't gonna kill us hon', he just didn't wanna leave us in there."

## Chapter 8

*Sheriff Helms*

Sheriff Samuel Helms enjoyed a deep dreamless sleep. Multiple law enforcement agencies and news correspondents stretched him thin the past couple days. Everybody wanted to know who the suspect or suspects were for the murder Erving "Chop" Belle. He wished he could have told them that Chop's killer would never go to jail much less trial because he's too busy protecting and serving this fair county. Where had the Long family gone? Where were they the night of Chop's murder? Were the Long's even suspects? Was there a hit man in Brunswick County? Did Chop's friends kill him? Is there a drug war going on? Was the murder a good thing or bad thing for Brunswick County? Fran Williams from the Wilmington news conducted a survey of the latter question to a hundred Brunswick county residents. She'd report the results on the evening news.

Some folks on Brunswick's south end were using the fireworks meant for Independence Day to celebrate Chop's death. Impromptu cook-outs and house parties dotted nearly every non-black neighborhood. Bars along the Intracoastal Waterway struggled to handle all the business thrown their way. Chop was the wicked witch of the east and folks celebrated like munchkins. For the most part, they were in no rush to find or punish Dorothy.

Chop's death was a prophecy come true. It rubbed a lot of folks the wrong way when he was acquitted in that big high school drug case where the kid died. Chop was guilty. Everyone felt it in their gut. Inflated ego and disdain for the victim's family seemed to drip off of him during the trial. A lot of people learned who Chop was through the State of North Carolina's narrative of that case. The disgust for Chop grew to its peak when the jury found him not guilty. The trial ended ninety days ago and people were still praying Chop got his good and hard.

Sheriff Sam Helms never saw such joy come from one man's death. Made him feel like a hero. People practically forced him to join in the festivities. His wife had scheduled a pig picking for the next evening. She was especially ecstatic.

"Baby," Diana said holding the ringing phone. The sheriff snored on. She shook him until he came to.

"Huh, what...what is it woman?" he asked scowling at his better half.

"The phone," Diana said hitting him in head with it. He snatched it.

"Sheriff Helms," he answered, it was Deputy Terry Long . In fifteen second the sheriff was sitting up and fully awake. "Who's over there now?" Diana hit him on the shoulder. When he turned to her she mouthed, *What happened* . "Good, don't call anybody till I get there." He hung up the phone.

"Sam what's going on?" The sheriff rushed to the bathroom.

"I gotta piss," he said. He didn't close the door.

"Did somebody else get shot? Is Misty okay?"

The sheriff put on the blue jeans he took off four hours ago.

"Hell no, Misty's fine woman. Somebody in Phoenix got found dead just now."

"My Lord," Diana said sitting up. "I don't know'em do I?"

"If you by crack in the Leland area you might," the sheriff cracked. Diana took a pillow and hit the sheriff in the face.

"If I wanted crack I'd just go to our daughter's boyfriend. At least I used to could go to him."

"Yeah." The sheriff turned down the color on his polo shirt in the mirror. "Seems somebody's taken it upon himself to rid our county of crack dealers." He turned to Diana. "Guess you'll have to kick your habit soon sugar."

Diana charged toward him with a grin. She punched him in gut. "If I was smoking crack, you'd best believe I'd have you out there selling your ass to get me some."

"Good Lord, I married a pimp and an addict."

Diana drew back to punch him again.

"Okay okay, you win!" The sheriff said turning his body sideways. "I can't work beat up sugar." Diana opened the drawer on the night stand. She pulled out the sheriff's .40 caliber glock. She loaded it and put it in the holster around his waist.

"Be careful baby," she said before they kissed.

He sped eighty miles per hour north on 295 from Southport. Early Long was a good earner and a great manager. Leland, Phoenix, Northwest and Navassa belonged to him. To shut the locals up he collaborated with the Narcotics Task Force that operated out of the Brunswick County Sheriff's Office to set up low level dealers with a small amount of drugs. They'd enter a cycle of small convictions while Early, the sheriff and select officers kept making money. Early would be damn near impossible to replace but he was on his way out anyway.

The sheriff belonged to a group of officers that spanned the state of North Carolina. This group had no fancy name and nobody outside of the group knew of its existence. They were a band of thieves who helped each other shake down big time criminals in various counties. The sheriff had come into a ridiculous sum of heroine that winter. He and his son Blake were getting rid of it routinely until the end of Erving "Chop" Belle's trial. Chop was a loyal customer. He had and so was a handful of other dealers, including Early Long. Chop told Blake to fuck himself and Early said he didn't want any more of their dope, said he was straight. The sheriff wasn't straight and he wanted to know who was supplying the biggest dealer in his county. Nobody had any answers for the sheriff. The heroine was better than the sheriff's. The bundles they discovered through various arrests were potent and plentiful. Sheriff Helms planned a sweep of every dealer on Brunswick County's south end that refused the drug supplying services of surrogates secretly representing him and his son. Chop had to be put down for a number of reasons. The others wouldn't be put down but definitely put away. Sam Helms owned Brunswick County, point blank period.

Pulling into Indian River loop the sheriff was relieved to see only Deputy Long and the man who called the police. Just two men in the middle of the night.

"Sheriff," Deputy Terry greeted shaking the sheriff's hand. "Sorry to wake you but you gotta check this out." The sheriff got a load of Indian Circle. Nobody was awake.

"I'm Sheriff Sam Helms," he said holding his hand out to the short wiry red haired man with Deputy Long. He took the sheriff's hand.

"Hey man, I'm Keith Arlen. I stay right over there." The sheriff took in the two story white home with grey work van and green Camaro in the parking lot.

"You got a nice home sir," he said. "So what happened out here?" Keith let out a deep sigh.

"Man, I went to Wal-Mart for some things and uhh...when I come, I saw a black pick up out there past hem trees on Lanvale. I ain't pay it no mind when I park my car and get out I heard a woman screaming. Screaming wild as hell and then two women run out the front door of that house." Keith pointed at Uncle Early's house. "One of'em was stark naked and seem like she had blood on her."

"Blood?" the sheriff said. Keith nodded.

"Yes siree, and they ran out to Lanvale down the road in that truck's direction. Then some big black some bitch come out the house and shot the gaddamn shit outta my work van."

"Calm down sir," Deputy Long said.

"Listen man, I ain't out here to raise no sand. I wanna know how I get my van fixed. How do I go about that man? Now Sheriff, I don't bother nobody. These big ass holes in my van ain't my fault so I know I ain't the one gotta pay fer'em."

"That's right," the sheriff said, putting his hand on the man's shoulder. "and you won't Pay for it. I promise you that. We're gonna call some folks out here to examine your van. Get the bullets out for evidence then we'll repair." The sheriff held his hand out for Keith. Keith shook it enthusiastically.

"That sounds great sheriff. I'm telling ya, I told mama to vote for you cause I knew you wasn't for no shit and you'd keep us a good county with morals and-"

"Okay sir," Deputy Long interrupted. "You can go to your home now. We'll be speaking again in a few hours." Keith nodded and trotted back to his home.

"Hold on Keith," said the sheriff. Keith stopped and turned. "Did you see the shooter's face?"

"Hell know, that some bitch raised that gun and started firing almost instantly. I thought Jesus had called me but the boy was only interested in killing the back of my van."

The sheriff nodded and Deputy Long waved Keith back to his house.

"Here you go sheriff." Deputy Long handed the sheriff two surgical caps.

"I've been inside," Deputy Long said on their way to Uncle Early's. "Early's in there blown to pieces. I'm talking about...like smithereens Somebody came here tonight just to kill him." They put the surgical caps on their feet when they reached Early's paved driveway. "You know whose truck that is?"

"Looks like Andre Long's," the sheriff said looking in the Rang Rover's windows. "What's it doing here?"

"Very strange business going on," Deputy Long said walking up the sidewalk to the front door.

"Somebody kicked it in," the sheriff said. Deputy Long nodded. The smell of blood was strong and fresh as they entered the hallway. "Good God Terry, why didn't you say something?"

Deputy Long chuckled. "I said he was blown away."

"Yeah but you didn't say all this. Sweet Jesus Almighty." The sheriff knew just looking at the room who *could* be responsible. Barring some out of town actor paying Early a visit, Julius Belle was the only person the sheriff knew this kind of propensity for violence. Did he think it best to pay the Long family back like this. Pound was absolute vengeance and Early's brains and guts splattered everywhere suggested just that. Operation Chop Down continues...maybe.

"So what do we do?" Deputy Long asked. "We go pick up Julius now or in the morning?"

"You go and question him tomorrow, late in the evening. He'll think we're not on to him. In the meantime let's get this place properly examined. Make sure the news cameras get all they can stomach of this."

"And *don't* arrest Belle?" Terry asked. The sheriff shook his head.

"Terry, if we arrest Julius Belle, we'll have to protect Julius Belle. Ike Long is still out there. Maybe he'll try to get Julius, then we get'em and whoever else wants jump in this. To take Julius now, even for questioning, would disturb nature's course. If we do bring Belle in, it will be because of the evidence he left in this room." Terry took a deep breath.

"Look at the women's clothes and the purses over there," he said, picking up a lime green patent leather purse off the floor.

"That ain't no women's clothes Terry, that's girl's clothes." the sheriff left the room. Deputy Long opened the purse as he followed him out.

"Well look a here. Cassandra Handler, eighteen years old. This is a West Brunswick High School ID."

"Yeah I bet," the sheriff said getting on his knees in the hall bathroom perpendicular to the bedroom. He started pulling out toilet bowl cleaners, air fresheners and soap scum cleaners. "Early always liked'em young."

"You should see the age of this other one," Long said checking the other purse. "What are you doing down there?"

After everything was taken from under the sink, the sheriff pulled up the bottom of the cabinet and sat it diagonally against the side of the cabinet. He stood for the benefit of his back and so the deputy could get a look.

"How much money do you think that is?" the deputy asked. The sheriff squatted carefully and picked up a plastic wrapped block of twenty dollar bills.

"We can count it later deputy. Come on."

They walked down the hall past the front door to the kitchen.

"This fool loved to eat, obviously. A pretty good cook too. He has, rather had his hands in that seafood restaurant in Leland. Built a walk-in fridge and freezer in here so he could store a bunch of shit in the house. Had delivery trucks coming to this house every week."

"He thought he was a king," the deputy said, shaking his head and stepping into the walk-in fridge behind the sheriff.

"He was, around here," the sheriff said. "Early controlled a lot of traffic, in and out of the county. Wasn't dumb, just loved to indulge."

Boxes of coconut shrimp sat on a metal rack against the left side wall. The sheriff knocked them all over. The shrimp were in plastic bags of twenty. Three rectangular squares of heroine fell to the floor when the sheriff knocked over the whole rack.

"Good Lord," said Deputy Long. "This is a career bust sheriff!" The sheriff chuckled.

"A career bust? Who are we gonna bust man? Early's dead." The sheriff started putting the kilos back into their shrimp boxes. "A lot more good could be done with these than showing them off to the public. Yeah, a lot more good."

## Chapter 9

*Twenty five years ago.*

*"Daddy!"*

*Billy didn't hear him over the lawnmower engine as he concentrated on the grass line. It was six thirty in the morning, he just cut the grass by the boy's window.*

*"Daddy!" Erving called.*

*Billy heard him that time. Once Billy's head turned, the boy raced to the lawn mower. Billy stopped so Ervin could hop on. He was half way there when Angela, wrapped in her house robe, stepped out to the front porch.*

*"Ervin, get back here!" she shouted.*

*"I got him!" Billy shouted as he turned blades off . Erving kept running and hopped on.*

*Sitting on his dad's leg, secured by his arm, six year old Erving enjoyed the ride. With both hands on the steering wheel he searched for pinecones, he liked seeing them fly all over the yard when they ran them over. While Billy drove, Erving swatted the mosquitoes away. Under the pine trees with low branches, Erving would grab them and hold them over his dad's head so they wouldn't hit him in face. Erving worshipped his dad.*

Sitting on Chop's brand new mower, one that can turn on a dime, he cut the grass around his old house, he just finished Marie's. Folks from all over were expected drop by until the funeral. A funeral for *Chop*. Marie and Misty planned to cook from nine to twelve. Billy was assigned all the heavy lifting and deep frying. He called Pound and Kiana for help and Kiana explained politely that Pound wasn't helping with anything. She offered to come by with Jared and help out. Billy stopped in front of the porch of his old home. He could still see Erving dart to him, eyes on his feet so he wouldn't fall. That was his little man.

Marie never visited Billy when he was incarcerated, never sent a card. When he called home for the holidays and she was in the house she wouldn't take the phone. He desperately wanted to speak to her to apologize for his situation; for whatever condition Angela, Pound and Chop were in because of his absence. It was Marie who convinced her husband Herbert to accept Billy's engagement to Angela. Billy Belle, no college degree, no house of his own and wasn't at all active in the church. The Lance family found him a job, helped build him a house and parked his behind in the church. When Angela passed away Billy sent letter after letter after card to Marie with no response. He spoke with Chop and Misty at length about it and they couldn't help the situation.

When Billy walked into Marie's house after twenty-five years her face glowed as she stood with her arms open. Billy cried like a small child as he and Marie swayed from side to side.

“I missed you son,” Marie said. “Don’t worry about nothing, you still got family right here.” Nathaniel could curse his soul, if Marie said Billy was alright then he was alright.

Billy put the lawn mower up at Chop’s and walked back to Marie’s. EJ, Chop’s lawyer and best friend, pulled into Marie’s yard. He parked his black Lincoln MKZ beside Marie’s Camry. At seven fifteen in the morning EJ looked ready for trial, three piece navy blue suit and a big Rolex hanging off his wrist. He stood a few inches under six feet with a close cut and no piercing. When Billy was coming up the folks who carried themselves like EJ were called squares. When Billy started his family he hoped his two sons and all their friends would become squares.

“What’s up Uncle Bill?” EJ greeted. They weren’t related. When EJ was a kid Chop’s parents were Uncle Billy and Aunt Angie. His parents were Uncle Eric and Aunt Sylvia to Chop and Pound. Billy shook his hand.

“Hey EJ.” Billy’s voice always raised an octave when greeting a young success, some kid who helped ease the pessimism about the future older people naturally harbored. Billy took off his work gloves they shook hands. “You doing alright son?”

“Yes sir, I just dropped by to see how Aunt Marie was doing.” EJ held a briefcase. Billy looked at it briefly.

“Yeah man she uhh…she’s definitely the backbone of the family.” Billy sensed a little apprehension in EJ. Most folks that he came across the past six months, who knew where he’d been, would get a little fidgety. Billy learned to act like he didn’t notice. “If she asks you how you’re taking things and how you’re family’s doing just let her be strong for you. That’s how she copes.”

“Oh I know,” EJ said switching his briefcase from his right hand to the left. “I hope she copes me up some banana pudding.” Billy laughed.

“You go on in and see Marie,” he said. “And if she has some banana pudding in there save me some.”

“Uncle Billy I love you but I can’t promise you all that,” EJ said heading to the side door.

”Man, you silly,” Billy said chuckling. EJ walked into the house. Billy sat in one the chairs Marie had in the yard. A minute later Nathaniel pulled into Marie's.

Billy, still smiling, crossed his arms and watched Nathaniel labor out of his Park Avenue. He looked ready for trial too, walking around his car.

"What the fuck you looking at?" he greeted. Billy shook his head.

"Nothing, absolutely nothing."

"You really think you did something sucker punching me huh. I'll whip your ass Billy, quick! Watch your back boy." Nathaniel strutted to the house. Billy put his gloves back on, he had weeds to pull.

"Aunt Marie," EJ greeted. Marie hugged his neck and kissed his cheek.

"Hey baby, come on to the dining room." To get to the dining room they had to walk through the kitchen. The smells hit him, a half dozen Sweet potato pies, a couple lemon meringue pies, a three layer chocolate cake, a three layer red velvet cake and four glass pans of peach cobbler cooling on the counter.

"It smells good up in here," EJ said ogling the counter as they walked by. "I guess you didn't get around to-"

"It's in the fridge," she said without turning around. "Got a dish going to Chop's house, got one staying here and got one for you and your family."

"Thank you so so much." EJ showed all of his teeth.

Chop had finished reflooring the house and painting the house two weeks ago. Hardwood for the living room, vinyl for the kitchen and bathrooms, carpet everywhere else. Marie chose royal blue for the dining room carpet to go with the white molding and beige walls. She took pictures from her old albums and put them in new frames throughout the house. They were pictures of the families of all Marie's children and her brother's children's families. Right there with them was a Dixie Youth Tee ball League picture of EJ, Chop and Andre Long. They played for the KFC Colonels. EJ opened his briefcase on the dining table as he sat.

Marie sat across from him.

"Okay Aunt Marie we got a lot of-"

"Mama!" Nathaniel called from the living room. "Mama where y'all at?" EJ knew who's voice it was but didn't want to believe he was hearing it.

"In the dining room!" she shouted raising an index finger to EJ to hold on a second.

"Mama you cooked all this mess?" Nathaniel entered the living room. "You don't need to be carrying on like this. It's plenty food in this house as it is."

Nathaniel tapped EJ's shoulder with the palm of his hand as he walked by. EJ stared at Marie.

"Hey Mr. Lance," EJ greeted. Mr. Lance used to be Uncle Nathaniel to EJ before he grew and understood who the man really was.

"Hey EJ," Nate greeted with little enthusiasm as he sat beside Marie. " So what's going on with Erving's estate?"

EJ looked to Marie, she looked away. This was supposed to be just a meeting between the two of them. Guess the banana pudding wasn't free.

"Yeah...well let's see," EJ said pulling papers from his briefcase. "This is Chop's Diner and Chop's barbershop."

"Barbershop?" Nathaniel said.

"Yes," EJ said, picking up the information from the table. "We planned to start construction on a building on the corner of Cedar Grove and Mt. Pisgah for the barbershop. The barbershop is still scheduled to be built." Nate took the paper from EJ's hands.

"No," said Nathaniel shaking his head reading the paper with his bottom lip turned up to his nose. "We're gonna cancel that and use the money for something else." Nathaniel dropped the paper and caught eyes with EJ, eager to make another change.

"Mr. Lance," EJ took a breath, "the barbershop wasn't Chop's alone. It was a partnership between him and me, fifty-fifty. My brothers Tony and Tim are graduating from barber school in the winter. When they come back from Fayetteville their going to cut in this new shop."

"No they're not either," Nathaniel said sitting back in his chair. "That land doesn't belong to you or Chop, it belongs to my family. Ain't nobody building over there without our approval. You need to tell them boys to start cutting on the porch until they find a place to lease." Marie's mouth dropped as she put her hands on her hips.

"Mr. Lance," EJ took a deep breath and gently bit his lip, " construction starts in August. The barbershop is on its way. Aunt Marie gave us permission to use that land a year ago."

Nathaniel turned to Marie. She seemed fascinated by the china set that had been sitting in that same corner for forty years.

"Mama what the-," he looked to EJ then back to Marie, "What the hell? How did you make a decision like that without saying something to me? Did you even talk to Evelyn or Cedric?" EJ crossed his arms.

"Evelyn is in Charleston and Cedric is in Winston Salem. What do they care about a half-acre plot up the road from here?" asked Marie.

"It's their land, that's why they care! It's why I care. We can do a bunch of things with that land. If not today then maybe in the future our kids might want to do something with it." Nathaniel took the papers about the barbershop. "And you can't be making decisions like this no more. These boys'll tell you anything."

"What's that's supposed to mean?" EJ asked uncrossing his arms. Marie put her hand on Nathaniel's shoulder and shook her head.

"What it means is y'all, you and Chop, fooled my mama into signing away her land for some barbershop mess!"

"Okay y'all," Marie said. "Let's just calm down." EJ took additional papers from his briefcase.

"To be clear Mr. Lance, neither I nor Chop fooled Mrs. Lance into anything. She offered that plot to us and we accepted. It's still her land, her's. I've seen the deed. There is no Nathaniel Lance on it. And she's fully capable of making decisions with her own property."

"No, you let me be damn clear!" Nathaniel bellowed as he stood. "The fact that she even gave you and my ignorant ass nephew that plot on the corner is proof she ain't got no damn business making these decisions!"

"You know what, you got a lot of nerve coming in here-" Marie lifted her hand up and EJ stopped talking. She turned to Nathaniel.

"Now Nathaniel, who is the mother and who is the son?" she asked. Nathaniel sighed.

"Mama come on now, you know what I'm trying to say. These boys took advantage of your kindness. They never ask you for nothing when I'm around."

"And why the hell would we!" EJ snapped pounding the table with his hand, he stood. "Who the hell are you for us to ask anything, except on how to lock black folks up?"

"That's enough EJ," Marie said.

"No, he tried to put his own nephew away for the rest of his-"

"He was a dope dealer, a killer and-"

"I know what he was!" EJ shouted. Marie held her chest, she never heard EJ shout. Nathaniel huffed. His blood was pumping. "He was my friend, my brother, my business partner and *our* family! He did a lot of shit he had no business doing but he was on his way out of it." Nathaniel, with a quizzical look, sucked his teeth.

"On his way out?" he said. "On his way out? On his way out to where? Everybody in this county, no, in this whole district knows who and what the hell Erving was."

"No shit Nate!" EJ snapped. "That's why he had to leave the drugs alone eventually. When your own damn uncle tries to put you in jail it's time make a change. I always wanted him to go straight." Nathaniel crossed his arms, his bottom lip got even closer to his nose. "I'm serious. It wasn't until recently that he decided to stop for himself. Chop quit selling drugs months ago. This barbershop and the restaurant and the mobile homes were only the beginning of his eventual change. A transformation Mrs. Lance here wanted for her grandson. Some of us think folks can change without jail."

"Oh yeah?" Nate asked. "Well that's a nice fairy tale. But ain't nobody shot that boy up like that because he stopped selling drugs!" Marie shuddered. She'd been doing everything, *anything*, to take her mind away from how the news described Chop's body.

"What?" EJ said. Nathaniel crossed his arms, pleased with the point the made. Marie leaned over and hit Nate's arm.

"Are you saying you know why Chop was killed?" Marie asked. Nathaniel popped his self on his forehead. He seemed to be the only undense one in the room.

"Cause he's was a drug dealer Mama! Drug dealers shoot people and get shot all the time. The jail in Bolivia's full of Ervings who survived their gunshots to get caught selling dope. When you living so low you'll sell poison to people, you'll find yourself in the company of people just as low. People who'll act like *your* friend, *your* brother, *your* business partner then stab you in the back. Or shoot you to damn pieces! That boy done shot and kidnapped people around here and even over in South Carolina. Y'all up in here trying to tell me he was saint in a gangster's body!"

Nobody said anything for a few minutes. Nathaniel planted his fist on the table standing beside Marie; Marie rocked left and right staring at the wall. EJ stared at Nathaniel. EJ hated to hear it but the truth was just spoken. Chop was an gangster, a smart, bright, funny, deadly gangster. He killed folks slowly and quickly. He did things that made EJ stop talking to him sometimes, like when he beat Andre Long within an inch of his life.

"Nobody said he was a saint," said EJ as he sat. "He was *our* family and it was *our* responsibility to give him every opportunity to be better. You got every right to think how you do you're here wanting to swim through his estate and personal effort is mind boggling to me." Nathaniel's mouth was fixed to say something especially vile. Marie tapped him and shook her head. "Mrs. Lance, I'll talk to you again later, and alone. I'm taking the pudding out of the fridge too."

Marie smiled and nodded as EJ entered the kitchen. Nathaniel looked up at EJ then back at Marie.

"You made some banana pudding?" He asked.

## Chapter 10

Less than two miles away from Marie's front door step sat an abandoned mobile home in the middle of the woods. Decrepit sofas, couches and carpet blanketed with dust and mildew exuded a musty odor that only ripened when it got hot. Ants commuted on the floors and decayed walls. Wasps flew in and out of the broken windows. Their nests inhabited the entire inside of the broken ceiling over the den area. Sitting on the kitchen floor, tied to the oven with jumper cables, Cassandra and Heather slept.

Before leaving them in the mobile home Pound asked the girls about the condo Andre Long owned in Myrtle Beach.

"The Sands," Cassandra said, hoping he'd let them go. "His room number is 1720."

"Are you gonna kill us?" Heather asked as Pound wrapped her wrists with jumper cables.

"Why would I do that?" he asked. That was seven hours ago. Uncle Early's blood dried all over Heather's naked body. The ant bites woke her up.

"Cassie!" she screamed over and over. She squirmed and kicked. The ants kept biting. On her neck, her under arms, her breasts, and legs were feasted upon. She screamed to the top of her lungs. Nobody could hear her.

The humidity inside the mobile home intensified by the minute. Heather's flesh crawled. The ants went about their business. She would have chosen death over another minute of suffering. Cassandra kicked awake by Heather, thought about the stem and bag of crack in her pocket. If she could just slip out of those jumper cables then maybe...

"You think he killed Dre?" Cassandra asked.

"I don't give a damn about Dre Cassie. These ants are biting me!" Heather whined as she twitched to every bite in and around her private area. Crying and twitching with each sensitive bite. Hell couldn't be worse than this.

"If he kills Dre he might could let us go," Cassandra said. Fully clothed and wearing sneakers, she attempted to stand. On her feet, her body was bent backwards. When she turned to face the oven her arms were awkwardly twisted. She practically stood over Heather.

"Heather I need you to stand up hon'. We might can get out of here." A small step to the side sent pain through her arms. "Hurry up hon'. You gotta get up now."

Heather pulled her arms down and lifted her hips. She stood on the balls of her feet but couldn't maneuver like Cassandra. She twitched as the ants kept to their work.

"Oww," she whined. Pity almost overwhelmed her.

"Okay okay," Cassandra said checking Heather's posture, it seemed hopeless. "Okay this is what we gotta do. I'm a try to put my knee up under you so you can..."

"So I can what!" Heather barked. The ants were finding new orifices.

"You're gonna have to somehow use my knee to flip up to the counter hon', I know it sounds crazy but we gotta try." Cassandra, despite the pressure on her arms put one knee on the floor and the other under Heather. "Come down on my knee."

The small of Heather's back met Cassandra's knee. She lifted her feet and slipped from Cassandra's knee.

"Oww!" Cassandra grimaced as Heather came down on her ankle. "Stand back up, stand back up." Heather stood again. Cassandra placed her knee closer to the oven. She grimaced as she twisted her arms further. "You see that hood over the stove?" Heather hung her head back to look over her hands. "Try to get it with your feet." Heather took a deep breath.

"Okay." She said eyeing the hood over the stove. Her shoulder blades sat diagonally across Cassandra's knee. She attempted the flip and her left foot easily found the hood.

"That's it," Cassandra said. "Get the other one up there and flip up on the counter."

Heather's other foot easily found the stove hood. Before she knew it she was sitting on the stove on her knees.

"I did it!" she said looking around. The ants didn't stop biting. "Now what?"

Heather's hands were straight out. Cassandra wondered if she could bring her pockets to Heather's hands to get the crack, stem and lighter out. The more she thought about it the worse the chances looked.

"Alright alright, open that drawer with your foot if you can." Heather looked over her shoulder to the drawer.

"Shit!" Heather said, pulling the iron drawer handle with her big toe. "I can't...it won't...it's stuck...maybe if you kick it we can-"

The sound of the back door froze Cassandra. Heather tried to be still but the ants wouldn't let her. The weed smoke reached the girls before Pound did.

"Y'all doing alright?" he asked.

## Chapter 11

*Treasure Dawkins, Sister In Love.*

Treasure Dawkins sat in a beach chair under the big pecan tree in front of her trailer. With a Beats by Dre Pill sitting on the cooler beside her, a blunt sitting in both ears and a Corona in her hand, she watched the open field across the road. She learned of Chop's death almost forty-eight hours ago and she was only feeling worse.

Nobody was closer to Treasure than Chop, Pound, her baby's father Tremaine and Billy Belle, not even her mother. Treasure's mother was Charlene Dawkins. When Billy and Angela separated, Billy and Charlene began seeing each other. When Billy had his sons he'd take them to Charlene's in Supply and they'd play with Treasure. In that brief time the three children became extremely close. Treasure became Chop's big sister and Pound's little sister. Together they climbed and swung on every branch of that pecan tree. Charlene was kind enough but Treasure really helped the boys cope with their parents' separation. Treasure still had childhood pictures in the house of her carrying Chop on her back at the Holden Beach pier. He was scared of water back then.

Treasure's father was a crack addict named Clifford. He never married Charlene and never had a hand in raising Treasure. He'd break into Charlene's home to steal money and various items when she was away, sometimes to feed his addiction and sometimes for spite. When Charlene began seeing Billy, Clifford got bold. He'd break in knowing Charlene and Treasure were there. Charlene would find herself on the receiving end of a beating for trying to stop Clifford. When Billy appeared Clifford couldn't be found. After calling the cops a number of times Charlene put a restraining order against Clifford. It didn't make a bit of difference.

One day while the front door was open Clifford, all two hundred forty pounds of his 6'2" frame, walked in and unplugged the TV while Charlene was watching it. Treasure was instructed to leave the house whenever Clifford came by no matter what. As her parents fought inside, the eight year old sat on the porch steps watching the open field across the road. When Billy's Thunderbird pulled into her driveway she leaped off the steps screaming.

"BillyBelle BillyBelle BillyBelle!" She bolted to the driver side door banging the window as if Billy didn't see her.

"What's wrong baby girl?" Billy asked stopping the car.

"Daddy's in the house stealing and mama-"

"Watch out," Billy said, leaving the motor running. Treasure backed up and he stepped out of the car. He was in the house almost instantly. Treasure was right behind him.

Clifford was in the living room holding the 27 inch Sony Trinitron television Billy recently bought for Charlene. She hung on his back, her left arm around his neck while she beat him with her right hand. Clifford's knees bent as Charlene leaned back. He tossed the T.V on the couch where it bounced to the floor. He slung Charlene from behind him to the floor. That's when Billy and Treasure walked inside. Charlene, writhing in pain, twisted left and right on the floor, groaning as she tried and failed to reach the pain in her back with her hands.

"Bitch you better hope this T.V still works." Clifford's voice was unusually soft and silky, it had a Nipsey Russell quality. He squatted and put his hands under the heavy T.V. When he stood with it, like a pitcher on a mound, Billy hit Clifford in the nose with an overhand right punch. Clifford fell on Charlene's legs, he never let go of the T.V. Billy jumped on the T.V and Charlene screamed. Clifford tried to block the punches but couldn't. As Billy hit him repeatedly in his face, he put his hands under the T.V and pushed Billy and it off of him while Charlene begged them to stop. Billy grabbed the T.V and placed it gently on the floor. Clifford took his baseball mitt hands and delivered a left hook to Billy's one hundred seventy pound body, sending him flying across the living room. Billy crushed the coffee table beside her couch on the way to the floor. Clifford jumped on top of him just as Billy turned on his back. Billy's upper body moved with every punch Clifford landed. He wouldn't let Clifford hit his head but after a few minutes his forearms felt as though they were being pummeled by cinderblocks.

"Stop!" Treasure screamed at the top of her lungs, tears making tracks all over her chubby cheeks. She balled her little fists and windmill punched Clifford on his shoulder and along his arm. He grabbed Treasure and slung her back toward the front door.

"Take your little narrow ass outside!" He ordered, rolling his neck.

In that time Billy pulled a switchblade from his pocket and flipped it open. Clifford turned to Billy and the entire five inch blade disappeared into his jugular vein. It didn't dawn on Clifford what happened until he saw his blood cover Billy's face and chest. He grabbed his neck, feeling the warm stream run off his knuckles. His wound didn't calm Billy's fear. Billy wasn't sure he was hurt enough. When Billy stood, he stabbed Clifford repeatedly in his ribcage. With blood in his eyes, on his face and on his shirt, he poked away making Clifford flap like a fish. By the time Billy stopped, because of exhaustion, Charlene and Treasure were outside with the police.

"Oh my god!" a neighbor shrieked when Billy walked out the house. "She done got that man to kill Cliff." "She in there shacking up with Angela's husband and got him to kill Cliff!" The ladies in that trailer park gossiped and sucked their teeth at Charlene. Billy didn't know then but as the police sent him to the jail in Bolivia, Charlene was writing a statement on her porch saying she witnessed him murder Clifford over jealousy.

Charlene, a registered nurse, moved to Wilmington when seventeen year old Treasure decided she'd sell dope with Chop. Months before Billy was released Charlene issued an order of protection from him.

Chop threw a coming home party for Billy at the Cedar Grove Improvement Center, a big impressive multi-purpose building n the middle of the neighborhood, only four years old. Billy and Treasure danced to Whitney Houston's "I Wanna Dance" just like they did when she was a little girl.

Treasure's pill played only 2pac, her favorite. She took a blunt from her ear, lit it and turned the pill up.

"Mama!" perfect timing.

Turning around in the beach chair Treasure fixed her eyes on her youngest daughter Lovely. She stood on the porch holding the glass door open, letting all the cold air out. Lovely didn't have the same father as her older sisters. Kenya and Charisma's dad was Tremaine, the owner of Anytime's in Little River. He'd come by in his Escalade and take the girls to the mall, the movies and the big water parks in South Myrtle Beach. He was a super hero in Treasure's house. Lovely's dad was dead. He was ten years younger than Treasure and had been shot four different times before dying the fifth. He was big and loved to eat, Lovely was her dad's child.

"What is it my Love?" Treasure asked, Lovely closed the door and walked to the end of the porch.

"Can I get some cereal?"

"Girl, get you some cereal."

"Carrie said no cause I just ate lunch."

Treasure saw Charisma's logic. At five years old Lovely's back, shoulders and belly were getting out of control, just like her father's. Treasure put the blunt out on the ashtray beside the pill. She was 5'7" and slender. The sun made her usual caramel skin a maple brown. Halfway to the porch Billy's S10 pulled into the driveway.

Parking his truck in his usual spot near the tree, Billy let his windows down. Only he, Tremaine, Pound and Chop were aloud to stop by unannounced, even Charlene had to call first. There were three trailers behind Treasure's and four beside it. She owned all of them. Each one served a purpose. One trailer was for cooking crack, one was for customers to smoke crack, one was a liquor house, it was in front of the trailer used for gambling, one was decked out for Treasure and her girlfriends to relax and smoke weed, one held her clothes and one was a place for her little cousin/worker Lucas to bring girls, he paid rent.

"Billy Belle!" she greeted, pronouncing it Billybelle. That's how she pronounced it as a child. Her daughters greet him the same way.

"Hey Babygirl." Billy got out of the truck. The heat immediately went to work zapping the coolness off his arms, the top of his bald head and face. He hustled past the pecan tree. He and Treasure hugged.

"This is crazy ain't it?" Treasure said.

"Yeah it is," he said. Kenya saw Billy through the blinds in the window. She went outside and raced Lovely to him.

"BillyBelle BillyBelle BillyBelle!" They screamed.

"Hey babies!" Like pint sized bullies, the girls patted Billy down and started going through his pockets.

"Quit that 'fore I beat y'all! Lovely, quit I said!" The girls kept digging. Kenya dug while bracing for a hit from her mother.

"It's alright," Billy said. "Kenya baby, I got a white bag in the front seat for you. Y'all split it down the middle."

Pigtails, elbows and four sandal bottoms darted to the truck. The girls loved Billy but adored Skittles and Starbursts.

"I hope they like that candy cause I'm beating'em when you leave." Treasure crossed her arms. The girls turned on the radio in the truck and enjoyed the candy right there.

"Babygirl, let'em live. You was the same way." Treasure shook her head.

"I been meaning to stop by," she said watching the girls. "It's just...how did this... why?" She didn't cry but her eyes welled. Lovely and Kenya stopped their munching session to assess the situation.

"It's unreal Babygirl I know. It's a... I don't know. I just don't... we just gotta be strong. I don't mean it to sound easy cause it won't be." Treasure nodded, her bottom lip poked. "I'm here for you, you hear me? We gonna get through this, it's gonna be alright." Treasure nodded furiously as the tears fell. She wrapped Billy up and squeezed him. He never doubted Treasure's trust in him.

"You know we gotta kill Ike and them," Treasure said. Billy took his arms from around her. He took a step back.

"Damn Babygirl, why you gotta do that?" Bill put his hands on his hips.

"Why?" Treasure said with a chuckle, no smile. "Chop is gone and they did it. They gotta go." Billy turned to his truck. The girls were dancing and munching.

"Babygirl, I never really spoke to Chop about um... you know, staying out of prison. I knew he was gonna do what he was gonna do, same with you. You're grown. But let me tell you that prison is no joke. You can't raise them girls from a visiting table. I tried with two boys and didn't reach neither one."

"I understand, but that ain't bringing Chop back or putting them niggas in the ground for me. Me and Pound can't let this pass. Niggas'll start thinking its open season on us." Billy never heard Treasure talk like this. He was under no illusion about what she was. When it came to treasure he naïve about everything, her penchant for being ruthless mainly. Such a pretty girl with a sweet voice. Like Chop, Billy still saw a child when saw Treasure.

"Well, let me tell you this too. That cemetery ain't no joke either. I never thought I'd have to bury a son. Don't make me have to bury a daughter." He checked his watch. "I'm late, gotta a lot of work to do." Billy and Treasure headed to the truck.

"You're still working at a time like this?" Treasure said.

"I'm working at Marie's. Y'all need to come get a plate. I'm a talk to Pound too. I don't want nothing to happen to y'all. I ain't been out but a minute and look what's going on." Billy offered his hands to Treasure. "Come on let's pray."

"Nope, I'm good," Treasure said walking behind the beach chair, shaking her head. "I just need to-"

"Lord, thank you for giving us..." Billy walked to Treasure and grabbed her hands. Like him she bowed her head.

"Kenya," Lovely said sitting on her knees in the passenger seat, munching a handful of Skittles. "What they doing now?

"Praying," Kenya said operating the radio.

"Huh?" Lovely asked.

"Praying!" Kenya snapped. "They praying, you know BillyBelle like praying." Lovely dug her hand into the Skittles bag.

"What they praying for?"

"Probably cause Chop got killed."

The Skittles in Lovely's hand hit the floorboard and her jaw dropped.

## Chapter 12

Marie's sweet potato pie was the first thing Misty ate since she found out. After the first bite the whole pie was grave danger.

"And you said you weren't hungry." Marie stood over Misty, rubbing her back as she ate. She kept Misty busy all day, cooking, cleaning and playing with children, she even laughed a little. Some folks didn't speak to her. She'd offer them certain items to eat and they wouldn't even nod or shake their head. One little boy, Nathaniel's youngest son, asked her what was white trash exactly? He also inquired about gold diggers and party girls.

"It's a real pretty white girl," she said in his ear as she rubbed his back. "One that'll kiss you everywhere and make your wee wee feel *so so* good." A tent grew in the boy's pants immediately. He left the kitchen and ran out the back door.

Going to a club, a restaurant, on vacation to an island resort, black girls would ignore Misty and flirt with Chop. Some would throw fits like Misty was guilty of wrecking a relationship they had with Chop that never existed. She'd even been stabbed once. The Lance family didn't know that, nor would it have mattered. They wouldn't speak to her but some would speak to each other loudly so she could hear them insult her. It was funny because she didn't know many of these people. Instead of thinking she was hurting over Chop's passing as much as them, really more, they spent their time in his house sniping to each other about the white girl who used him. How many of these "loved ones" wrote Chop off when he was on trial for his life? How many trifling women, black chicks and other colors, would've stood by Chop through that?

"Hurry up with that pie girl we gotta go." Marie patted Misty on the back and disappeared in the sea of people in the living room. It was three o'clock in the evening, Marie had gone to Wal-Mart twice and had to go again . Misty begged her to go.

Misty, finally bathed and looking decent, put on her sunglasses and flower hat. She took her pocketbook from the table and followed Marie out the back door. So many cars, the grass was barely visible. Misty's Lexus was blocked in by three cars.

"We taking my car baby, come on," Marie said, stepping around vehicles. Misty struggled to catch up.

Misty caught up with Marie in the driveway as Diana Helms pulled in. Misty stopped. The heat pressing her skin let her know she wasn't dreaming.

"Girl what are you doing *now*?" Marie asked turning back to Misty. "You trying to burn up out here?"

Diana parked her Ford Expedition in the middle of the driveway.

"Here goes nothing," she said putting on her sunglasses on. She got out of the SUV and walked to the passenger side and pulled out a three layer strawberry shortcake in a glass holder. Strawberry shortcake was Misty's favorite. Diana closed the door and hit the alarm button on her car keys.

"Hey Marie!" Diane waved and Marie waved back smiling. Misty's teeth clenched as she balled the strap of her pocketbook in her hand. Marie walked on to her back yard.

For the first time in four months, mother and daughter stood face to face. They just stood there quietly. Between Misty and the sun, Diana didn't know where the heat was coming from.

"Well hey Ms. Missy," She greeted with her hand on her hip. She instantly regretted bringing the "Ms. Missy" business up so soon. Diana took her hand off her hip. "Um...I made this for ya."

Misty, with her arms crossed, looked away. Marie pulled her Toyota Camry behind Diana's SUV and let it run on idle with the a/c on.

"Look," Diana said, "I'm sorry about what happened, very tragic." She didn't mean to sound condescending. She looked down at the ground. "But since it *did* happen," then she looked up at Misty, "I don't see no reason for you not to come home and-"

"You *wouldn't* see!" Misty snapped. "How could you see a reason and you ain't seen or said nothing to me in God knows how long?"

On the drive over, Diana pictured this going in a totally different direction. First, Misty would let her in the house. After greeting a few smiling black faces, she'd let Misty cry into her bosom and say how wrong she'd been and how right her loving mother was. They'd eat some cake, talk about better times and they'd pack some of Misty's things in time for the pig picking on the fourth. Now Diana felt like boxing.

"Honey, we both know why we weren't talking to each other, but that's over. You're hurting right now. I can still feel it when you hurt. I wanna be there for you." Diana smiled. She didn't mean for it to look as fake as it did.

"Oh okay so that's why you come here, to show how fucking glad you are he's dead!" Misty balled her fists by her sides and shook with every word.

"Hold on now, you watch your mouth." Diana turned pink, the cake holder trembled in her hands as perspiration spotted her Capri pants and neon green tank top. "I was trying to be nice. I ain't glad that black drug dealing son of a bitch is dead. I *am* glad you didn't end up dead with him."

Misty took a deep breath and chuckled as she shook her head.

"Drug dealing son of a bitch huh? That's all you ever saw. Funny how you saw such a monster in Chop but keep looking right past that drug dealing son of a bitch you sleep with every night!"

"Dammit Misty!" Diana shrieked. She looked left then right. There were no eavesdroppers. "Honey, think about the life you're living. Money and drugs baby? The people you grew up with is disgusted with you. But you don't care do you? Why should you care, especially now when everybody you ran from got proved right!"

Marie beeped her horn. Misty attempted to walk off. Diana grabbed her arm, hard.

"What are you doing?" she asked as Misty tried to break away. "You're gonna live out here by yourself, in *Cedar Grove*? This is what you want for your life? You think these people give a damn about you?"

Misty yanked her arm away.

"They may not give a damn about me but Chop did. And I don't give a damn about you!" With that Misty slapped her mother's cake holder out her hand before walking off.

The cover saved a little over half the cake while the rest spilled over the rocks in the driveway. The front of Chop's house had seven windows. Kids, adults and old folks filled every window watching the drama unfold while eating pie. Diana, shoulders sunken, picked up her cake holder. By the time she got her SUV, Misty and Marie were gone.

"Could we take Empire Road instead of the highway please?" asked Misty as

Marie turned off Cedar Grove Road onto Mt Pisgah.

"Sure," Marie said accelerating. She started to turn on the radio then decided against it. "You know, if I was your mama, I'd have beat you with that cake cover. Beat you like the eggs she used to make that cake with."

Misty reclined her seat and sighed.

"Ms. Marie please, I don't wanna-"

"So," Marie said, "You're gonna." She turned on Empire. "I know y'all ain't the best of friends and I know it's a hard time for everybody but that's your mama."

"But you don't know her. I promise if you knew her-"

"I don't have to know her. I know she's your mama." They stopped at the stop sign on the corner of Empire and Holden Beach. A cemetery sat on their right. Marie's knuckles turned white. She shook as she gripped the steering wheel.

"Oh my God Ms. Marie, are you alright!" Misty placed a hand on her shoulder, the vibrations were unnatural. "Okay you're gonna have to let me drive."

Marie had a dream about a cemetery the night before. Billy was digging plot after plot. He didn't have control of his hands. He was crying as he watched his hand go about their work. It hurt Marie every time he finished a plot. She wanted the leave but she had to keep living and enduring the pain. She took her hands off the steering wheel and rubbed them together.

"Girl, get off me!" she snapped batting Misty's hand away. Looking both ways, she took a right on Holden Beach. "Everything good in you came from your mama so don't give me that if you knew her stuff ok." Marie was still shaking but it was coming down. "Nobody and I mean nobody loves you more than that woman Misty, nobody. I know Chop was your Superman but he couldn't take the place of a mama to her daughter. I don't know who you think you fooling. Right now you gotta be strong enough to see past your own bullshit and do the right thing."

Misty, looking out of her window with her arms crossed, sucked her teeth.

"Now all of this is my fault," she whined. Marie shook her head frustration.

"See what I'm saying? I'm telling you to cut this mess out and do what's best for you and all you hear is me pointing blame."

Misty took her shades off and wiped her eyes.

"Well that's what you're doing."

Holden Beach Road ends on Main Street in the town of Shallotte. Wal-Mart is to the right. Marie drove straight through Main Street, heading to Highway 17.

"I thought we were going to Wally World," Misty said.

"I lied," Marie said. Main Street brought them to Highway 17, five miles south of The Long Asphalt plant.

"Ms. Marie I'm sorry." Marie turned south on the highway. "I...I don't know what to do." She screamed with her face in her hands, Marie rolled her eyes. "He's gone...I miss him...my sweetheart is gone."

Marie was tempted again to turn on the radio but she'd just chastised Misty on being rude to her mother. She stopped at a light and looked at the cars at the Dodge dealership to keep from looking at Misty.

"Let me ask you something. Why do you think somebody owes you anything?"

Misty looked to Marie with her mouth open.

"I don't think...what are you talking about?" Misty whined, tears flowing.

"If you didn't notice already a lot of people are mourning Chop right now. A lot of people you don't even know that has given more to him that you'll ever know. The difference is you think somebody's supposed to treat you like some kind of hero or something for sticking it out with him."

Misty stopped crying.

"What?" she asked. Her voice a little deeper than usual. The light turned green.

"You heard me," Marie said pressing the gas. "It's easy to be with somebody when it's all good and trust me, you two didn't never go through a damn thing."

Misty's arms were crossed again. Her face managed a smirk.

"I guess that trial the whole family just suffered, including myself, was just a smooth ride huh. Chop wasn't really about to go to jail for life, them attorneys was just playing around huh."

"Like I said, it's people in this world that truly looked out for Chop, better than you ever could. And ain't none of them carrying on like you."

Misty looked out the window and shook her head.

"Why are you saying this Ms. Marie?"

"Cause you act like you can do this, this grieving the man you loved for the first time in your life by yourself and you ain't got to consider nobody cause you feel bad. I was the oldest child in my family Misty. I buried both my parents, a husband, a daughter and now a grandson. Death is a part of life. Know it and accept it cause you can't change it. Carry it in your head everyday. Not just to cope with losing Chop but so you can quit wasting your life."

"How is my life a waste?" Misty's voice squeaked, her shoulders tried to rub her ears.

Marie stopped at a light.

"Are you serious? You really want to empty bed pans and wash old people all your life? Listen, this is me and you. You're not slow baby. You're young so you still got options. And you got some money somewhere, I know this. That house you and Chop built in Lockwood Folly is done right? Go ahead and move, *call your mother*, then get into school and start getting your life together. The sooner you get to work on that the sooner that weight of grief'll start to lighten. I'm not telling you nothing wrong." Marie accelerated.

"Ms. Marie, I appreciate your concern but just let me handle my life alright. I can handle more than you give me credit for." Misty looked to her right and it felt like the biggest kick in the gut.

"Is that right? Well we gonna see," Marie said pulling into People's Funeral Home. Nathaniel Lance stood outside with Harriett. Cedric Lance, Marie's youngest son stood by his car with EJ. Kiana stood by herself in the shade by the front door.

"Why are were here?" Marie almost barked.

"Well...I know people doubted your intentions with Chop. I'm sure your family questioned his intentions with you. I happen to know you two shared a genuine love. You was his *wifey*, right?" Marie said giggling. She parked at the front door and cut the engine. "Well Ms. Wifey, the funeral is coming in a few days. You gotta pick a casket, a suit and some shoes. And you have to see him today too baby." Misty shook her head furiously.

"No, not today, not yet," she rambled.

"Oh you're going in there and you're going to see him right now. We're burying that boy on the fourth, two days from now." Misty screamed again. She stomped her feet and pounded her legs with her fists. Marie shook her head. This girl was so spoiled. "It's gonna be fine sweetie. Look, think about Chop and what he'd have you do right now."

"No," Misty said, sobbing. "I can't today. Let's just go back and finish cooking or something, please." Marie opened the door.

"I am sick of playing with you." Marie got out and took the keys. "Stay here while I make arrangements to bury *your* fiancé!"

## Chapter 13

"Eric Johnson," Pound said swatting mosquitoes from his face, standing on his front porch in a wife beater house shoes and boxers. "His office hours is eight to five at the muthafuckin Briar Plaza in Shallotte."

"Listen," said Deputy Long as calmly as he could lookin yp at Pound from the front yard. "Just tell me where you were last night between eleven o'clock and one o'clock."

"You really wanna know where I was?" Pound asked leaning over his front rail.

"I need to know so I can confirm it and be on my way." Deputy Long held a pin with a pad. There were six people of interest on Brunswick's south end in the murder of Early Long. Julius "Pound" Belle was the only real person of interest. It was five o'clock and Deputy Long still had three people to see, for nothing.

"If you really gotta know then you know where to go. Eric Johnson, attorney at muthafuckin law. I ain't saying shit on my behalf Terry, you know that." Pound got a kick out of incensing Deputy Long. They went to school together. Terry Long was a wrestling state champ, 185 pound division. And an All-State linebacker. In the spring, they would play hooky together by going to the beach or some girl's house. Back then Pound was still only Julius and on his way to North Carolina A&T University. Terry was going to be a hydroponic gardener.

"Julius, the sheriff told me before I came to call if I couldn't get an alibi from any person of interest."

"Interest for what, what the hell happened?" Pound asked.

"Hold on man. Just tell me where you were last night so I can go. If not I'll have to call the sheriff and stay here while he acquires a warrant for your house. Man, I'm trying to go." Billy pulled into Pound's driveway. "That's good, I can get two out of the way."

"Terry I was right here last night, all night." Pound opened his front door "Kiki, come out here!" Deputy Long nodded. He approached Billy as he got out of the truck.

"Evening Mr. Belle, I'm glad you're here." Billy looked to Pound, Pound rolled his eyes. "I just need to know where you were last night between eleven o'clock and one o'clock last night."

"I was at home man. I stay on Mt. Pisgah."

"Okay, I need somebody to confirm this. Were you home alone?" the deputy asked as he scribbled.

"No, I was with my friend Carol Gore. But I'll tell you what, call my parole officer Shamika Mitchell. She called last night at midnight I think." Deputy Long scribbled her name down.

"Damn, you got Shamika? I heard she don't play man."

"No, she don't and she calls every five minutes it seem like." Terry put his pen and pad away. "You okay Mr. Belle. I didn't mean to do that you yesterday." Billy shrugged.

"You did it though. It's already done so I ain't worried about it. The soreness should disappear in a while."

"Yo Terry," Pound called from the porch, "Tell him Kiki."

"He was here all last night Terry," Kiana said. Deputy Long scribbled Kiana's name.

"Well I'm gone then. Julius, you take car and keep your nose clean. Y'all have a good evening."

"Alright now," Pound said. Deputy Long got in his sheriff's car and pulled away.

"Hey Billy," Kiana greeted. "You want something to eat?"

"I'm alright Kiki," Billy said stepping up the porch. "Pound let me talk to ya."

Pound looked to Kiana. She walked in the house and shut the door. Pound stood there with his arms crossed.

Pound was the only child Billy and Angela meant to have, Chop came unannounced. Pound used to be so scared of people. Couldn't get little Julius to say hey, bye or wave his hand. The only thing that made him smile was being in the bed with his parents or being alone with the radio on. Young Julius was never comfortable with Billy alone, he clung to Marie and Angela. They thought something was wrong with him but Billy knew better. He was just a late bloomer. When he entered the second grade he was promoted to the academically gifted class. Everything came easy to Julius then. He wasn't very emotional. He was the model child before Billy and Angela split.

Billy never talked to Pound about why he locked up. Pound pieced it together the best he could. Billy left Angela then Pound took Billy going to prison as him leaving the family completely. The sense of betrayal burned in Pound. He stopped visiting Billy long before he became an adult and wasn't especially happy when Billy got released. When Pound went to prison for five years, he made good and sure he wasn't at a unit with his dad. Billy kept reaching out, Pound kept leaving him hanging.

"What he say happened last night?" Billy asked looking up at Pound from the yard.

"He ain't never say but it's probably got something to do with that shooting in Phoenix," Pound said looking down and away from Billy. "Been all on the news." Billy stepped onto the porch.

"Yeah, people at Marie's say it was Ike Long's little brother. Said he was in charge of the whole north end. They didn't tell me but I know they think somebody around here did it cause of Chop." Pound looked at his dad and shook his head. "What's going on with you, how you holding up?" Billy leaned on the porch railing.

"Shit I'm good," Pound said leaning on the porch railing across from Billy. "I'm fucked up but hell, ain't nothing I can do about that." Billy pulled out a Newport and lit it.

"Me too," he said, taking a pull. "Know who did it?"

Pound looked down shaking his head.

"I'm a know in a minute. These niggas round here can't hold water."

"Well I just came by to see if you was good,"

"I'm good." Pound studied his dad. "When I find out what you want me to do, tell you?"

Billy looked out to the road. "I don't know if wanna know. I don't know what I'd do," he said, taking a pull.

"Shit, you gonna have your ass in the house before Shamika call, that's what you gonna do. Why shit away the rest of your life?"

"I lost a lot but I didn't shit away nothing." Billy flicked his cigarette butt. He looked his son up and down.

"Hey, you ain't even got to come up here with that funky ass attitude. I was just saying. Ain't like I'm lying." Pound always said what he was thinking, never had trouble doing so. "And you shitted away plenty. Marriage, fatherhood, freedom, all that got flushed when you killed that man. It was the right thing to do but hell, you ain't gotta be right all the time."

"I learned that the hardest way son." Billy looked out to the road. Everything was peaceful a few days ago. Now his world felt like a teapot, it was boiling quietly. Soon it would whistle and there was no telling where he'd be when it did. "Here's something else I learned. You have to consider the ones you love before you act. That keeps you right in your heart if nowhere else. Anger is natural but not always right. If we, you and me, use our wisdom better we can do right by the ones that depend on us at least. I know when it come to you and Treasure and some these knuckleheads it gets more complicated but it's the same rules in place. Do what's best for who you love. Cause if you die, that's who's gonna hurt the most and when you're locked up that's who'll miss you the most." Pound just stared at his dad like he was a fool. Billy stared back. He wanted to humble his son right there at his own house. They had fought once. Marie had a birthday dinner at her house and wanted him to attend with the rest of the family. He didn't come and when Billy called him he hung up on him. Billy rushed over to Pound's house and beat him up in the back yard. Never hit him the face, all body shots. He had to give his son credit, he never stops. Pound was known to black out and feel no pain while brawling in some of the toughest youth prisons in the state. Billy was the only person still in his life that could beat him, or even contend with him "Whatever you do be safe. I love you boy."

Pound chuckled a little, pushed off the railing and went in the house. Billy got in his truck.

In 1870, the blacks living near Holden Beach attended Sunday morning service at Piney Grove Missionary Baptist Church. They attended service by standing y side windows and listening to the white pastor preach to his white congregation. Fed up with having to worship like that, they decided to make use of the many cedar trees a couple miles north of the Piney Grove church. The church they built was Cedar Grove Church. Around the church, they built their own community prompting other groups of blacks in the county follow suit.

As the community grew so did the congregation. They added wings and brick to the church and they renamed it Cedar Grove Missionary Baptist Church. One hundred five years later Billy Bell married a lady from the Cedar Grove community named Angela Hill. Billy has been part of the church and community ever since.

Billy entered the huge red brick house of worship through the front glass doors. He just got off the phone with Shamika. She allowed him to break curfew for choir practice but he had to call first. It was eight o'clock and the young adult choir had already begun. The off white walls in the foyer boasted pictures of former and current pastors and deacons. Rev. Otis Brown was the first pastor and co-founder of Cedar Grove Church, him and Deacon Richard Lance. Angela always mailed Billy the church's monthly newsletter. Ninety percent of current events in the community involved the church and/or a church member. Billy knew about the new audio system, new pastor, paved parking lot and the big new dining hall in the back when it happened. If the newsletter didn't include a Cedar Grove success, tragedy, birth, or death, Angela would include it in her letters. The news that made Billy miss the church more than anything else was the news about scholarship awards and the life saving surgeries being bought for those in need. Billy intended to come home and be with his wife on the front pew but cancer took Angela. She'd be proud that he came back to the church.

He walked through the wooden double doors and down the aisle. The choir sang a song Billy usually lead on Sundays.

*I am. A living testimony*

*You know I could've been dead and gone*

*Lord you let me live on...*

When a choir member was late they would just step into choir stand, grab a hymn book and start singing. Billy made his way up there.

"Hold up, hold up y'all hold up," said Deacon Harvey Gore, Billy's girlfriend's brother. The choir and piano player stopped. "Billy we're practicing for the funeral service. You won't be up here then."

"Yeah I know," Billy said, holding his Chop's Diner hat in his hands. "I just... ya know this where I be on Tuesdays."

The choir laughed. They represented Brunswick's working class. Two teachers, a bus driver, a janitor, a nurse assistant, a truck driver, a social worker, a correctional officer, a store clerk, a mechanic, a power plant worker, a landscaper, a school lunch lady, a bank teller, a line cook (Billy), a barber, a retail store manager and a sheriff's deputy. Mabel Gore was going to lead Billy's song.

Billy didn't know he could sing until he attended church services in prison. He joined the choir inside, performed every Sunday and every holiday service. Billy sat at the front pew behind the piano. The light resting on the choir, even when they weren't in their robes, was a celestial sight. Billy sang along and clapped his hands. Some of his choir members had suffered more than him. His twenty five years in prison were rivaled by some losses and setbacks some of his choir members endured. They all had faith that tomorrow would be better than yesterday. By the end of the fourth song everybody took a break. They sat down and talked and joked around. Billy had been on his feet since five o'clock that morning. His feet, legs and arms got heavy. He was thinking about how Mabel would fare singing lead during the funeral service for the first time when his chin hit his chest.

"Yeah girl, I told her right there in my classroom if she don't do nothing else with her son, make sure he takes a bath before coming. Well she got to rolling her neck-" Mrs. Bryant, the elementary school teacher and Cedar Grove tenor, caught Billy in the corner of her eye, "Hold on girl." She left the choir stand to Billy's pew.

"Billy, Billy!" Billy stirred then his eyes popped up. "Hey Denise, was I snoring." She laughed.

"No, not yet. You need to go home and rest. We'll make sure everything's tight for the service." Billy stood and stretched.

"Well I'll see y'all later, take care." Everybody said their goodbyes to Billy as he left out the side door. Sleep had been scarce since the day Billy raced to the Long Asphalt Plant. He was gonna skip dinner and go to sleep.

The parking lot stayed well lit. The lights came with parking lot expansion. Billy pulled out his keys when a Mazda3 pulled up behind his truck.

"Billy!" Kiana, sat in the car, it tickled her to see Billy startled. Billy looked around and walked over to Kiana's driver side window.

“Hey Kiki. Is everything alright?” he asked.

“Get in,” she said. Billy couldn’t help but notice Kiana’s dress just barely covered her waist. Long brown legs glistened in the church parking lot lights. Her pregnancy was showing but she was a long way from dropping. And she had the prettiest brown eyes.

“Why, what’s going on sweetie, is Pound in trouble?”

“Me and you gotta go somewhere,” she said as her right leg moved her whole body. Billy had heard about Kiana. In his day they would have called her fast. He wanted to talk to Pound about it but he didn’t want to whoop his ass over the conversation.

“Girl I’m tired, I’ve been on my feet all day. Carol just called and told me to come home early so she can-“

“Billy,” she said, furrowing her eyebrows. “Listen boo-boo, I got something that belongs to Chop and you got to come get it.”

“What’s that?” Billy looked around the church yard. He felt guilty for some reason.

“It’s at my mama’s house. Are you getting in or are you gonna follow me over there?”

Billy looked to the road and saw Terrance’s Ford F-150 fly by. It looked like Pound was driving it.

“Can this wait till another time Kiki?” he asked.

“The sooner the better,” Kiana said starting her car.

## Chapter 14

***March 17$^{th}$ The Deal***

**“Are you for real?” Chop asked.**

**“We gotta go see,” Marie said turning the TV off as she stood. Chop sat.**

"I ain't trying to go to know prayer meeting. Can't we catch him at the house or something?"

"Maybe we can catch you at Tabor City Prison," Marie snapped. "They might not let you leave Scotland when they get you in that prison system." Chop stood and left with Marie to church.

Chop had it all. He broke his dependency on Ike Long and Blake Helms to supply him heroine for a more trustworthy supplier with considerably better product. He owned three dozen mobile homes throughout Brunswick County's south end that he rented for a five hundred dollars a month a piece. He capitalized more than anyone from Brunswick County's illegal gun sales, prescription and recreational drug consumption. He could only guess at how much money he was making, it was coming so fast and from so many streams. He concentrated only on who owed him and there were no outstanding debts.

Chop was on the verge of losing it all. A kid at West Brunswick High told the police he sold ecstasy at school for Chop Belle and a another kid dies from the drugs he sold. The state gave the jury a number of charges to convict Chop of. With the right combinaton, Chop could spend the rest of his life in prison.

The prayer meeting hadn't begun yet. The choir hadn't entered, nor had Reverend Greene. Folks were socializing, mostly about Chop's trial. They might really have him this time. His goose was cooked. He might run and leave the country, he doesn't have any kids. His uncle should broker him a deal where he could give up his many drug dealer secrets for lenience on his sentence.

Some were afraid of what may become of the community when Chop went to prison. He forbade every drug dealer from Cedar Grove to sell their product inside the community. Drug users inside the community bought their drugs away from Cedar Grove Road in surroundng neighborhoods and mobile home parks. People didn't complain as much as before about the community going to hell and didn't think about drug activity if it wasn't in their home.

Folks thought it was really over for Chop when he walked into the church with his grandmother at six o'clock at night. He's trying to get religion at the last minute. Should've thought about that when he started selling that shit. I bet he won't go to church when they slam that prison door behind him. I just hate it for Marie, she can't catch a break. She'll be alright, Chop's the one that's got her rolling in that brand new Toyota.

The piano player entered and began playing a hymn. The choir stood and sang as Reverend Greene. After a very long prayer, announcements were read and then there was testimony. Everybody cut eyes at Chop. He cut eyes right back.

"Get up and say something," Marie said in his ear.

"What, I ain't here for all this." Chop looked straight ahead as somebody else got up.

"When she gets done you get your ass up," Marie said. Her whisper was as vicious as her bite.

"Anybody else wanna get up and testify?" asked Reverend Greene.

"Get your ass up!" Marie whispered. Chop looked at her in disbelief as he stood.

"Hey everybody, I um…I just-"

"Hey!"the church resounded. Chop took a second to look around.

"Yeah well, as y'all know I'm going through a trial right now. My side should be done in a few days. I did not do it y'all. I need y'all to know that and to pray for me."

The congregation looked around at each other for a minute.

"Okay Chop." they said. "You got it Chop." "We gonna pray for you boy!" "God's gonna make a way Chop!" "You gonna make it through this Chop!" "God's gonna work it out!"

"Hold up now," Reverend Greene said standing, the gold and burgundy robe flowing over his huge chest and shoulders made him look like a holy super hero. "Erving Belle, you're a good boy, got a good family." He came down from the pulpit and stood at the altar. "You're in trouble now though, big trouble."

The congregation nodded in agreement. Chop was in deep trouble. The reverend left the pulpit and stood at the altar.

"Let's just say this trial goes exactly as you hope and we hope. God gives you your life and spares your from bondage, how will you go forward?" Amens sounded from the congregation and choir stand. "See a lot of us is just living. We turn away from a lot of opportunity for the sake of immediate comfort. I'm just as guilty as anybody else. But you Erving, I imagine if somebody could get out from under the mess you're in they'd straighten all the way up."

"Amen," The congregation seconded.

Reverend Greene walked to Chop's pew. Chop's heart wanted to jump out of his chest. "So what's it gonna be son? What are you gonna do tomorrow that you're not doing today?"

Chop just stood there, clueless as to what to say. Marie had the most evil grin on her face. She was in on this. Chop could've jumped out his skin he was so nervous. Reverend Greene shook his head and smiled. He made his way back down the isle.

"I'll put the dope down," Chop said. The reverend stopped in his tracks. The congregation gasped collectively then went into a talking frenzy.

"Everybody please," the reverend said patting his hands downward to quiet everyone. "What did you say son?"

" Ain't no secret what I do. I been doing it for a long time. I know it ain't right and I let a lot of y'all down but it's over. I get out of this, it's over."

Jesus Christ could've walked through the wooden double doors and the congregation couldn't have been any louder. They just witnessed a miracle. Chop was changing his life. No more drugs in Cedar Grove, that's what the congregation thought they heard. Some didn't believe a damn thing Chop said.

"Okay Erving," said Reverend Greene, nodding with his hands on his hips, "Come with me to my office." He turned to the piano player he played a few key that made the choir rise and sing.The whole congregation stood and sang and clapped. Marie followed Chop down the side isle and to the back to Reverend Greene's office.

Once inside his office, the reverend hugged Chop, lifting him off the floor.

"I'm proud of you son. You made a big commitment to the folks who really love you and I know you'll make good on it." He hustled around to his desk. Chop and Marie made themselves comfortable on the big black leather sofa along the wall.

"So," Chop said rubbing his hands together. Marie was very excited. Chop was eager for the feeling. "What am I doing here exactly?"

The reverend hung his robe on the coat hanger. He pulled a manila folder from the file cabinet and sat.

"Let's see, Ms. Gertie Fields. She's on the sick and shut-in list. The doctor says she needs more help than her family can give her. That dementia has really taken hold. She needs some professional in-home assistance. Her family and them can't handle all the bills they got Erving. They are deep under water and now this." Chop turned to Marie. She swayed left to right, her eyes were closed.

"Hold up Rev, haven't I done enough?" Chop asked, sitting up. Reverend Greene sat the papers on top of the folder. Chop at on that sofa a great number of times to send money where the reverend saw fit. They met at the reverend's house and visited those in need together. He did a great deal in the past. It felt good to help people. Chop had no problem doing whatever the reverend asked.

If Chop didn't rattle the reverend, he would go about his business with Chop in a lackadaisical way. Saying something borderline disrespectful or doing something that gave Reverend Greene pause would was Chop's way of keeping him sharp and better engaged. Reverend Greene couldn't get as familiar as he'd like with Chop. Chop constantly criticized, berated a few times, the reverend for being to trusting of people. A young lady told the church one Sunday morning that mother was sick with no insurance and needed medicine she couldn't afford. Reverend Greene called Chop and gave this lady two thousand dollars. The girl just moved to the area and was an orphan. She had no mother but had a healthy appetite alcohol and new clothing. The egg on the reverend's face rolled off his back. Chop took it upon his self to help the reverend to keep his self in check.

"Sister Marie can you help me out?" Marie opened her eyes smiling.

“What’s gonna happen is you and me are going to see Gertie and her family tomorrow after court and get them straightened out.” The reverend nodded, Chop looked at his grandmother as if to say, ‘Oh Really?’.

“Look, I ain’t got a problem helping nobody, you know that. Right now it feels like I’m being handled.” Reverend Greene’s mouth fell.

“Boy hush, ain’t nobody handling you.” Marie said hitting Chop. Chop turned to Marie.

“It feels like I’m getting handled in here.” Chop turned to Reverend Greene. “And do you know for sure that these people are gonna do what they say with this money?” Marie hit him again.

“Well,” Reverend Greene said leaning back. “I know all the good you’ve done Erving. I don’t ever want you to feel like I or anyone else takes it fore granted. But my job and my joy is to help my flock and the community as much as possible. You’ve been instrumental in bringing me a lot of joy over the years.” The reverend stood and walked around the desk. He sat on the front of his desk. “You know that even if you weren’t in a bind I’d have had you up in here like I’ve been doing for years. You’re the backbone of this community Erving. This situation is proof that good deeds pay off. It’s not good that this lady is sick but what have you and I been coming together to do for so long? Help the sick people in this community, feed the hungry in a number of communities. Together we make God smile. Now life has thrown you a curveball and the clearest way out of it is doing this righteous work you’ve been doing the whole time. That’s God son, plain and simple. Are you gonna help the Fields family out? I know without a shadow of a doubt that they are in such great need.” Chop nodded. He looked to Marie and back to Reverend Greene. If this was another con by somebody targeting the reverend’s soft heart...

“Yeah, I’m a see’em tomorrow. I got that, they good.” Marie put her hand on Chop’s knee.

“You’s a good boy,” she said as she stood. “A good man. My Lord wouldn’t have nothing happen to you. Come on, everything is done.” Chop stood. He the reverend shook hands and hugged.

"It's done," Reverend Greene said looking Chop in his eyes.

"Come on boy," Marie said. "fore we miss this offering." Chop looked at the Reverend and nodded as he backed out of the office.

"Hold on," said Reverend Greene. "What you said outside about putting down the dope. If you don't put it down you'd be insulting God. We live by God's word son and he takes us for our word. Don't play with him." Chop nodded as Marie rubbed his back. When he closed the door Reverend Greene got on the phone.

"Gregory...hey man this is Fred...yeah Rev. Fred...look, you remember what we talked about last week...yeah...what she say...she said she would...now that's alright right there Greg. Yes...oh he fitna take care of that...he fitna get y'all straight tomorrow...I'm a put him on some more sick and shut-in folks that's hurting...oh he fitna kick out, all the way out...so she gone do it... you sure...alright then, thanks again brother...alright."

Reverend Greene was speaking with Gregory Cobb. Gregory's daughter was Tara Cobb of Leland, juror number four in Chop's trial. Once Tara was selected, Marie and the reverend went about the work of persuading her to make sure the jury found Chop guilty of nothing. Tara Cobb didn't know Chop or his family and she'd been talking to her dad about the case against the judge's orders. The state's case seemed weak, she reasoned but seeing the victim's family everyday was starting to wear on her. She had a fiancé named Antonio Knight from Cedar Grove. They met in Winston-Salem at Winston-Salem State University. They had been a couple for six years and engaged for two. Every time they set a date to marry Antonio had to bail his family out of an emergency, keeping him from buying a house and starting a family. He just got his credit back in order when the doctor caring for his grandmother, Gertie Fields, said she had to be put in a home or get in-home care. Gregory shared this bit of info with Reverend Greene and Sister Marie. After Gregory got a confirmation from Tara that she'd do what he asked regarding the trial he called the reverend to finish the deal. Chop agreeing to stop selling drugs wasn't part of the deal, more of an unexpected perk. Reverend Greene handled him. At his desk, he prayed prayed Chop would stay on the path he promised because the good fortune they stumbled upon with Gregory Fields wasn't promised for the future.

## Chapter 15

*Anita, Kiana's Mother, Safe Keeper*

Kiana's mom stayed in Shell Point, a small community between Holden Beach and Shallotte. Relief fell over Billy when saw Kiana's mother's Cutlass in the yard. And the lights were on in the small brick house.

"Anita got something cooked in there?" Billy said as he and Kiana walked to the front door. Kiana shrugged, putting her key in the knob.

Cinnamon air freshener and a strong undercurrent of something deep fried came out of the walls.

"Shoes," Kiana said kicking off her Air Force Ones. Billy kicked off his Reebok Classics.

Thirty eight years ago Anita married Arthur Brown from Cedar Grove. He used to be one of Billy's good friends. He worked for the state Department of Transportation for years, then he started getting high. Arthur lost his job and Anita kicked him out of the house. He moved into his mother's house and became a runner for the hustlers in and around Cedar Grove. One night, in the middle of a fistfight with a kid who claimed Arthur broke into his house, Arthur had a heart attack and died.

Anita sat in the living room on the couch. Wearing a blue sheer night gown, her snores rivaled some of the old lifers Billy left in prison.

"What business did Chop have with your mama Kiki?" Anita used to be the finest woman in Cedar Grove, light brown skin like Kiana's with dimples in her heart shaped face, big brown eyes, long black curly hair and a rump that used to snatch eyes out of sockets. Even after marriage Arthur had to fight for Anita. Kiana shook her mother awake.

"Girl what the hell you doing!" Anita barked. Kiana stepped to the side so Anita could see Billy. She tied her robe and stood. Her teeth used to be straight, white and perfect. Now they had spaced out while gravity ravaged her body. Didn't stop her from smiling.

"Hey Billy," she greeted as they hugged.

"Hey now," Billy said. Kiana took Anita's seat.

"What brings you here this time of night?" Billy tried but didn't respond. Anita turned to Kiana and back to Billy. "You alright Billy? Do you know why you're here?"

"He's here to get Chop's stuff mama." Anita turned to Kiana and back at Billy.

"Good," she said, leaving the den and going to closet in the hallway. Kiana came up and nudged Billy.

"Come on," she said. Anita pulled a dirty bucket out of the hall closet from under a bunch comforters. She took a respirator mask out of the bucket and handed it to Billy. She handed him a Tyvek coverall to protect his shoes and clothes. She took two flashlights, a box of moth balls, a can of spray wrapped in duct tape and marched to the front door. "Come on," she said.

The opening for the crawl space on Anita's house was in the back under the master bedroom. The light on the side of Anita's house was out.

"Kiki you didn't say nothing about crawling under this house," Billy said.

"I know," Kiana said. "But it be best if you just take Chop's safe now."

"Yeah," Anita said, pulling a cigarette from the pocket on her robe. "Cause if you don't get it now I'm calling the police and I'm letting them get it." Once at the back of the house, Anita lifted the tiny hook on the door and opened the crawl space. She turned on a flashlight, gave it to Billy, then she lit her cigarette. "He got the safe at the other end of the house under the kitchen. Chop cleaned it up down there Billy, new insulation, fresh thick plastic on the ground and no mold nowhere." Billy nodded taking the other flash light . He squatted down in front of the opening and shined the light inside. "But you gotta take these mothballs cause he got two big ass copperheads in there."

"What!" Billy stood and flashed the light in Anita's face.

"And they big too Billy. Chop's ignant ass got'em down there for protection he say." Anita looked at Billy like 'what's the big deal?'. "He got mothballs down there already around the safe. Be careful now."

"Please Billy," said Kiana. "Chop had a lot of important stuff in that safe. You have to get it now please. Chop would want you to have it." Billy wanted to hit something. He wasn't scared of much but he feared snakes. With a balled up face he put on the Tyvek suit.

"Here Billy," Anita spraying Billy with a sulfur infused repellent. "Them snakes ain't gonna fuck with ya now. Chop would stay down there for hours and wouldn't see the snakes."

"But they down there though," Billy said.

"Oh yeah, they down there," Anita said nodding. Billy took the mothballs and the flashlight. He shook his head and crawled under the house.

The crawl space was immaculate. It looked as if Billy was under a newly built house. He crawled on his hands and knees. Various pipes forced him to move on his forearms. He could hear the snakes. They rested on rocks stored in the corners of the house. They were moving. Were they approaching Billy or going the opposite direction, Billy wasn't sure. Anxiety plagued him but never overcame him, he prayed silently until he reached the other side of the house.

A grey safe sat between a number thick white industrial strength trash bags. They were filled with something that made them sit higher than the safe. Billy, laying on his stomach shook the safe. It wasn't bolted to anything but would be a force to negotiate. He rolled on his back and was about to spin his legs to the safe. He moved one the bags beside safe. They were filled with foot long rectangular squares. Billy shined his light on six bags. He opened one and pulled out a square.

"Oh Lord have mercy," Billy said, turning back on his stomach, resting on his elbows.

The squares were plastic wrapped stacks of dollar bills. Billy held a foot tall stack of twenties. He put it back and grabbed the safe.

"You coming out?" Anita asked, hearing Billy's grunts get closer as he labored over the plastic. Billy pushed the safe out into the yard then got from under the house.

"Where's Kiki?" he asked, picking up the safe and walking to the truck.

"She had to get back to lil J. That son of yours been gone all day. Sent one his friends by the house for some clothes so he can go out tonight from wherever he at. Can you believe that shit?"

Billy put the safe in the bed of his truck. He pulled off the mask and took a cigarette from inside the driver side door. He gave one to Anita.

"Well," Anita said through deep. "There it is."

"What's in there?" .

"I guess money, shit. The last time he was here he was putting some in." She leaned on the truck.

"Why didn't y'all get Pound to take this?" Billy asked flicking cigarette ash.

"Cause it don't belong to his sorry ass," Anita said, rolling her neck. "I know that's your son and everything Billy but that nigga ain't worth shit. He treats my daughter like a dog and don't spend no time with Lil' J."

"Well," Bill said between pulls. "I told him to do better by J but all he say is Lil' J ain't-"

"So what he ain't his, shit!" Anita shouted. "That nigga can do *something* with the boy, with his sorry ass."

Billy's lady friend Carol called his cell phone.

"Hey baby...I'm over here to Anita's...yeah Anita Hill...Chop left a safe under the doggone house and Anita just wanted it gone 'fore somebody come and...Oh I'm about to leave in while so you can...well don't warm it up yet, I'll call when I'm on my way...well don't worry about it, just go to sleep and I'll warm it up when get in...ok love you too."

Anita threw her cigarette in the yard. "You gonna help us when this baby come right Billy?"

Billy crossed his arms.

"Sure, I'm a do everything I can for me grand boy." Anita nodded.

"That's good Billy cause um...that baby's your grandchild but Pound ain't the daddy." she took a cigarette from her robe pocket, she kept her eyes on Billy.

"What?" Billy said. He was as disgusted with the messenger as he was the message. "Are you sure?" Anita nodded. "How the hell you know?" Anita lit her cigarette, she took a deep pull and exhaled.

"Billy, your late son and my daughter been at it for a long time. They been spending a lot of time right there in Kiana's old room," Anita pointed the two fingers holding her cigarette at the window on the right of the house. "I thought for a minute she was bringing your old ass back to the room. Pound don't even touch her."

"Does Pound know?" Billy uttered softly, looking over his shoulder.

"Fuck that nigga if he *do* know!" she snarled. "What he gonna do about it?"

"Anita, does he *know*?"

"I don't know if he know. He ain't said nothing, hell. Kiki ain't in the hospital shot the hell up so I guess he's still in the dark about it." Billy opened his car door for another cigarette.

"Well listen," Billy said grabbing the respiratory mask from the ground. "Chop left some more stuff down there I gotta get."

"Go 'head," Anita said walking to her front door. She stopped and turned to Billy. "you need me?" she asked flicking her flashlight on and off.

"No I got it." Billy flicked the flashlight she gave him on and off.

"And um...my mortgage is six hundred dollars a month. Chop, God bless his soul, was late on this month's payment. When you crack this thing open, you need to get at me."

## Chapter 16

*July 3rd Midnight*

*Andre Long Ex Best Friend.*

"Andre Long, you sorry son of a bitch, where's my baby!"

"Ms. McKinley, I swear I don't know," said Andre over the phone. "I haven't seen her in a week, honest."

"No Andre, something's wrong. She usually sends a text message er' something. My sister's daughter was with her too and she ain't from her neither. I know you know something." Ms. McKinley mumbled and growled through tears. Andre rolled his eyes through the phone. "Is there anybody you can think of Andre, anybody who might know where she is?"

"I've been calling everybody I know since we talked last night. Nobody's seen her. She usually calls me too. We're gonna find her, I promise."

"Find my baby Andre, you *better* find her." Ms. McKinley she hung up her phone.

"Fuck that bitch," Andre said after the call ended. Who knew or cared where those little sluts were? Uncle Early had them but he was killed. Those little pieces of shit probably set him up.

The toilet flushed in the bathroom of his condo. It was time to take Bree, a blond seventeen year old junior from North Myrtle Beach High School back to the mall. He'd drop her off in the mall parking lot to her dad's car was. Her dad was a dentist and her mom was a realtor. Bree worked at American Cookie in the mall. The mall closed two hours ago. Her butt, mouth and pussy was sore and she was high out of her mind.

"Damn!" Pound said letting the shovel fall. He stood straight and planted both hands on the small of his back. A weed break tempted him. One hour digging and he was barley six feet into the earth. The Gatorade he bought from the store was all gone. He grabbed the shovel and gave it twenty more minutes.

After flattening the bottom of the hole he climbed out went to the truck. The girls were lifeless, neck snapped and naked. Heather was a little heavier than Cassandra so Pound grabbed her first. The hole was further than fifty yards from the truck. Due to the trees and thick briar patches, Pound couldn't drag her in a straight line. Every stump and tree root he pulled her over seemed to add ten pounds. After kicking her in the hole Pound grabbed two handfuls of his jeans by the knees, sucking air as his black tee soaked in sweat. Pound should have brought Mack T with him. He could have toted both girls on his shoulders and they'd already be done.

When it came to body disposal, Pound preferred to be alone. He didn't tell Mack T about Uncle Early or the girls and they watched the afternoon new about Early together. God forbid the feds put Mack T in a cell for the rest of his life and he realizes he can't take it. Mack T was no snitch but neither was anybody else until they snitched. During his five year stay in prison, Pound found that it was the friend who did the most damage.

The truck sat behind a pink and white trailer in St. Helena. St. Helena is a rural town in Pender County, two counties away from Brunswick County. The trailer used to belong to Kara Webster, a girl Pound used to see before she moved to Greensboro. Nobody moved into the trailer yet. It sat a hundred feet from the road with a couple miles of thick woods in the back. The pole at the road shined away from the trailer making it invisible at night. After pulling Cassandra through the woods and in the hole Pound took off the gloves and lit a blunt, casually kicking dirt over Cassandra and Heather's face. He shoveled what he felt was enough dirt and hit the highway. Once he reached Wilmington it was midnight. He called Mack T.

"What's up nigga?" Pound greeted. "You get them clothes?"

"Yeah I got everything. I got the chains and the rings and earrings too. Where you at?"

"About twenty minutes out. You get the deodorant and cologne and toothbrush and shit?"

"Nigga I said I got everything. Kiana put all that in the bag. You're good, now come on. The shit done started two hours ago." When the phone call ended, Pound pulled into Mack T's driveway in Winnabow.

Winnabow is a rural community on Highway 17 between the towns of Bolivia and Leland. Mack T had a place in Cedar Grove and also stayed with his baby's mother Porsche in Winnabow. She was nice enough. She knew when to be quiet and kept the kids and house clean. The only problem was Porsche let the kids stay up all night long, even on a school night. Tasha, 14 and Jalil, aka Lil Mack, fifteen, would argue at the top of their lungs over the phone, the TV or just for practice. Mack T often had to threaten bodily harm to his kids in front of Pound. They would settle down but not out of fear of their dad. Mack T to them was as soft as a teddy bear. A teddy bear that carried around a lot of money and didn't hesitate to spoil his children, unless they were disrespectful. Pound drove up the long bow like driveway and parked in the back yard. The little wooden house had lights on in every window. Pound would bet money that everybody was in the den watching a movie.

Sitting on the steps, Mack T stood when Pound cut off the truck.

Mack T was the oldest son of Cedric Lance, Angela and Nathaniel's youngest brother. Mack T was born when Cedric was in high school. Marie raised him while Cedric went to college. When Cedric graduated he married a lady who wasn't Mack T' mother and moved to Winston Salem, North Carolina. Cedric took his son with him but six years Cedric's wife couldn't tolerate him. Mack T ran with the wrong crowd of kids and he was constantly suspended from school for fighting. Cedric's wife hated embarrassment but was afraid to discipline Mack T. Cedric sent him back home to Marie.

"Come on nigga, we ain't got much time," he said giving Pound a pound. The T in Mack T's name meant Tonka. He was barely five feet tall, hence the name Tonka (Tonka Truck), but strong as hell, like a Mack truck. He also owned a tractor trailer that drove to Texas once a month.. He resembled a husky turtle without a shell, his thin side burns connected to the close cut beard on his pug like dark brown face. Pound followed him in the house where the family sat watching a movie from the Saw series on an eighty inch flat screen.

“Hey Pound,” greeted Porsche and Lil Mack, their eyes never left the screen. Pound and Mack walked on by. They went into the hall bathroom.

Mack sat on the sink while Pound undressed in the shower.

“We on that kush tonight boy! OG,” Mack T said, pulling out a blunt as slim as an ink pen. Pound turned on the shower and Mack lit the blunt.

“Treasure called today,” Pound said, lathering the shampoo in his dreads. Mack took a long pull from the blunt.

“Fuck Treasure,” Mack said, trying to speak while keeping the smoke in his lungs. He’d been trying to get into Treasure’s panties since high school. She said he was too short.

“Anyway,” Pound said. “She said Neil came through today on some bullshit.”

“Dry your hand,” Mack said. When Pound put his hand over the shower curtain Mack handed him the blunt. “Shit, I liked to spent my whole knot with that little nigga the other day. He had every pair of Js in a bunch wild colors. *And* his Js is real. I got some Space Jam Js, some Melo Js, CP3 Js, some Blake Js. I got the youngins’ school shoes for the whole year.”

“Word,” Pound said passing Mack the blunt back. “He came at Treasure today saying...the boy say he the future now.” Having a coughing fit, Pound passed the blunt back.

“The future? He fitna open a Foot Locker?” Mack asked before taking a hit.

“Goddamn that shit hit. I don’t even want no more,” Pound said. “But yeah, that’s what I’m saying. What else is this lil’ nigga talking about? But no, he say he got bricks now. He’s the future, now that *Chop’s* gone.”

“No, hell no, my lil’ cousin ain’t said no shit like that.” Mack T hit the blunt gently, practically peck kissed it.

“He must of did. Treasure ain’t gone lie about no shit like that.” Mack got off the sink, his pudgy face screwed up.

“So you saying Neal...my little sneaker pushing ass cousin is *happy* about Chop being gone? And telling niggas he got designs on filling his shoes?"

"Mack!" Mack looked up to see Pound's dry hand hanging over the shower curtain. He passed him the blunt. "That ain't all." Pound continued after giving the blunt a peck kiss. "He told Treasure that he already got Lavelle and them buying a brick and a half a week. I called Lavelle and he said Neal got some good boy. He said it's just like the shit he was getting outta Leland for a while." Mack jaw dropped.

"Oh my fucking God!" he said. "Neal was with them niggas who got Ike's brother!" Pound turned the water off and grabbed the towel.

"That's what Lavelle was thinking. He got Neal to give him some dope on credit. He just gave the nigga a free brick and a half." Pound put on some boxers. They left the shower and went into Porsche's room.

"I ain't know the nigga was moving like that though. What Treasure say when the nigga said all this?" Pound put some black jeans on and some grey socks.

"Nigga, Neal came through there on his white Kawasaki Ninja. After hearing that bullshit Treasure took the little nigga's helmet and beat him all in the head. Had him stuck in Supply drunk. One of his baby's mamas had to come get him. The Ninja's still sitting in the yard."

"Man," Mack T said putting his head in his hand. He relit the blunt. "I'll be in the den. Hurry up nigga, we late."

"Chill out nigga, we always late."

Pound put on his baby powder, white tee, and black jeans. His black belt had a black skull buckle. Neal sold him the pair of white canvas Nike Hyderdunk sneakers with the black check. He put diamond earrings the size of Peanut M&Ms in his ears. The oversized gold watch had a thick diamond bezel. Diamonds encrusted the thick gold chain in Ziploc bag. His charm was an Egyptian hawk, the symbol of Horus. The wings, the body and sun disk on its head were covered in diamonds. Pound left Porsche's room.

"Lil Mack, come outside with me," he said walking past everybody. Lil Mack, like a rookie anxious to get off the bench, sprung from the sofa and followed Pound out the door. On the steps, Pound pulled out his bankroll. "I want you to wash this truck." He handed Lil Mack a hundred dollar bill. "Wash the inside windows, the seats, wash the floorboard, the dash, the doors, the outside windows, the hood, especially the bed, the whole outside, the tires and the bumpers. Do it tonight, right now."

"I gotcha Pound," Lil Mack stuffed the money in his pocket and ran off to fetch a bucket.

"You ready to ride homie?" asked Mack T. He had another blunt between his lips. Pound nodded.

Mack T kept his car in what Pound called a tent garage. It was a Carport garage canopy big enough for a SUV, made of polyurethane and assembled like a tent. Mack T unzipped the doors. He and Pound pulled the doors to the sides. The black and chrome 79' Chevelle had been perfectly waxed and buffed. The moonlight made it look like marble. The interior was two weeks old, light grey leather with black trim on the bucket seats. The stick shift handle was a big black and grey marble sporting the letters DGB, Dem Grove Boys. Pound got in on the passenger side.

"We riding light or heavy?" he asked, as Mack T pulled one of four iPods from the glove compartment. He turned it on and hooked it up to the stereo.

"Heavy and light," Mack said. He pulled two glocks from a compartment behind the passenger seat. "I got two compact forty cals."

"What I got?" Pound asked. Mack did something with the left side of his seat and two compartment opened, one behind the driver seat and the bottom of the back seat.

"Shit, we gonna share these to 40s and we gonna share these." Pound grabbed the M16 from under the back seat. He admired it and put it back. He pulled the 12-auge automatic shotgun out of the back of the driver seat. He pumped it once and put it back.

"Cool," Pound said, taking the blunt from Mack T. "I feel better."

Mack T pushed the start button beside the steering wheel. The 400 small block engine roared to life. The white LCD screen showed the speedometer, the RPM meter and a full tank of gas.

"We don't need to be heavy tonight," Mack T said, backing out of the tent garage. Scarface's "Untouchable" album played through eight speakers, two in the trunk were twelve inches. Before putting the iPod in the custom stand in front of the stick shift, Pound selected the Scarface song "Smile". Mack T took the blunt and pulled out of the driveway.

Highway 17 connected everybody in Brunswick County to each other and the county to everywhere else. From Cedar Grove to North Myrtle Beach, South Carolina is thirty eight miles south on the Highway. From Cedar Grove to Wilmington in New Hanover County was thirty six miles north. Pound and Mack T used to walk fifteen miles to the Mulberry neighborhood of Shallotte to go to the club. As Mack T sped toward the state line Pound reclined his seat and closed his eyes.

Due to their dad being locked up and their mom working all the time Chop became Pound's responsibility and only disciplinarian. He never hit Chop with a belt, he'd take his TV and video games, lock them away and forbid him to go outside. Chop would try to fight Pound and Pound would whoop him every time. Then he'd extend the punishment he'd already put in place. It was always Pound who did the punishing because Angela was often too tired to deal with him. Pound was his mother's enforcer and the family's protector. This is why he went to prison.

Angela began seeing Ike Long. Between the two brothers, Ike courted Pound first. He bought him clothes and video games and even talked about buying him a car. If Marie couldn't drive him or Angela was at work, Pound took his bike to Holden Beach where he worked as a stocker at the supermarket. Pound sold crack for Ike because he needed a car. He left Chop at home with Ike's son Andre while he stayed out all night and day. It was all good until Ike started hitting Angela.

She had plans to be Mrs. Long. Ike had a Mrs. Long already, he needed a girlfriend. Arguments lead to fights and to Pound attacking Ike. Angela and Pound fell out over the situation. To Angela, Pound was butting into "grown folks" business. He was confused. How was he was supposed to ignore her black eyes, welts and humiliation. He started hating his mother for accepting such treatment. Ike stopped hitting Angela but he never stopped abusing her with words. He stopped taking her out, giving her money, paying bills, and calling before breaking plans. Somehow he was able get Chop to hustle for him. The kid was eager to get from under his big brother's authority. Money, to him, could provide that.

The trouble started when a young Chop and Andre Long gave Tito, an older hustler from Cedar Grove, an ounce of crack on credit. The day he was supposed to have the money came and went. Days turned to weeks. After a month of constant threats, Chop and Andre took action. They kicked in Tito's door, dragged him outside and beat him like a dog that just bit a child. They punched, kicked and stomped on him while cursing his soul. Tito's jaw was broken in two different places, his front teeth were kicked out, eyes were swollen shut, and his face was swollen with bruises and fluid. He had three broken ribs, one lung was on the verge of collapsing. His right leg was broken at the knee and he suffered a fractured skull.

And they pissed on Tito.

Chop bought a semi automatic 9mm a week before. He shot the windows out in front of Tito's trailer, startling his girlfriend and his daughter. The girlfriend called 911 and an ambulance came in time to save Tito's life. When the cops asked him who did this he said he didn't know. His girlfriend, not a Cedar Grove native, told them Chop did it over drugs. The cops arrested Chop that day for shooting in an occupied dwelling and inflicting serious injury with the intent to kill, fifty thousand dollar bond. Andre Long got the same. Ike bailed his son out.

Pound continued selling drugs, just not Ike's drugs. He washed his hands with Ike and Angela. He rented a trailer on Holden Beach Road and became a DJ, DJ Jewels. To keep him off his ass, Chop bought him a eight channel mixer, an amp, four speakers and all the CDs from the store. Pound, nineteen at the time, bailed fourteen year old Chop out of jail and got him a lawyer.

Chop plead not guilty, but his lawyer informed him that he'd have to do some time. Despite this being Chop's first offense, the district attorney's office didn't want to deal, they wanted a trial. Pound visited Tito in the hospital and told him to tell to the police that he beat him up by himself, not Chop and Andre. He told Tito to convince his girlfriend to recant her statement and write a new one saying what Pound wanted it to say. Pound forgave Tito's debt to Chop and paid him a thousand dollars to do as he said.

Tito's girlfriend didn't want to do as Pound said. Chop had gotten out control. Tito wasn't his first victim. Chop had a habit of shooting somebody's car, nightclub, house, or neighborhood. People, mostly kids around Chop's age and older folks in the streets, were getting hurt. The bullets that he sent through Tito's house were a few inches from his daughter's head. She felt it would be for the best if Chop went away for while. Pound told the girl, thirty seven at the time, that if Chop did one day in prison behind the incident involving Tito he was going to personally kill everybody she loved, starting with her ten year old daughter ,then Tito, then her. She left the hospital, five hundred dollars richer and with a new statement for the district attorney's office. Her new statement said she never claimed to see the beating or shooting. She only knew that Tito owed somebody money for drugs and never intended to pay it back. She remembered hearing Pound's voice outside though.

The last thing Pound wanted to happen is for Chop to become a convict like their dad. Without telling a soul he turned himself in to the Brunswick County Sheriff's Office in Bolivia. The detectives didn't buy it at first. The crime fit the narrative that had already been growing of young Chop in Cedar Grove. He was angry, violent and quick to shoot. Pound gave them specific details of the crime and circumstances around it. Details Tito, at Pound's insistence, corroborated. Pound accepted a plea for ten to fourteen years in prison on various charges.

As a youth in prison Pound had to fight every day. He was big but easily overmatched by many experienced brawlers who came up since preadolescence in the justice system. He got in shape and practiced his hand speed. His wins eclipsed his losses 7 to 1 by his second year. This was the first time he was referred to as Pound. Julius became a feared knock out artist from nowhere. Nowhere because most youth inmates came from North Carolina's cities. Even inmates from other rural areas had never heard of Brunswick County let alone Cedar Grove.

Treasure would visit Pound any time Marie didn't. Chop and Angela was still on Billy's visiting list. Over the phone Pound used to talk to Treasure's then boyfriend

Tremaine Gore. He was the owner of a new club in Little River, South Carolina called Anytime's. He also had cocaine by the carload. Treasure wanted Chop to leave Ike alone and buy from Tremaine. Pound said he'd talk to him. It sickened him that his little brother had embraced Ike like a surrogate father. As Pound did time with older inmates, some of them from Brunswick County told stories of Ike Long's betrayals and setups. He had the Sheriff in his pocket and over the years he worked with four different head district attorneys targeting low level dealers. Ike Long, Sheriff Helms, a few deputies and two district attorneys collaborated with a handful of judges who paid them to produce defendants they could punish with prison time. Prison officials throughout the state bankrolled a number of operations like this. Ike shared this with Chop and offered him protection from it.

In the middle of his fifth year, Pounds' lawyer EJ convinced the judge to consolidate Pound's sentences, giving him only a few months to serve. By the time he was released Ike and Angela's relationship was on the rocks. Chop owned Cedar Grove but Ike owned Chop. Pound took the role of instigator, showing up to his mother's house unannounced to get in cursing matches with Ike. One day Ike pulled a knife on Pound and Pound broke his jaw, cracked his eye socket and broke his ribs. Ike's face was never the same. When Ike recovered he took it out on Angela, slapping her around and even spitting on her. Angela, for the first time called Chop for help. Chop came to the house and dragged Ike out, threw his stuff out of the house into the road and forbade him to come back. They actually carried on a business relationship after the incident. Heroine had come to Brunswick County in a major way. Ike began diluting Chop's heroine while he gave his son Andre the best dope available. That's when Chop came to Pound, becoming the forth and last person to deal directly with them. Treasure, Tremaine Gore, and Bucc, a fellow Cedar Grove gangster were the other three.

In prison, Pound became friends with a couple Mexicans from Dallas, Texas. When Pound was released he and Mack T took a trip to Texas and became buyers of premium heroine for a wholesale price. Money poured in. Pound owned a landscaping business and bought contracts for his company in New Hanover, Pender and Horry Counties.

Chop, with the help of his longtime girlfriend Misty, created a business relationship with the sheriff. Sheriff Helms wanted Chop to make money setting up dealers from Cedar Grove. Chop wanted to pay the sheriff to keep him in the loop about future raids and every confidential informant in the county. On the strength of his daughter Sheriff Helms gave Chop his wish. Chop paid the sheriff well for it. Ten thousand dollars a month and Chop would know of any heat approaching him before it got to him.

The “Last of A Dying Breed” album started when Mack T crossed the state line. Anytime’s sat on a narrow back road in the Little River woods with only moonlight shining on the street. Cars filled the dirt and grass parking lot and lined the road on both sides. People were walking up the road to the club. Some women wore dresses so short and tight they looked like long baby-tees. Some people were laughing and some were crying, especially the women. Everybody had a fifth of something and a blunt as they walked. They were mourning and celebrating Chop’s life. Two parking spots in the front of Anytime’s were reserved for Pound and Mack T. They pulled into the parking lot.

“Hold up Mack.” Pound tilted his head to see the side of the club. “Go to the oak tree.”

Mack rolled to the side of the building where a huge oak tree stood. Club Anytime’s was a one-story white cinderblock building. There was a plain white and black hand-painted ply wood sign in the front saying Anytime’s. A group of guys sat and stood on a couple scaffolds painting the side of the club. Some painted, most called to the women coming from the road. Some smoked weed and bounced to the bass thumping through the walls. Pound got out of the car.

It looked like somebody took a picture of Chop and blew it up to fit the side of the building. Two big words ran down the back side the building, R.I.P CHOP. Chop was painted in color. He wore his gold chain with the big butcher’s blade charm Misty bought for him. They had the diamonds just right. He stood in front of tall cedar trees painted forest green. They seemed to reflect a light shining from Chop. Pound was almost overwhelmed. That picture was taken in Anytime’s with Pound along side Chop and Tremaine eleven years ago, it was Pound’s release party. At the time a lot of things were up in the air between the brothers. Chop made a lot of ridiculous promises in the V.I.P that night, the most important was to stop dealing with Ike Long. He came through on that.

"Damn," Mack T said. The building looked like a billboard for a movie. "Them niggas *did* that."

"Yo!" Pound called to the painters. "Who the fuck told y'all to do that?"

"Tremaine!" they said. After double parking, Pound and Mack T skipped the whole line and entered the club. The guard let them through with a hug and a dap, no pat downs.

Anytime's walls were all mirrors. Green and red lights bounced off of them as the five foot speakers and blunt smoke battled for the atmosphere. Silver banners with Chop's name hung behind the bar and along the front of the club. Various flyers with Chop's face and a bucther's knife were floating everywhere. They said, "We Miss You Chop," We Love You Chop," "Chop Belle The Don," and "Chop Forever". Guys were giving drunken salutes to the hanging pictures, some drunken women cried and talked to the pictures, trying to hug them. There was barely room to move. The fire marshal had shut the club down before for having too many patrons. They were from all over Brunswick County's south end, Cedar Grove, Royal Oak section of Supply, Mulberry, Shallotte, Seaside, Pine Crest, Longwood, Ash, Calabash, Airport, Thomasboro, Ocean Isle beach, Holden Beach and Sunset Beach but mainly Cedar Grove. It looked as if people were on top of people. Some were dancing, barely anybody held up the wall. Two people along with Tremaine's brother, Sean, tended the bar.

Pound made his way to the bar giving daps and hugs. He could feel the grief from everybody. His little brother was missed. It came from being fair with people. He couldn't be crossed but he wouldn't cheat anybody. If anything, he'd bless whoever he dealt with. That's how his clientele grew so fast. That's the real reason why those folks visited Pound that evening. Pound took notice of who was there and who wasn't. Aside from Mack T, the DGBz, Tremaine and all his people, there weren't many folks in the club he wouldn't put a hole in. Sean's tip buckets were overflowing with money. He was sweating and screaming orders over the music. Pound found a spot at the bar, Mack T was on the floor with a red bone freak.

"Pound, my nigga!" Sean greeted. He and Pound lifted themselves over the bar to hug. "I loved Chop, man. You hear me? That was my brother. Hearing about that nigga being gone hurt my mama nigga! My nieces, my kids, my baby mamas, everybody fucked up." Pound nodded to everything and hugged him tighter then sat back down.

"Where Tremaine at?" he asked when Sean came back and gave him a fifth bottle of Hennessy Black.

"He in the back. Probably got one them hoes in there! You see how he got Chop on the side of the club?" Pound nodded. Sean pointed behind him. "Here he come now!"

Tremaine, fifty five years old, strolled through the club. A tall slim dark skinned brother with no grey hairs in his thumb thick dreadlocks stopping at the small of his back. He looked like he was Pound's age. The women loved them, that's why he and Treasure couldn't make it. Everyday he was with at least a couple girls while giving at least twenty apologies to the rest. He always had a new girl. The last time he spoke to Pound he introduced him to Dalia, Dalia introduced Pound to Carmen.

"Tre, what's good boy!" Pound and Tremaine hugged and laughed like they hadn't talked in years.

"Everything good my brother," Tremaine said. "Let's go to the office." Tremaine wasn't patient with his patrons. His quick gait came with shoves and pushes, all with a smile and Pound backing him up.

The office had another bar, gray marble floor tiles and two purple pool tables. Two fichus trees sat in the far corners of the office. The neon blue lighted bar sat between the trees. Paintings of black Egyptians hung on the peanut butter colored walls. Dozens of African Paintings sat on the floor and leaned against the wall. Tremaine and his mom sold paintings and other items on weekends at flea markets all across north eastern South Carolina. He sat behind his student desk, sporting a computer and a paperweight resembling the Anytime's sign out front. Tremaine sighed.

"You gonna be alright man, cause I'm fucked up," he said. Pound took a big swallow of Hennessey.

"I don't know man. I just...I'll worry about me after I kill Ike and them." Pound took another big swallow as Tremaine shook his head.

"Now that's what I wanted to talk about," he said. Pound sat his bottle on the floor and sat up in his chair.

"You know where he at?" he asked.

"That ain't what I mean. Pound, if I thought for a second Ike killed our brother, I'd be hunting for him myself. He ain't the one that did Chop though." Pound stared his friend in the eyes. *He's supplying Ike and Ike's bringing him a lot of money*, he thought. *That's why Tremaine is buying so much dope.*

"How the fuck you know he ain't do it?"

"Same way you do. That nigga won't shoot shit how is he and his son gonna do Chop like that man?" Pound sucked his teeth and picked his bottle up. "And Andre wants to talk to you too." Pound shot to his feet. His mind raced to the M16 in Mack T's car.

"What the fuck you mean talk? My brother dead and you want me to talk to *them*? Where this nigga at Tre?"

"Chill yo ass out man. Andre's on his way here. I told him y'all can talk right here and figure this out."

"Ain't shit to figure out Tre!" Pound screamed. "That nigga's dead on sight! Ike too!" Tremaine lit a Newport and rubbed the temples of his head.

"Think about what you saying and who you saying it about. Them niggas ain't no killers and you know it. Plus Ike's still plugged in to them boys up there. If something goes down they're gonna get you. Ike's already pushing them to get you and your pops over his brother Early."

"What the fuck you mean they-"

"Did you hear me? He trying to twist your pops and you over his little brother being killed the other night. He said the sheriff's bullshitting him, talking about he gotta investigate first." Pound sat with his arms crossed.

"So...so what is you trying to do here? What's your play in this huh? What the fuck you think I'm fitna do when-" Tremaine stood.

"Pound," Tremaine said calmly. "You can't make money locked up. I feel what you feeling right now but them niggas you're after is the wrong niggas. Think about your brother. Where the hell was he at the other night *alone* with Ike and Andre? Matter fact, where was he?" Pound knew where Chop was the night he was killed. He wasn't telling Tremaine. "Who ever killed him knew he was beefing with Ike and them. You think Ike and Andre would really shoot Chop to hell and then leave him on they property? You know how much land them niggas got? Ike owns part of that new casino they take out in the water here on the weekend. Why not dump the nigga in the ocean? Somebody's out here playing you brother."

Pound sat down. He guzzled his Hennessy, it helped some but not much. Missing Chop would never go away, neither would the guilt. He was Chop's brother and part time father. Pound used to wake Chop for school, cook his breakfast, taught him to iron his clothes, play basketball and fight. They were both *good* boys, always said yes ma'am and yes sir to grown ups. They made sure their yard and Marie's looked decent without asking. They considered Angela and Marie when they were away from home and behaved accordingly. When Chop got older and gained his boss status, Pound was more proud than anyone. He'd have been more proud if Chop got a scholarship to college or a contract to play a major sport. Chop didn't ask for all the problems in his family to and he certainly didn't ask for Ike Long to come into his life. Chop became strong, became a leader and Pound felt he was more responsible for that than anybody. Was he, at all, responsible for Chop's death is the question that couldn't escape his mind?

He didn't pull the trigger, but in some situations doing nothing is the same as doing the wrong thing. Chop followed Pound's drug dealing example and may be alive today if not for that fact. There was never an effort to steer Chop away from drug dealing. Maybe because he was in such firm control of his business and those around him, Pound saw no need for worry. Maybe Pound saw his brother as a means to his own end. The more dope Chop sold the richer they both got. Chop was old enough to make his own decisions and could be stubborn so why even try? Chop was loved and respected by everybody, maybe he didn't detect insincerity in folks as well as he should have.

Tremaine threw the hard facts in Pound's face. Ike and Andre Long weren't capable of doing what had been done to Chop. They weren't that stupid to leave him out in the open either. Pound always hated Ike for mistreating his mother and turning him and Chop out to the streets. In prison he wondered if Billy ever felt the same sickness in his stomach knowing Ike Long was guiding Chop's future. Pound had always meant to kill Ike, just on general purpose. If Chop didn't keep his promise of distancing himself from Ike, Pound would have already. Ike didn't kill Chop but he helped make him into someone where this kind tragedy was too likely for comfort, Pound reasoned. Pound knew he helped Ike in that same effort. He guzzled the Hennessy again. It didn't help as much as it did before.

He was going to kill Ike and Andre, it would help his feelings. Fuck'em. They cheated Chop and tried to turned the police on him. Sabotaging Chop was supposed to prove that he couldn't thrive in the drug game without them. They were wrong, Chop eclipsed them. Hurt pride is a great motivator so maybe they weren't capable of killing Chop but they were capable of paying to get it done. If that was the case and they had someone leave Chop at Ike's asphalt plant Pound couldn't just shoot them. He had fantasies of chopping off toes, fingers, ears, lips, noses, and private parts and one at a time. Fuck what Tremaine was talking about.

The music stopped.

Screaming and hollering sent Tremaine out the door. Pound regretted not bringing a gun into the club. Everybody seemed to pile up in the front of the club. Security wasn't in sight. Montana, one of the underage DGBs in attendance, brought a bottle up over his head, jumped in the middle of the crowd and brought it down hard on somebody. The closer Tremaine got to the middle of the conflict the closer Pound got to the bar.

It was Andre.

The crowd was trying to rip him apart. His face was so disfigured it gave Pound pause. Tremaine got to him at the same time Mack T did. Mack hit Andre with an uppercut causing him to double over. He coughed up blood as Mack T punched him in the side of his head. Andre threw up on people holding his hands up in surrender. Two security guards got off the floor and grabbed Andre. They pulled him like a tug of war rope from the crowd out the front door. Tremaine closed the door. People cussed Tremaine while Pound ran back in the office. He went out of the office exit and ran to the front of the club. The ground tilted on him. He tried to anticipate it but kept running into cars and scaffolds. Blood and footsteps lead away from the front door, around Mack T's car and to the road. Pound took a 40. Cal out of the car. He heard a car door slam somewhere up the road. The Hennessey kept tilting everything. Car lights came on up the road and rolled slowly. Pound raised his gun. He ran to the car's brake lights, shooting trees, ditches, parked car windows and doors. He ran out of bullets before the untouched car sped out of sight.

Tremaine checked his desk. The .45 caliber glock was still there. He left it and ran out the door Pound left open. He could barely see Pound walking down the road.

"Pound man, what happened?" he hollered, jogging to the front of the club. "Was that you doing all that sh-"

AK -47 rounds charged through Tremaine's back and legs. He fell nose first into the dirt. Andre Long stood over his shaking body.

"You set me up nigga?"

Tremaine turned his neck to see Andre as he limped away down the road.

## Chapter 17

Billy Belle's alarm clock usually sounded at 6:30 am. Before brushing his teeth or taking a shower, he'd do a thousand push-ups, five hundred squats and sit-ups. After cleaning up he'd turn on the news and prepare his breakfast. Scrambled eggs with cheese, onions, green peppers, grits, toast, and gourmet coffee with a shot of one of his five different creamers. He'd have sausage patties, sausage links, bacon, fried fish, salmon patties or corn beef. Helping people and walking with God was his daily aim but Billy's mornings belonged to him. His six month long tradition stopped with one 3:30 am phone call. He wiped his face and put on some clothes. By 3:35, he was out the door, Carol was sound asleep. Chop's vault and bas of money were was still in the back of the truck. Billy sat it all at the steps behind his house. After the Newport was ablaze, he got in his truck and rolled down the windows.

Treasure was on her way to jail and needed Billy to get the girls, Charlene wouldn't pick up the phone. When it rained it poured and Chop's death alone was a tsunami. Driving around at this time of night seemed ungodly to Billy but obviously not to a lot of other people. Cars zipped around Billy and roared by going the other direction. Sirens blared and police lights flashed down every road he passed. *At 3 in the morning?* The Kangaroo gas station resembled a carnival. People sat on the sidewalk in cuffs while others drove away. Billy had a curfew. Waiting at the highway light, Billy called his Parole officer and left a message.

Ten sheriff's deputy cars filled Treasure's yard, one of them parked in Billy's spot. He drove past the trailer and parked behind a police car on the side of the road. He walked to the driveway.

"Hey!" a deputy shouted as Billy approached. "Get outta here, this shop's closed for good."

The deputy, a six foot white boy with a barrel chest and huge arms stretching his uniform, held a 12 gauge pump action shotgun and wore a bullet proof vest, all for little Treasure. He planted his meaty index finger in Billy's chest.

"I come to get my granddaughters sir," Billy said as he looked behind the deputy. "Treasure just called and said she was getting locked up. She said their bags was already ready." The deputy put his hand back on his shotgun.

"Stay right here," he said before marching up the driveway. There was a Kawasaki Ninja motorcycle in the yard, Billy never saw it before.

Billy lit another Newport and sucked it like a milkshake. He felt like he forgot to do something.

"Mommee!" cried Lovely. She stood along side her sisters in the living room while Treasure sat handcuffed on the sofa.

The Brunswick County Narcotics Task Force invaded her home. They turned over beds,

ripped up carpet, pulled the vents out , emptied cereal boxes, emptied the freezer and took apart

the washer and dryer. They raided the seven trailers and discovered nothing. Treasure Dawkins

would be charged with maintaining a dwelling for unlawfully keeping or selling controlled

substances. They discovered a Ziploc bag in a dresser drawer of her bedroom containing a

quarter ounce of weed and one rolled blunt.

.

Pound's Texas drug connection was having problems eight months ago leaving Chop, Bucc, Treasure and Tremaine in need of a supplier. Chop, through is girlfriend Misty, secured a supplier in her brother Blake Helms. When Chop bought heroine from Blake, he bought to supply his friends. Chop and Blake became somewhat close. Blake would visit Chop and Misty at there home in Cedar Grove to drink and hang out. Blake often made statements about being the "New Man" in Brunswick County. When Pound's connection came back three months ago, Chop dropped Blake for his brother. Chop always shared his dealings with Blake with Pound. Chop was concerned about the eminent fallout with the sheriff because of his abrupt dissociation with Blake. Chop depended on the sheriff's information and Pound, through Chop, appreciated it. Pound never told Mack T but his cousin Neal was a confidential informant against a number of drug dealers in Brunswick County. He was a person whom the sheriff recruited to bolster the state's case against defendants for grand juries. When Treasure called Pound about Neal claiming to be the "New Man" of Brunswick County, the points connected instantly.

"Lovely Lovely," Treasure sang. "I'm gonna be gone just for a minute okay. I promise I'll see you in a few hours."

"Then why we packed our clothes then?" Lovely cried.

"Just in case, alright? I'll be back to get you early in the morning, I promise." Lovely nodded furiously. She went to hug Treasure and a deputy walked between them mushing the child back toward her sisters. The tears rained down.

"Aw come here baby." Lovely rushed to Treasure and squeezed her neck.

Kenya and Charisma looked on. They held four pieces of knock-off Louis Vuitton luggage Treasure bought for a trip to Six Flags. Charisma held hers and Lovely's.

"It'll be okay my Love." Treasure kissed Lovely's temple. "Charisma!" she barked.

Charisma stood at attention.

"When you get to Billy Belle's you better not touch nothin', take nothin' or break nothin'. If I find out any of y'all gave him some trouble I'm kicking *your* ass first."

"Okay," Charisma said as Treasure looked at her like she'd failed the mission already. "I'm gone do everything right." Treasure released her with her eyes and grabbed Kenya.

"Don't make me get out and beat your ass." Kenya trembled and nodded her head.

"Hey!" Treasure leaned all the way to her right, looking pass Charisma to the front door. A deputy poked his head inside. "The girls' granddad is here."

"Alright y'all, come give me hug." Lovely went back to squeezing Treasure's neck. Kenya had to hug them both. When Charisma attempted a hug Treasure leaned back. "You remember what I said do?"

"Yeah," Charisma whined as Kenya and Lovely picked up their bags. "Call Daddy."

"And tell him to get me out now!" With her mother scowling at her, Charisma stole a hug and followed her sisters out the door.

They followed the deputy down the driveway to the road. Billy flicked his Newport in the ditch.

"Hey babies!" Billy wiped the smile off his face, the girls weren't in the mood. He took the suitcases. Kenya and Lovely looked at each other on the walk to Billy's truck.

"You," Kenya mouthed silently.

"You," mouthed Lovely.

"Billy Belle, you got some candy?" Kenya asked. Charisma drew back to hit her but put her hand down. Billy snapped his fingers.

"I knew I forgot something." The girls got in the truck. First Kenya, then Charisma, they pulled Lovely inside and shared the load on their laps. "How 'bout I get y'all some tomorrow, it's too late now ain't it?"

"We going right by the sto' BillyBelle," Kenya said with Lovely sitting back on her face. "*And* our mama locked up? I know you ain't gonna do us like that."

"Kenya stop begging," ordered Charisma, her head pressed to the window. Billy crawled by the house. Deputies were still coming. Two deputies dragged a struggling Treasure down the steps and through the yard, Billy stopped the truck. The deputies opened the back of car and Treasure kicked back on the steps. An officer wagged his finger in Treasure's face then she spit on him. They slammed her on her stomach and drove a knee between her shoulder blades.

"Mom-mee," Lovely whimpered.

"Why they doing that?" Kenya said, her voice fluttered. Her stomach tried to jump through her chest. The deputies pulled Treasure's limp body into the van.

"They killed her?" Lovely asked barely. Billy put his hand on her shoulder.

"No...she'll be alright babies. I'm a wait and follow'em to the station." Billy's phone rang. "Baby, get my phone out the glove compartment."

Charisma handed Billy the phone. "Yo phone is old."

"So," Billy said before hitting the send button. "You old."

"Ha!" Kenya shouted. Lovely managed a smile behind her tears.

"Hello," Billy answered.

"William James Belle." It was his parole officer Shamika Mitchell. "I know you ain't outside your house tonight. Especially not tonight!"

"It was an emergency, I had to get my grandchildren because their mother-"

"It ain't my problem to see about no grandchildren! You're supposed to be in *your* house so can stay out of *our* prison. If you don't answer your house phone in five minutes I'm sending a car up there to get you. Do you understand me Billy?" Billy looked for Treasure. She was in the car. The girls looked at him wondering who that was screaming at BillyBelle.

"I'll be there Shamika, thank you for understanding." He hung up before she could respond.

"Billy Belle yo girlfriend *mean,*" Charisma said. "She talk like she yo mama."

"I know," Billy said.

"Mama told me to call Daddy. Can I call him?" Billy handed her the phone. She dialed the number, it went to voice mail. She called it again, same thing.

"Call Grandma house," Kenya said.

"Mama gonna beat the shit outta us for waking Grandma up." She tried

Tremaine again. Voicemail.

## Chapter 18

*Blake Helms. The would-be King.*

Blake Helms pulled in to the Waffle House parking lot off the highway in Shallotte. It was five in the morning and he'd just come from North Myrtle Beach. This was the time of his chubby little life. He must have bought a hundred drinks for people he didn't even know at the Spanish Galleon nightclub on the beach. He had sex with one of his old classmates in the parking lot. It was a great night.

Last night was the night Brunswick County became his kingdom. His dad purged Brunswick County's south end of every significant drug dealer that wouldn't buy heroine exclusively from him or someone selling for him. Just one night! There was so much money to made and the idea of it made Blake giddy.

Neil was Blake's top lieutenant. He was twenty three years old like Blake and just as ambitious. A tall mixed race pretty boy with cornrows down his back, he never tried to impress a girl his whole life. They always fought for him. Neal sold clothes (men's, women's and kids), sneakers, hair care and black hygiene products, CDs, DVDs, magazines, bottled water, incense and candy. His flock of ladies ensured his ventures succeeded. Blake used to envy Neil but now Neal worked for Blake.

The sky was slowly changing from black to coral blue as Neil pulled into the Shallotte Wafflehouse in his white and neon green Camaro. He looked beat up, black eye and busted lip. Strutting to Blake's Acura, he was beaming. He was helping usher in a new empire. Blake unlocked his door.

"Man that shit was crazy last night," Neil said when he got in and closed the door. "Man they fucked Longwood up, Supply too. Somebody in Airport shot a cop. It's about to be crazy."

"I heard that too. Dad still has a lot of warrants to serve. He's waiting on us to stake our claim in Cedar Grove before he moves forward with those warrants." Blake flipped through pictures on his phone. "Look at this." Neil leaned over.

"Ew, you fucked Clarissa?"

"What, Clarissa's a dime man." Blake continued flipping through the pictures showing Clarissa in every imaginable position. Neil snatched the phone and turned it off. "What the hell man!"

"Blake you gotta cut this shit out. You're a boss now. These slut ass bitches ain't worth your time no more." Blake turned the phone back on.

"So she used to be with Lucas, so what?"

"She never used to *be* with Lucas, she was that fool's slave. I'd come to his crib and she be opening the door butt naked. It be like fifteen niggas in that little ass trailer putting fingers and bottles up her ass and don't none of'em leave without a blowjob or some backshots. You gotta cut that trash off." Blake sighed.

"What about you, did everything go smooth? I mean, except for Treasure?"

"That shit ain't funny," Neal snapped. Blake chuckled. "I should've punched that bitch in the face. Anyway, a lot of people said they were down but Lavelle from Johnson Town really liked it. He bought a brick and a half and said to see him again in a few days."

"That's great man, for real," Blake said. "We own it all now. All the major hitters are dead or on their way to jail. Put all their money together and whatta ya got, us!"

"You sure it's gonna be just us?" Neil asked. Blake flipped through his phone pics of Clarissa.

"Man, every dope boy that doesn't buy from us is going down, even if they're not doing too much. We're not thinking about a big picture but the *whole* picture. You know we got three dozen informants in the district ready say whatever confidentially to clear our way. Compared to Chop this'll be a small hurdle."

"Yo, y'all got lucky with that. The fool was supposed to be untouchable?" Neil started enjoying the Clarissa pics too.

"I don't think so. That guy thought he was Superman yo. We proved he wasn't faster than no speedin' bullet." They laughed and soon parted ways.

Elroy's Country Diner was *the* place for a down home breakfast in Shallotte, North Carolina. Sheriff Sam Helms enjoyed a hearty discounted breakfast there from time to time. Ike Long and Sheila ate there at least three mornings a week. This was the first time he or the sheriff saw the back of the restaurant, old cracked asphalt bursting with weeds leading to an open field. At eighty thirty in the morning, they positioned their cars so the two drivers could talk face to face.

"So is he in jail?" Ike asked. Sheila was inside making their morning order.

"Ike, he's not on the list. We only swept up dealers our informants can identify. Julius ain't no hustler man. I think he's crookeder than a sum bitch too but I can't get to him right this minute." The sheriff turned down the police radio and worked the grits out of his teeth with a toothpick.

"What about my brother Sam? That piss ant nigger killed my brother and y'all ain't locked him up yet."

"Come on Ike, you don't know if he did or didn't. And if you know he did it you must know what for. Please don't let me find out you had something to do with Chop Belle." Ike looked up to the ceiling of his Cadillac.

"Sam, I ain't had nothing to kill him for. My son didn't either. I don't know why he got killed but he did so fuck'im."

"Well that's what I'm saying about your brother, not that last sentiment but the first. What reason would Pound have to kill your brother? Since you know Julius or Billy Belle killed him then you know the cause behind the killing. Tell me what that is Ike." Ike furiously swatted at a fly that buzzed into his car. He became more aggravated with every swat.

Ike felt like swatting the sheriff. He didn't want to hear about motive or logic. He wanted to hear that Julius and Billy Bell were in a jail cell at the Brunswick County Government Complex in Bolivia for the murder of Earl Long. Ike wanted hear the sheriff's ideas on building the case. It didn't have to be logical, truthful or credible, just convictable. Ike Long knew that the sheriff knew him as someone who paid well for whatever service he requested. Why the sheriff had become distant infuriated Ike.

"You don't know him like me. I know that sorry son of bitch did it cause I know him. He ain't got no damn sense. Killing my brother just cause his brother got killed makes perfect sense to him. He's a psycho. You remember that time he almost killed Tito Graham with his bare hands?"

Sheriff perfectly remembered Julius taking the rap for his brother's assault of Tito Graham. Statements like that were why Sheriff Helms considered Ike Long just another puppet in Brunswick County show. The sheriff didn't appreciate be taken as a fool or a product to buy. He controlled the game. In recent years Ike Long masqueraded as a reformed dealer who spent his days in his plush beach home praising the Lord and helping the community. The truth was he still directed a lot of heroine traffic in Brunswick County, north and south end, through his son Andre and his brother Early. He also invested in dump trucks, front end loaders and mobile homes. The town of Shallotte gave him a small contract to help out with that big snow storm a couple years back. Since then Ike tcarried on like we was the mayor of Shallotte. He became more opinionated about civic matters than any drug dealer before him. Ike Long was a clown. A clown who thought Brunswick County's real leaders like Sheriff Helms were supposed to jump for him when he snapped his fingers. For a clown, insulting the sheriff's intelligence was a part of the snap.

"Julius paid his debt to society for that. He's been home for better than a decade now without so much as a speeding ticket. Maybe he isn't who you say he is." Ike shook his head.

"This kid is...he's the devil Sam. He got a lot folks fooled. You know his daddy got a brain full of squirrel shit too. The whole damn family-"

"That reminds me," said the sheriff, holding up a finger. "The night of Early's murder he was with two teenage girls from Sunset Beach. Their things were at the crime scene but they were gone. We plan to share that with the media today. Any idea what they were doing with your brother?" Ike shook his head.

"Come on Sam. He was probably...it don't matter what he was doing. He didn't deserve to get killed for it. And if you know they was there, make those girls tell you-"

"Nobody's seen'em since the day your brother was killed." The sheriff watched Ike's pecan colored face turn pale in front of him. "Their mothers called me personally last night and told me things I didn't wanna believe. I'm mean tales of drugs, underage sex. They believe your son drove the girls to various residences for the purpose of sex for cash. Andre's vehicle was at Early's house the night of the murder. The more time these girls go missing the closer these details get to the light of day."

Ike sat and thought about what the sheriff said. He'd been getting calls of condolences from friends and colleagues who saw him a reformed pillar of the community. At the moment to them, Early was only Ike's brother. The sheriff insinuated a dreadful proposition. Basically his son and his brother were pedophiles, crack smoking pedophiles. These girls could be probably dead. If so, the news would be all over it. The mothers of the girls would describe Ike's son and brother to the world as Brunswick County's worst excuses for human beings. People would instantly mention Ike Long along side Andre and Early Long. A small empire hung in the balance. Now just wasn't the time.

Too much work had been put into creating a different Ike Long narrative. Huge donations to various churches were only the start. He supported the right commissioners and committees in Shallotte, Ocean Isle Beach and Calabash, the ones Sheriff Helms supported. West Brunswick High School received new football equipment, a refurbished field, a new gymnasium floor and ten scholarships a year in the name of Ike's late mother. After a couple years of giving, Brunswick County gave back. Contracts for his dump trucks and front end loaders became endless. Town councils and golf community planners threw money at Ike Long, the country philanthropist. He turned his profits into a commercial landscaping company, and a heating and air company. The companies employed and were supervised by friends and family of commissioners and other movers and shakers of the county. His legitimate empire was formidable but a scandal the size and scope of two dead white girls could bring it all down. The wave caused by Chop's body being discovered at his asphalt plant hadn't even finished rippling yet.

Suddenly, Pound was a significantly small fish to fry.

"I don't know nothing about all that Sheriff. Them little girls could be dead now. That means whoever killed my brother killed them and I'm telling you-"

"Okay Ike. I can see you got it hot for this boy. Until I have something that smells like probable cause I'm not gonna touch him. These girls need to be found and found fast." The sheriff backed out into the field and drove off. Ike parked around the front of Elroy's and joined Sheila.

## Chapter 19

Still no answer.

Billy left two messages on Tremaine's phone, Charisma said he always answered. They called the Sheriff's office. Treasure's bond was a two hundred and fifty thousand dollars. Billy called Pound to see if he'd been locked up. Kiana said he was still in South Carolina and would try to get Treasure out when he got back. Billy offered to help pay some of the bond. Kiana laughed and said Pound would take care of it. She told Billy that Tremaine Gore got shot and was in the hospital. Billy told the girls they couldn't call him anymore until he called back.

When he came home with the girls last night, Billy woke Carol up and put fresh sheets and a comforter on his bed. He gave the girls his bedroom, Carol almost went to her mother's. When the girls fell asleep Billy told her what happened, including the part about Tremaine.

"This is too much baby. I don't even wanna think about it right now," she said as Billy pulled out the sofa bed. "I guess you're not working tomorrow cause you gotta watch these kids."

"I gotta see how Charisma acts before I leave her in charge." Carol put the sheets on the bed while Billy sat on the couch smoking a Newport. Carol got in bed and fell asleep.

This *was* too much. Something very bad was happening. Chop, Pound, Tremaine and Treasure hung tough. One was dead, one was in critical condition and the other was locked up.

Billy feared that Pound was on his way to be with one of them. This wasn't a coincidence and it wasn't over. Billy held no illusions about his sons. They were both rough individuals, gangsters. These tragedies were the fruit gangsters reap.

They plod along while Kiana, Jared, Misty, Marie, Carol, Charisma, Kenya and Lovely hang in the balance. Billy understood himself to be part of the cause because he wasn't around to guide Chop, Pound and Treasure the right way.

He put the cigarette out and checked on the girls. Lovely was in the middle, Kenya on the right, Charisma didn't have a pillow. Billy took his out of the den and put it on the dresser just in case she woke up.

Chop wasn't in the ground yet but he was long gone. Billy tortured himself with memories of him as boy. How they'd play all day long, how he use to act a fool when he had to leave the visitation room in prison. Marie told Billy to enjoy the memories and don't allow them to be a hindrance. People were counting on Billy to help them through this. Marie was right, it was still on her and him.

He didn't want to own Chop's Diner but he did want to work there. He didn't know if Marie, Misty or Pound were going to own it. Chop promised Billy his house back when he moved to his new home in Lockwood Folly with Misty. What would become of that? What if nobody could get Treasure out of jail? What if she received a long sentence? What if she didn't want Charlene having the children? Nobody knew if Tremaine would survive the shooting. If he didn't, would his family be up to the task of caring for the children? Would Treasure want that? What if something happened to Pound? Kiana and Anita spoke as if it were a forgone conclusion. They were already looking to Billy to help with Kiana's baby went it came. And *Chop's* the father. How would Pound react when he found out? Would Billy hurt his own son to protect Kiana and his newborn grandson? Billy made a phone call.

Andy Stahl was an old friend of Billy's. He served fifteen years in prison for midnight burglary. He could get into anything. In prison, he watched inmates put their canteen items in their lockers then steal all of it when they went to the yard. One day, Andy stole from the wrong inmate. A six foot five, two hundred seventy pound, rock hard psycho named House discovered all his snacks and marijuana were gone.

House didn't ask Andy about his stuff. He assumed it was Andy because he made Andy take items out of other lockers under threat of bodily harm and/or sodomy. House gave his snacks to other inmates for sexual favors and sold the weed he didn't smoke. Andy stole a good two weeks worth of favors and a month's worth of weed from House. House attempted to take Andy's manhood in front of Billy's bunk.

House didn't have his pants down yet and Andy screamed like a boiling cat. He knew the consequences for violating House. Blood and shit left on the shower floor served as stark reminders that House was never to be played with. Andy didn't want to take from House but he owed some Indians a lot of money. They told him about the package of weed House just received. Andy took it the next morning.

Billy put his book down and got up from his bunk. House held Andy with one hand as he tried to run away. When he got himself aroused he punched Andy twice in the head. Andy's brain rattled in his skull rendering him limp. Before House could see him, Billy delivered a flurry of uppercuts to his ribs. House's ribs poked his vital organs. He tried to turn around but it hurt too bad. The officers put Billy in the hole and shipped House to another facility. It turns out that House was the target of a gang that had designs on the numerous rackets he controlled. He would have been dead soon if Billy hadn't attacked him.

Andy was beyond grateful. He brought Billy two paper bags full of iced honey buns, Billy's favorite. Andy stole every one of them. They became friends and Andy ran to Billy every time he got into trouble. Sometimes Billy would help him out of it, other times he'd make Andy wear the beating. He used to tell Billy stories about breaking in big houses, taking safes and cracking them. He proudly boasted of a supermarket job where he broke in through the roof and ceiling. He silenced the alarm and took fifteen thousand dollars from the safe. Took him a half a month to blow through the money. Andy Stahl was drug addict from Oak Island North Carolina. He was release eight months ago and never touched drugs again. Billy received money, magazines and books from Andy until he was released.

Chop's safe, in Billy's opinion would be simple for Andy. At eight o'clock am Billy called him and headed to Oak Island, twenty miles east of Cedar Grove. Andy, 5'6", late forties, slim, had freckles and short red hair. Even in prison he woke up wearing a baseball cap. His apartment was on the first floor of a two story four unit wooden building. It sat inland, surrounded by pine trees. Big Wheels and beer bottles littered the small rock and oyster shelled parking lot.

"Billy Bob!" Andy greeted as he stepped through his sliding glass door. "Wauz say man!" He and Billy shook hands.

"I'm doing good. How you been getting along?" Billy asked.

"Man, I been roofing non stop. I been all the way to Jacksonville to back round your way. Ain't drinking or smoking or nothing."

"That's good Andy." Billy pulled out a Newport. "I knew you was sick of seeing that fence."

"I ain't bullshittin' Billy Bob. They made a believer outta me." Andy followed Billy to the back of his truck.

"Check this out for me." Billy pulled a bed sheet off the safe.

"Hmm...Gardall makes a good safe. This is a six digit electronic. This here's a big dick safe, a media safe's what they call it. You can put a stick of butter in there, set the safe on fire and the butter'll be as you left it." Andy hopped into the bed of the truck. He turned the safe on it's side and sat it back. "Billy, um...you stole this?"

"Hell no, it was my son's. The people he kept it with didn't want it in the house no more so they made me take it. Hurry up and open it."

"This ain't no safe you can just open. I'm a have to take it to my friends shop. If it's even possible that it can be open he'll have the tools for it."

"Is that right?" Billy said, He sat his cigarette on the side of the truck.

Andy pulled his cell phone out as a white Impala with a North Carolina Employee license plate crept into the driveway. Andy shoved the phone in his pocket, covered the safe with the bed sheet and hopped off the truck in one and a half motions. Billy looked over his shoulder and almost shit himself.

"Shamika Mithcell's your P.O?" Andy nodded and put on a big fake smile.

"That bitch don't play neither," he said threw his teeth. "I'm a try to get her in the house. You take off." Shamika cut the engine and opened the door.

Billy felt as if a guillotine had been put in front of him. The passing cars, the trees, the road, even the sky seemed to be staring at him accusingly.

"It's too late for that. I ain't even supposed to-"

"William James Belle," Shamika greeted with a smile. A tall, shapely, high yellow, extremely cute professional of twenty nine, she wore white open toe sandals, white capri pants and a sherbet colored blouse. Billy's heart beat louder and quicker with every step she took. "I knew you liked jail. You weren't really feeling this freedom thing were you?" Billy kept his eyes on his feet.

"Hey Shamika, I was just up here to get some oysters for the Fourth of July and-"

"You broke curfew last night," Shamika said looking at her watch. "Now, not even six hours later I catch you with a known felon. I knew today was going to be like this." Shamika pulled her phone from her hip and hit one button.

"Hold up Shamika, come on," Billy said. "I'm sorry alright. You know I don't want to go to jail. You know what I'm going through."

"Yes, hello," Shamika said into the phone. She saw the defeated look in Billy's face. He was one of the good ones. Paid a big price for a freak accident. Still, she couldn't stand to be not taken seriously. Arresting Billy Belle felt like a mistake.

"Get in your truck and leave," she said putting the phone on her hip. Her gorgeous face balled into something terrifying. "Now!"

Billy put the tailgate up on his truck. He grabbed his Newport and moved to his driver door. He was going to say something to Andy but waved instead.

At home Billy went to the bathroom to wash his face.

"Billy Belle," Charisma brushed her teeth from the bathroom to the living room. "You ain't got nothing to eat in here. We want some Hardees biscuits."

"If you got some *Hardees* biscuits money with a *Hardees* biscuits car then go get some. And close the door if you're using the bathroom baby."

"You gonna let us starve?" Charisma whined.

"What are your sister's doing?"

"They in the room watching T.V. Daddy still ain't picking up." Billy checked on the girls. He walked back to the bathroom.

"Put some clothes on. Me and you are going grocery shopping." Charisma's big brown eyes lit up. She rinsed her mouth and raced into the bedroom..

They left Food Lion with more cereal than anything. Charisma, usually the young adult around her sisters, ran around the store asking for everything that caught her eye. And she couldn't stop talking.

"Billy Belle, can we get some ice cream on the way home? And we need some movies to watch too." Billy put Charisma on the back of the truck and handed her the grocery bags to place at the front of the truck bed. "Ooh, you know what we didn't get? We need some drummets. I know how to fry'em and bake'em."

"Put that sheet over that milk baby." Charisma did as she was told. "I got some chicken in the freezer. I'll teach you how to barbeque some." Billy held Charisma's hand as she jumped off the truck.

She got in the truck and rolled down the window. A lot of families moved around the shopping plaza. Boys and girls Charisma's age ran around minivans and SUVs, they reminded her of Lovely. Their mothers, most of them wearing visors, sunglasses and fanny packs, let them act silly and play. One boy ran up to his mother and hugged her before hopping in the minivan.

"Punk ass kids," Charisma mumbled as Billy pulled out of the parking lot.

Holden Beach Banking and Trust Bank was across the street from Food Lion. Billy pulled into the bank.

"I gotta go in here real quick." Billy got out the truck and went into his pocket. "Take this five dollars and get some ice cream next door." Charisma took the money and marched to the small ice cream stand beside the bank.

Billy was one four customers in the bank. The air was cooler than Food Lion's.

Two tellers joked behind the counter.

"Mr. Belle?" Billy turned around to a young lady in a blue pants suit, red heels, and a big American flag bow in her flowing auburn hair. Her nametag said Simone Bryant, bank manager. It took a minute to place her.

"Hey Simone, how you doing?"

Simone's dad was Lamar Brown, property manager for Chop Long's rental properties, baritone for the Cedar Grove Young Adult Choir. Her mother was Faith Varnum, a nice white lady from just outside of Cedar Grove. Simone was always mistaken for an Indian. Her tan skin, dimples, straight teeth and easy smile often sent loan applicants out the door with a smile and no money. Her husband was Travis "Big T" Bryant of Bryant Auto in Shallotte. His garage was across the street from Chop's Diner. The Bryants were some of Chop's closest friends.

"I'm doing okay," Simone said with that smile. "I've been meaning to stop by the house but you know how it is."

"Yeah," Billy said looking around. "Can we talk in your office?"

Her office was the size of Billy's bathroom, the walls were glass with the beige blinds pulled up. Simone closed the door as Billy sat.

"What can I do for you Mr. Belle?"
As she moved to her desk Billy fumbled his thumbs. He took the key with the Holden Beach Bank Logo tied to it and put the rest in his pocket.

"Well uh...Chop...he did a lot of business here right?" Simone nodded.

"He got his loan to open Chop's Diner here." With a shake of her computer mouse the screen came to life. She started typing away. "He has a savings account and a checking account. Mr. Belle, you understand we can't give his money to you. If he didn't have a will then his estate may have to be settled in court."

"Okay," Billy said. "I'm not here for all that. I just came into a lot of money and I wanted to know um...what would happen if I did this with it or that with you know what I'm saying?" Simone, with big eyes and a closed mouth smile shrugged.

“I’m trying to understand Mr. Belle. Exactly what did you have in mind for the money?”

“Well…I had two things that I gotta do with it. First I gotta give some the church. Second, I wanna do five college funds. Three granddaughters, a grandson and one on the way.”

Simone nodded and began typing away on her computer.

“Mr. Belle we custodial accounts. The funds you put into these accounts grow tax free. However, if you choose to exceed thirteen thousand dollars in the accounts they will be subject to federal gift tax. Church donations are tax free.” Billy nodded. He looked out of the office window, traffic was picking up. “Mr. Belle, this money you’ve come into, is it cash?” Billy looked out of the window again. He nodded. “Okay, well I’ll tell what I told Chop, put in a safe place. If you don’t have an income stream or assets to justify having a significant amount of cash then hide it and use it on small items, nothing big and gaudy.”

“Okay, how about a loan you give some money like already have I can pay you back-” With a brilliant smile, Simone shook her head. Billy nodded and stood.

Billy stood.

“Thanks Simone. You been a big help.” Simone stood and moved to the door.

“Anytime Mr. Belle.” She opened the door.

Simone watched Billy walk out the front door before she marched back to her office and picked up the phone.

The sun was approaching full force. Charisma sat a picnic table under a huge umbrella in front of the ice cream stand. She walked to truck when she saw Billy.

“Girl, what is all that?” he asked. She had a cone of ice cream the size of her head.

“It’s triple scoop,” she announced as if she invented the concept. “It’s a strawberry, blackberry cobbler and-” she licked the yellow scoop, “banana pudding cone.” She pulled two quarters and a few pennies out of her pocket. “You want yo change?”

"You keep it," Billy said as a burgundy Cadillac XTS screeched to halt behind the truck. Billy looked at the drive then back at Charisma. "And don't drop that ice cream in the truck."

Ike Long, with a pint of Jose Cuervo gin swimming in his gut, stepped out of his running car. He strutted almost like George Jefferson around the hood of his car to the driver side of Billy's truck. He held a .22 caliber pistol by his side. His clean shaven pecan colored face was stone. The fifty nine year old man trained his gun on Billy.

"Get in the car nigga," he growled. Billy put his hands in the air.

"Man are you crazy?" Billy's eyes never left the gun. It moved but didn't shake, the trigger was hugged tight.

"You driving so take the wheel." Billy looked down at Ike's white ostrich loafers to his off white khakis to his sky blue shirt to his round sweaty face. Ike sweated profusely. His eyes were moist and serious. Billy's heart thumped like a stampede of elephants. "Now!" Ike screamed.

"I haven't done nothing to you man so I don't see how-" Ike shot Billy in the thigh. He fell backward to the pavement. Ike looked around, trying to find the cause of that loud bang. The bullet planted it self in Billy's le and felt like fire. Ike's eyes found Billy, then he remembered. Charisma's ice cream fell cone first to the pavement as she rushed to Billy. His tan khakis were crimson on the outer right side. Ike watched the front door of the bank.

"Charisma, listen to me," Billy said pulling off his shirt and wrapping it around his leg. "Call Kiana and tell her to come get you." Charisma shook her head.

"You going with him?" she whimpered. Billy nodded. He stumbled up. Ike kept the gun trained on him.

"Do what I said baby and don't call the police, you hear me? Don't call the police. I'll be fine, it ain't that bad. Just don't cry and make sure Kiana come and picks you up." Charisma face scrunched into a ball. She looked to be losing her footing. Billy grabbed her and picked her up amplifying the fire in his leg. "Listen, you ain't no little girl so you gotta do something important now okay. Make sure you do what you're supposed to do and you'll see me again in an minute alright." He put her down. Charisma, like the little girl she tried not to be, nodded, wrapped her arms around Billy and buried her face in his stomach.

"I ain't got all day and you ain't got but two legs," Ike said snapped. A car pulled up and he held his pistol to the side.

"Remember what I said sweetie. Go 'head, call her now." Charisma nodded furiously as she jumped in the truck. Two old folks walked around the truck, oblivious to the situation. Billy limped over to Ike's driver side door.

Marvin Sapp professed his love for the Lord through Ike Long's stereo system. Ike told Billy to drive to Cedar Grove. Andre told him the old house would be vacant.

"What's this all about Ike?" Billy asked, his right eye twitched. He wanted to cry, fight, he wanted rip Ike apart. Ike didn't say anything. He kept the gun trained on Billy. Billy hit the brakes just before turning on Stanley Road.

"Hey!" Ike said. "Keep going, I ain't playing!" Billy put the car in park and pulled the key out of the ignition.

"Not 'til you tell me what your problem is." Billy put pressure on his leg and rocked back and forth. "I can wait."

Ike lifted the gun and put it to Billy's head.

"Billy, I know me and you got a little history but you need to trust me when I say this is the day you shut the fuck up and do what it is I tell ya. Now *drive* this mutherfucka!" There was no strain in Ike's voice. Billy started the car and put it in drive. Ike relaxed, never taking his eyes or gun off Billy. "That's the problem with your whole damn family. Y'all ain't got no understanding but your own. Can't be wrong about shit, especially Chop's grown ass."

"Ike," Billy said ready to turn the car over in the ditch. "Did you kill my boy?"

"Yeah Billy, I killed that sassy mutherfucka! Then I dumped him in my asphalt plant for the world to see. You really think I'm that dumb?"

"Ike, did you kill my-"

"No I ain't kill him. What I'm a kill him for?" Ike asked as Billy turned on Cedar Grove Road. "I know *this*, he deserved every bullet his ass got." Billy took his eyes off the road. "What? Karma's a bitch and she faster than Carl Lewis, ain't no getting away." Billy turned onto Cedar Grove Road, he drove past the church when Ike told him to slow down. "There we go, pull on in there." Ike's old house couldn't be seen from the road. A long dirt driveway took them past the thick cedar trees.

"How do you keep karma off you?" Billy asked. "You feeding the needy?"

"Prayer and good works, that's how I roll, shit. I am the needy, I ain't no saint though. You put me beside your son, God bless his soul, I'm a look like Mr. Rodgers standing beside Dark Vader. Always had to get somebody back for something." Billy parked the car on the side of the house. It was the only two story house in Cedar Grove. It had four pillars in the front like a town hall building. A beautiful home only visitors saw.

"He ain't never do nothing you didn't teach him," Billy said, his chest heaving. Ike shook his head and rolled his eyes.

"Bullshit. I ain't never teach him to kill people. That was the fruit staying close to the tree I suppose." Ike said with a snicker. "Him pushing pills at the high school wasn't none of my doing either. And I ain't never in my life got high. Chop *and* Pound was on that powder. Now get the fuck out."

A cobblestone walk way lead to the walnut side doors. Pine Sol and Lemon Pledge scents greeted them as they crossed the threshold. Ike hadn't been inside the place in a year. Andre did God knows what with God knows who there and that's how it smelled. After dropping Sheila off in Delco North Carolina, Ike came to the house and was almost lifted off his feet by the putrid odor. He wiped down the walls, mopped the floors, and dusted the furniture. He even cleaned the toilets then opened all the windows.

"To the back," Ike said stepping inside after Billy. "In the laundry room."

Behind the kitchen sat the washer, the dryer and the ironing board. Ike had both machines running. He found towels and washcloths that could stand on their own and bed sheets that really needed to be thrown away or burned. "Go through that door in the back." The garage was full of old clothes, Christmas decorations and tools. There was no room for a car. The garage doors were electric. Ike hit the button on the wall and the doors went down. "Here." Ike handed Billy a pair of handcuffs. "Run them cuffs over that garage rail."

"What's going on Ike? What did I do to you?" Billy asked.

"You ain't done nothing yet, just do what I tell you."

"And what if I don't?" Ike took a step back, he looked Billy up and down.

"Then I'm a shoot your ass." Ike trained the gun on Billy's other leg. "I need you here for a while. When I come back you'll be free to leave but you need to do what I say right now."

The garage was stifling. It wasn't even noon yet.

"Listen man, if you got to leave me then leave me in the house. This garage is too hot." Ike shot a hole through the front window of the garage. The sudden report shocked Billy's nerves and made his ears ring.

"Billy, I'm not fucking with you. I'll be back in a minute. Cuff yourself up there!" Ike pointed the gun at Billy's chest. He stayed six feet away because Billy looked ready to pounce. Billy cuffed himself to the garage door rail.

"I'll be back in a minute," said Ike before disappearing into the house.

He put the gun on the dryer and headed to the master bedroom. Pound was going to submit, today. He was going to confess to killing Early, today. He was going to tell Ike where those girls were, today. Ike was going to rush back to the bank and hope Kiana hadn't picked that little girl up. Once she arrived, he'd take her and the girl. He'd contact Pound and make him confess it all under the threat of letting his woman, his dad and the girl die. Andre offered to let him and his buddies handle it but Ike happened to know that they weren't bright enough to pour piss out of a boot.

After seeing his little brother with his head blown off Ike couldn't sleep. The drinking returned big time. He hadn't been this out of it since burying his mother.

That was the day he understood that he was fully on his own. Protecting Early and Andre from harm were his only responsibilities. Ike taught Early how to sell drugs so he could have a decent living. He tried to teach Early common since. Early had always been a royal fuck-up. An alcoholic, he couldn't even keep his driver's license. He usually hired a drug addict to drive him to his daily rounds. All he did was eat and get high. Ike put the Leland police in his pocket and Early was only doing so much. He made his little brother's life charmed, but he fucked *that* up. Ike wished Early was alive so he could kick his ass and make him go straight. He wanted to kick in Pound's front door and kill everybody like Doc Holliday, maybe even kill Marie. She never liked Ike and the feeling was more than mutual. Sheila tried to help Ike see that being irrational wouldn't solve anything.

Ike turned the fan on standing near his old night stand, still worked. He didn't want to give a damn about Billy being hot but Billy wasn't his primary target. Ike unplugged the fan and headed to the garage. In the living room, he heard metal scraping and a thud from the garage, Billy hollered. Ike dropped the fan and rushed through the kitchen. He heard the door to the garage shut. The gun still sat on the dryer. Ike entered the laundry room and went for the gun. He never touched it.

Billy snatched Ike from the floor. Ike watched his own feet kick. The chain of his own handcuffs squeezed his throat. Sweat and blood from Billy's wrists dripped down the cuffs and on Ike's neck. Ike kicked Billy's shins repeatedly with the hard heels of his shoes. He tried to push Billy's head back, gouge his eyes out, hit him in the nose. Billy stared straight ahead. His shins bled as the pain rippled all the way up to his knees. Shamika Mitchell sat on the washer scribbling in her damn pad and Angela stood in front of him pleading with her eyes. Billy shook his head and they disappeared, he squeezed tighter. A frog's croak came out escaped Ike when stopped trying to scream. He tried to get a grip on the handcuff chain but it seemed to inside his throat. He struggled for almost a minute. Billy squeezed as hard as he could, a good minute after Ike's ghost had given up. Billy threw him to the floor. Every vein in Billy's body swelled. A dark hunger had surfaced, it wasn't satisfied.

## Chapter 20

"What!" Pound looked like the confusion physically hurt him.

"Treasure's daughter Charisma, she said an old black man in a brown Cadillac took Billy at the bank in Holden Beach. The man shot Billy," Kiana said listening to Charisma through the phone and driving her car south on Highway 17.

"Somebody took him?" Pound said. "And what he do with the kids?" Kiana listened to Charisma

"Charisma was the only one with Billy. Kenya and Love was...oh, I meant Lovely was at Billy's house. They're still there. Charisma is with Billy's truck at the bank in Holden Beach."

"Simone just called me," Pound said calling Simone back.

"Holden Beach Bank, Happy Fourth of July, this is Simone Bryant, how can I help-"

"Simone, do something for me," Pound said before burping. He just finished a chicken sandwich from Wendy's. He bought a Frosty but didn't touch it. After hearing what happened, Simone brought Charisma to her office while she checked the security camera.

"That was Ike Long who took your daddy. Your dad got shot in the leg too." She whispered through the phone. "I gotta call the police and report this so-"

"No," Pound said. "Don't do that. I'm sending somebody at Charisma and the truck." Pound punched his knee as he looked out the window. "I don't know what my daddy is up to. I'm a find out just do that for me."

"You sure?" Simone asked.

"Yeah, just look after Charisma for a few minutes. She ain't no trouble."

"Okay." Simone hung up. Pound and Kiana just passed the *Welcome to South Carolina* sign. Pound called Mack T.

"'Sup nigga!" Mack greeted.

"Change of plans, go to the Holden Beach Bank and get Treasure's daughter before you pick Treasure up."

"That's what I'm fitna do. Daisia already up at the station bonding her out. I'm five minutes away from the station with the money, I can't-"

"Nigga get down to that damn bank and get that girl. She was with my daddy when Ike kidnapped him." There was a pause.

"Say what?" Mack T asked.

"Ike kidnapped my daddy at the fucking bank and left Charisma up there in the truck. Go get her, *then* you get Treasure."

"Alright." Mack T turned into a driveway and turned around. "Yo, my cousin Neal want to see us today." Pound pulled the phone from his ear and looked at it. He put it back to his ear.

"Fuck that lil' nigga man! Go get Charisma and-"

"I got that homie but check it. Neal think we interested in spending with him. We need to find out what he's really got going on." Pound's frustration threatened to overtake him.

"Bring him by Bucc's house. If he come don't let him leave 'til I get there. But right now-"

"Nigga I already turned around," Mack T hung up the phone.

"Shit!" Pound punched the dash. "Shit! Shit! Shit! Shit!"

"Calm down." Kiana trembled. The madness surrounding the family was taxing her pregnancy. Six weeks from her due date, her head was pounding and her feet were trying to bust through her sneakers. She boiled inside when around Pound. She had to be the mother, the cook, the maid, the butler, the chauffeur and she had to do it all silently, while pregnant. It was hard for everybody but nobody seemed concerned about Kiana. Even Marie had her running back and forth to Shallotte for things she could get herself. Earlier that morning, Kiana suffered a huge cussing out by her mother Anita. She wanted to go to Wilmington to see the doctor and to shop but didn't want to drive. Kiana had to drive Pound to North Myrtle Beach to visit Tremaine in the hospital. He wanted to stay last night but Kiana had to beg him over the phone to leave the ICU. He had to change his clothes and get the gun residue from his hands and arms before the cops showed up. Then Marie pulled her typical guilt trip about Kiana not being available to help cook *all day* for visitors. She hoped Billy was okay but felt a little irritated that he had Charisma call *her* to come to the rescue. Why not Carol or the child's grandmother?

"Calm down? Bitch, Treasure's in jail, my nigga got shot and my daddy got kidnapped and I gotta calm down?" Kiana's head pounded.

"I'm just saying, calm down so you can think and figure this out. Everybody's feeling-"

"Bitch quit talking," Pound snapped. He scrolled down his cell phone directory for no body in particular. Kiana's hands twisted on the stirring wheel like a motorcycle, her pink bottom lip quivered. They were close to the hospital.

"You need to do better by me," she said. Pound turned from his phone.

"What?"

"You heard me, I know shit's fucked up but ain't none of this my fault. I'm in fucking pain with a baby and you acting like I'm one them little niggas that gotta jump every time you want'em to. I ain't even supposed to be driving or nothing. Can't you see that?"

There were no parking spots at the Seacoast Medical Center in Little River. They couldn't even enter the parking lot. Tremaine's family and homeboys lined the sidewalks and posted up on cars around the entrance. Some wore *Chop Belle R.I.P* t-shirts. Kiana, under Pound's orders, pulled up to the hospital entrance and parked the car n the middle of all those people.

"Can't see? My whole clique is getting twisted and you giving me fits and shit. You getting on my damn nerves. Now ain't the time," Pound said as Kiana cut the engine. Tremaine's mother stepped out the back of an electric blue Lincoln Town Car. It was daughter's car, Tremaine's sister. Tremaine's mother surveyed the parking lot then waved Pound to her. "That's your goddamn problem right there, you think I don't see shit. Guess you thought I didn't see you creeping with my brother huh. Guess you figured he wasn't man enough to tell me you a ho huh. Guess you figured you was *that* slick. Guess you figure I give a fuck about you and that baby in your stomach huh."

Time stood still. Kiana couldn't look in his direction. Her nerves grew sensitive like an unsuspecting victim in a horror movie. She didn't know if she should open the door and run or brace for the hit. Pound opened his door and planted his feet on the pavement. He took the cup full of melted Frosty turned to Kiana. "You gotta a lot a damn nerve talking to me crazy when we both know you 'sposed to be face down in a fucking ditch."

He took the lid from the Frosty and threw it in Kiana's face after he standing and slamming the door. The windshield could only muffle Kiana's screams. The whole car shook, pound didn't turn around.

Kiana wiped the chocolate gunk from her face. Pound stood with Tremaine's mother fifteen away from the car. The lady hugged and talked with Pound like she didn't witness him splash Kiana with a beverage. She could've killed Pound, he *knew*. She and Pound had been at it for two years. Pound stopped having sex with her four months ago. She was scared for the baby. It was boy, healthy and ready for the world. What world awaited the boy? Would he have a chance with Pound as his dad or his uncle? That poor child. The burdens waiting for him made Kiana ache. It was up to her give that baby a fair shot at life. She wasn't sure if she could save Jared. He watched her cry too many times all night after being beaten by Pound. He spent his days watching the TV or staring at the wall in silence. When Billy or Marie came by he didn't speak, even after Kiana or Pound spanked him. Jared wouldn't even cry.

As Pound spoke with Tremaine's mother and sister people started rushing to the front of the hospital. Somebody ran to Pound and said something. Treamaine's mother hollered and collapsed. Pound rammed his way through the front entrance. North Myrtle Beach Police cars entered the parking lot's two entrances. They parked where they could rushed to the entrance. Kiana felt like somebody took a hand and squeezed her heart.

"Tremaine's dead," she said to herself. The police ran into the hospital. The people outside went nuts. Police cars became targets for a half dozen assault rifles. Main street traffic headed south came to a halt as people ran into the street. Small children ran around unattended in the parking lot.

Pound ran out of the hospital, the police on his heels. He ran by Kiana's car and through the parking lot. The police officers sitting in their cars got out and apprehended Pound. Kiana shook her head and pulled out her cell phone.

"Mommy mommy mommy!" Lovely tackled Treasure as she entered Billy's home. She kissed Treasure's cheeks and ears and nose. Treasure, with her back on the floor squeezed her baby and smiled.

"You missed me my Love?" Lovely nodded. "Can I get up?" Lovely nodded and helped her mother up. Mack T and Charisma entered the house. Kenya stood in the living room with a half smile. It felt good to know Treasure was out of jail. She made up the bed and made sure Lovely was clean. Although she was hungry she didn't eat anything. Billy didn't say she could cook anything and Kenya refused to get out of line away from home, the cost was too high. Treasure ran to her and lifted her off her feet. "You better not have been acting up," she said as she kissed Kenya.

"I didn't do nothing," Kenya said while still in Treasure's arms. "Mama, I'm hungry, me and Lovely."

"Here go the groceries right here," Mack T said as he and Charisma sat the bags on the kitchen table. "That milk ain't cold enough for cereal. Here, bust open these cookies."

"Where Billy Belle at?" Lovely asked.

"We was at the bank and-"

"Charisma!" Treasure snapped, she turned to Lovely. "He'll be back in a little while." She went into the kitchen and started taking groceries out of the bags. "I'm gonna fix y'all something right now."

Charisma got Billy to buy ingredients for the girl's favorite, lasagna. Treasure opened the cabinets beside the oven when Mack T's phone rang.

"Stop playing," he said, eight eyes turned to him He put his back on the wall beside the door and slid to the floor. His face contorted from the agony of the news. "Man, no man."

"Mack, what's going on?" Treasure asked. The girls turned to the TV.

"Come on we gotta go," Mack T said. "Come on Treasure, we gotta roll, right now."

"Why nigga, what happened?" Mack T stared at Treasure until it hit her. He walked out the door.

"Charisma, you and Kenya get over here right now." The girls were in the kitchen and at attention. "Fix this lasagna. Y'all know how to do it. Don't rush it and don't leave the kitchen until it's done and the stove is. All. The. Way. Off." The girls nodded and manned their stations. Treasure hit the door. "Mack!" she screamed. Mack T was almost to the road. He backed the Chevelle back to the house. Treasure got in. "Tell me it ain't Billybelle."

Mack T took the blunt from his lips. "It's Tremaine, I'm sorry Treasure. It happened not even a hour ago during surgery." He held the blunt out for her. Treasure's head hung. She couldn't take another blow this big after losing Chop. The girls were going to flip, how would she them. Kenya's face wouldn't leave her mind. "We gotta go down there. Pound done ran up in the operating room, beat the surgeon down. The police chased him out of the hospital and caught him across the street."

"What the fuck is going on?" Treasure asked. They were flying down Mt. Pisgah heading to the highway.

"I don't know but-"

Mack T stopped the car.

"What, what now?"

"Billy just shot by us." Mack T did a three point turn in the road and followed Billy, rushing to Holden Beach.

"I didn't see no truck," Treasure said as Mack T accelerated.

"Girl, you just parked his truck at his house. He's in Ike's car." Mack T put the blunt in the ashtray.

Billy accelerated the closer he got to the bank. Mack T didn't try to keep up. Billy shot back and forth in oncoming traffic as he passed cars.

"He thinks Charisma's still at the bank," Treasure said. Mack T nodded.

"What the fuck is up with him him with Ike?"

Billy parked at the bank where is truck used to be. He never cut the engine and didn't get out. The Newport smoke escaped when he let the window down a little, still in handcuffs. His wrists were raw from jerking the garage door rail out of the ceiling. Blood spotted the collar and bottom of his Chop's Diner uniform. His blood would be on Ike when the cops discovered him. At least Ike couldn't hurt his family. Billy was fine with going back to the pen feeling like he made his family safe.

"BillyBelle!" Treasure called as Mack T pulled up to the Cadillac. "Charisma's at your house with the girls. We took the truck back too. What in the world happened?" Billy felt relief seeing Treasure free.

"Baby girl, y'all follow me." She watched him et in the car. Treasure started to say something but Billy was already on the street and at the light.

"Damn," Mack T said as they stood over Ike Long. He kicked Ike's leg. "Ole snake ass nigga. Got what he deserved."

"That's my blood on him. Can we get it off?" Charisma and Mack T looked at Billy and then at each other. They stripped Ike naked and put his clothes in a trash bag. Billy stripped naked and took a dress shirt and slacks from Ike's closet in the master bedroom.

"What about your neck?" Treasure said. "How did you get scratched like that?" Billy pointed to Ike. The vision came to Treasure and she shuddered.

"It's in his fingers," Mack T said before going to the kitchen. Billy stood over Ike while. "Look at all this. Uncle Billy, you done fucked up, all this bleeding. You know they got what they call a protein signature for blood. You scrub this muthafucka down and they still gonna know you was the one who did it."

"Oh Lord," Billy said looking down at Ike Long.

"Well...after seeing this, ain't nobody gonna think it's open season on us," Treasure said. Billy put his head in his hands. Mack T came back and shoved Treasure out of the way.

"Y'all back up," he demanded.

"What you gonna do with that butcher's knife?" Billy asked. Mack T got on one knee and moved Ike's left hand away from his body. Treasure turned away, Billy was still clueless.

"Oh Lord!" Billy shrieked as Mack T brought the knife down on Ike's fingers. Blood splattered on Mack T's face, shirt and on the dryer and clean floor. He hacked away with cold purpose until all five fingers were severed. It was beyond off putting to Billy. Treasure crossed her arms and shook her head.

"Damn Mack, why don't you just cut at the wrist? All that extra shit." Fresh blood seemed to swallow the tiled floor, approaching Billy's feet. Treasure rubbed his back.

"It's alright Billy Belle, we gotcha," she said. Mack T hacked away at Ike right wrist Treasure grabbed the bottle of bleach from the on top of the dryer. "fuck that shit Mack sayiny. This bleach is gonna clean everything in here. Then we'll set it all on fire okay." She grabbed Billy's hand. "I'm a take him to the car, you hurry the fuck up." Mack T gave Treasure the finger without looking up.

Billy was light headed. He told himself he'd protect his family no matter the cost. The idea of heading back to prison for the rest of his life was paralyzing. He wanted some water but didn't want go back inside. Mack T walked outside holding a plastic shopping bag.

"Alright Uncle Billy," Mack T said after carefully placing the bag in the trunk. He pulled out a gas siphon. "Get me a bucket out the garage." Mack T and Treasure took the gas from Ike's Cadillac and soaked the inside of the car. They put gas on the garage door rail and started a tral through the laundry room and kitchen. They doused Ike's whole body before busting almost all of the windows. The connected the gas trail from the house and the car. Mack T pulled out a lighter and tore a piece of Billy's old shirt. "Light this," he said. Billy took the lighter and lit it. Mack T dropped it on the connecting trails. Ike Long's residence was engulfed in ten minutes.

Lasagna baked as the girls cried. Charisma and Kenya screamed at their mother for the first time. A smack couldn't compare to losing their father. Treasure had to be wrong, sadly mistaken. Their dad would never die like Lovely's, he'd live forever. Charisma called Tremaine again and it went to voicemail, again. His voice message was like part of a bad dream. Treasure tried to suck it up and be strong for the girls, it didn't work. She apologized over and over and cried with them. They were walking into the chairs and into each other, unable to see through their tears. Treasure, wearing Charisma's clean clothes, didn't have any answers. Her defenses were done for the day. Mack T returned, showered and wearing brand new sneakers, a white t-shirt and blue jeans.

"Let's ride Uncle Billy," he said leaving out the back door. They went outside and left Treasure with the girls. "All the clothes and fingers and shit is burning up as we speak. I gotta go get Pound, you coming?" Billy shook his head as he walked to his truck. "Well where you fitna go then?" Billy stared at Mack T. Mack T realized that he sounded like he was questioning a child. "Sorry Unc, it's just that shit is getting crazy. We gotta know what's going on with each other until this shit blows over."

"What you mean we? *We* didn't get kidnapped today. I go where I damn well please ain't checking in with nobody but my PO." Mack T's door was already open. He closed it, looked to the sun and got in Billy's face, nodding and biting his bottom lip.

"I understand you ain't in these streets like me, I really do. But I can promise you this, ain't a soul around here that you consider family that I don't consider family. They hit Chop, they hit *my* brother. They hit Tremaine, they hit *my* brother. They hit anybody Pound love's then they hitting *my* loved ones too. Yo wife was *my* aunt, and yo kids is *my* brothers and that's how it go. I don't talk to talk neither." every time Mack T said my, he hit his own chest. He stood to Billy's side while still talking in his face. "I spilled enough blood so muthafuckas know where I stand, okay? Now I don't know what you had going on with Ike but today it ain't important. So please unc, if you can help it, don't jump into nothing else cause if you do you gonna have at least twenty niggas jumping in after you. Cause you're *my* family whether you wanna be or not."

Billy took the short gangster in. Billy couldn't remember the last time he was someone else's responsibility, Mack T was right. Because of who he was, Billy's actions carried unique consequences. If Billy got himself killed Pound and his DGBz would retaliate excessively to send a message. Whose son or father would Billy cause to be killed because of his knee jerk reactions? Billy nodded and limped in his truck.

"Hold up Billy Belle," Treasure called. "Let me fix your leg up. You got some alcohol?"

## Chapter 21

*April 15th*

**The courtroom was packed. The constant chatter of a hundred people bounced off the four walls. Cameramen stood beside the witness stand. They were to begin shooting when the jury came back from deliberation. Chop sipped water and cracked jokes. EJ tried to feign amusement. Behind them, Marie and Billy bowed their heads with Reverend Greene in prayer. Citizens in support of Erving "Chop" Belle filled every seat behind the defendant's table and the back half of the prosecutor's side. Pound, Treasure and Mack T stood at the door. Misty sat with Marie, her head also bowed.**

**It was the Brunswick County trial of the century. News stations from Raliegh to North Myrtle Beach gave their viewers daily updates. They all had a link on their respective web pages dedicated to the trial. Chop and his relationship with the sheriff's daughter made for juicy commentary. The sheriff had egg on his face after telling the Brunswick Beacon Newspaper and the Myrtle Beach Sun Newspaper that his daughter saw the error of her ways and would separate from Chop before the end of the trial. Star News of Wilmington reported Misty Helms actually proposed to Chop the day the state rested it's case. It was all**

theatre.

Against EJ's advice, Chop spoke daily with the press. He granted one on one interviews with reporters over meals at Chop's Diner. It was spring and his Easter suits were tailored and colorful. He didn't appear to have a care in the world. He often spoke of his spirituality and grief for the family of the child who overdosed from ecstasy at school. Chop felt as sorry as humanly possible. If there was anything the family needed he'd be happy to provide but he couldn't take responsibility. He constantly professed his innocence.

He spoke of the daily specials Chop's Diner offered. Reporters giving the interview got a free meal. Carol had to hire more help for the influx of customers. Some days Chop had guests for the camera. Marie interviewed with him twice, once on the first day of trial and the day of EJ's closing arguments. Reverend Greene spoke to the Wilmington news station on the court house steps. He said that if Chop was guilty of everything the state accused him of the federal government would have tried him. The more severe indictments were a result of Chop's reputation in the county. The state was picking on him. At the restaurant, Billy Belle even spoke about his incarceration and being unable to raise his son the right way. Chop's image got a much needed boost after the public learned he procured his dad a home, car and job when he was released.

EJ was masterful throughout the trial. He hammered away on the cloud of reasonable doubt hanging over the state's case. The state had a weak case to begin with. They were confident that their case against Chop was sound enough to garner a conviction. That was until the preliminary hearing.

The kid who implicated Chop was Emmanuel Cook, a fourteen year old Cedar Grove resident. He was known by classmates as a DGB, a group of boys from the Cedar Grove neighborhood who hung out together at school. Emmanuel also sold drugs for clothes and video games. He sold the toxic ecstasy to Marshall Hamilton, a sophomore varsity basketball player.

Within the month of Marshall's death, the district attorney's office arrested Chop four times. He was on trial for four charges stemming from the same incident. EJ attacked the lack of real evidence, really the lack of any evidence. Emmanuel's parents weren't present when the police questioned him. The state offered to drop four charges if he would plead guilty to the least severe charge.

He would serve thirty six to sixty months in state prison. Chop refused the plea bargain and the circus began.

Marshall overdosed on the drug and died in the locker room. He was discovered by his best friend, the one who told the police about Emmanuel. Twenty pills were discovered in Emmanuel's locker. In the principal's office, the police lead him to believe that if didn't he give up Chop they would tell his parents. Emmanuel's parents were notified and were on their way to the school an hour before Emmanuel implicated Chop as the person who gave him the drugs to sell. That's when Sheriff Helms stepped in.

The way the sheriff saw it Chop was his golden goose. Twenty thousand dollars a month and he bought ridiculous amounts of drugs from Blake. If Chop were to go away, just for a minute, the sheriff's cash flow would diminish. So he visited Judge Conley one night. It was under the judge's discretion whether or not the statement Emmanuel made to the police in the principal's was admissible. If the judge admitted it, it would the foundation of the state's case. Emmanuel had already received five years probation for a MDMA trafficking charge. Emmanuel explaining in detail his business relationship with Chop in front of the jury, should Chop take it to trial, was part of his deal. Chop was definitely taking it to trial.

Nathaniel Lance was one of the assistant district attorneys who visited Emmanuel and coached him on the questions he would have to answer on trial. When he left that evening, teenage members of the DGBs crept through Emmanuel's window to find out the state's strategy against Chop. They never forgot to promise pain, death and suffering if Emmanuel did what the state asked him to.

The Judge announced during preliminary hearings that Emmanuel's statement was inadmissible and the state was forbidden to mention the event in front of the jury. For this favor, Sheriff Helms offered the judge ten thousand dollars up front and a promise to ramp up drug convictions so the judge could better benefit from the "cash for prison time" racket he'd already been a part of. Emmanuel still had to testify for the state.

The boy flipped the script. On the stand, he said he didn't sell Marshall any drugs, he shared some drugs he found with him. Under EJ's questioning, Emmanuel told the court about Nathaniel Lance's visits to coach him for the stand. Objections seemed to sound from everywhere. The judge struck them down. After learning of the state's case engineering plot, the Chop supporters went into a frenzy. The news stations aired special investigative programs aimed at rumored corruption in the Brunswick County District Attorney's Office. For a day the judge lost all order in his court. For the foreseeable future, the state lost the faith of the public.

It was eleven am when the cameramen started shooting. The jury entered the coutroom and sat. Tara Cobb, the jury's forewoman, stood.

"Jury, do you have a verdict?" the judge asked.

"Yes you honor," said Tara. The district attorney stood when EJ and Chop stood.

"What say you?"

"On the charge of contributing to the delinquency of a minor, we find the defendant not guilty." The court roared in jubilation. The judge banged his gavel to no avail. If Chop was innocent of contributing to the delinquency of a minor he couldn't be guilty of anything else. "On the charge of conspiracy to commit murder resulting in death, we find the defendant not guilty." A lady sitting behind Marie and Misty shouted and praised God. "On the charge of manslaughter, we find the defendant not guilty. On the charge of second degree murder we find the defendant not guilty." Tara smiled and the court was in pandemonium.

Chop got up and invited everybody to the cook out he planned at the Cedar Grove Public Park in Supply. Balloons, picnic table covers, napkins, plastic forks and paper plates awaited all who wanted to come. Pound set up his music equipment on the basketball court. Every cook from Chop's Diner stood inside tents rented for the occasion and grilled pounds and pounds of meat. The weather was seventy five degrees without a cloud in the sky. Raleigh, Lumberton, Fayetvilles, Wilmington and North Myrtle Beach news stations reported the cookout as breaking news. Children ran around with hot dogs and cake. Smiling faces from Supply north Carolina came into thousands of homes on the six o'clock news. Tremaine planned another party in Myrtle Beach for the night.

"Will you bring your ass, damn!"

"Wait up, Jesus." Misty almost fell stepping onto the sidewalk. She felt naked. "This dress is too small and these heels are too high." Chop stopped walking. He looked to the star filled sky and asked God why. "Cause my feet hurt and my butt is out, that's why." Misty stopped when she got to Chop.

"First off, you gotta have a butt for it be out. Second, you the one that picked out the dress."

It was chilly. Chop was acquitted of all charges ten hours ago. Tremaine's club was undergoing renovation so he brought the party to the House of Blues in North Myrtle Beach.

"You know what, I'm not even feeling it tonight. I'm just gonna-"

"No the fuck you ain't," Chop said grabbing her as she attempted to stumble back into the parking lot. "They throwing a party for us." Misty shook her head, rubbing the goose bumps on her arms.

"Their throwing a party for you. I wasn't on trial."

"This is our engagement party girl. This ain't 'bout no trial. The whole world know I'm untouchable. They fitna find out I'm engaged." Misty rolled her eyes.

"If they watch the news they know already." Chop put his arms around her waist.

"These niggas don't watch no news." A pack of beautiful girls long legged black girls strutted by. They were younger a decade younger than and Misty and their bodies were unbelievable. "Oh that's why you're not feeling it tonight. All them big booty sistas got you shook. Ooh ooh, now you know you're too grown for that."

"I don't care about no big booty *sistas*. My feet hurt and I-"

"Oh my God." Chop lifted Misty like a new bride to carry over the threshold. "Every time we go to the club you pull this shit."

"Chop put me down right now." Chop carried her around the line for the door.

"Don't drop that snowflake," said a slim cinnamon skinned girl standing in line. She bounced in place to keep warm. "You know white skin bruises."

"So do black eyes bitch!" snapped Misty over Chop's shoulder. The pack of girls exploded and approached Misty while Chop carried her.

"Tonya," Chop said to one of the girls. She was from the Seashore neighborhood. She and Chop were real good buddies, she didn't want to mess up his flow. Her home girl was out of line but Tonya really didn't like Misty. "Y'all go'head. Now ain't the time." Tonya cut eyes at Misty before pulling her girlfriends away from Misty. Chop walked on. "Better be quiet 'fore one of them hoes jump on you," Misty sucked her teeth. She took her shoes off and held them. At the front entrance, Chop told Misty to bang on the door. An average height wide body bouncer opened the door in a huff.

"Ain't ready yet, forty minutes." Marv was from Brooklyn, New York. He had ten jobs. He was a bouncer, bartender, barber, bail bondsman, radio DJ, car detailer, song writer, studio engineer, wedding singer and he sold weed on the side. Marv knew everybody. "My man Chop, Teflon Don of the country. What you do, pass the jury some chickens, a burlap sack of pig feet?"

"Nigga let us in this muthafucka 'fore I call some New York niggas and tell'em where you hiding." Marv showed Chop and Misty his nine gold teeth and opened the door all the way for them.

"Hey!" shouted someone in line behind Chop. "What the hell y'all doing?" Marv went around Chop and Misty to confront the young man.

"One more outburst and I'll make you stay out here all night. Got that playboy?" the young man looked away and nodded. Marv went back to the door. “Get up in here Choppa Stylez. What’s good white chocolate?” Misty waved.

“Bout time,” Chop said stepping inside, “My fiancée’s getting heavy.” Misty smacked him upside the head. “What?” he asked.

“I like her,” said Marv as he followed them down stairs. “She wears the pants, ain’t that right Choppa?” Chop shook his head, Misty nodded.

“Shit, she wears the ring though, show’em that rock baby.” Chop stopped walking. Misty put the twenty carat cluster right in Marv’s face. “Bam!” Chop shouted.

“Damn, Carrie Underwood in here shining on’em. I can’t compete with that, you ruined her Chop.”

“No, not yet,” said Chop. He took the steps down to the main area. Only thirty people were inside, all Cedar Grove natives or affiliated closely with Chop, Pound and Tremaine. South Carolina folks were veteran hustlers who sold heroine for Tremaine. The past year, most of them cut the young hustlers they were grooming because of Chop’s situation. They were got drunk and making as much noise as the place did at capacity. They cheered and rushed to Chop when he turned the corner. He put Misty down and headed to the bar.

He was right, it wasn’t a party just for him. A big gold banner hung from the stage curtain. It read “Chop and Misty Happily Engaged”. Misty put on her shoes and went to the dance floor for a closer look. Identical banners hung on all three sides of the second floor rail.

“Misty, get over here!” Chop barked. Misty put her hands her hips and turned to a smiling Chop. She strolled leisurely to the bar. Chop grabbed her hand and held up her ring finger.

“Dayum!” somebody said.

“That’s a crazy ring,” another said.

“She deserves it,” Chop said. He kissed her in front of everybody, something he rarely did. People from the outside began funneling in. “Come on.”

**Chop and Misty walked hand in hand upstairs. Their weren't any turned up noses or off hand remarks for the rest of the night. Only smiles greeted them. Pound stood and gave his brother a hug, lifted him off his feet. He took Misty's hand and hugged her too.**

**"Congratulations little sis," Misty could have died.**

**All night they drank and danced smoked and drank. The DJ played songs from a list of Chop and Misty's favorites.**

**People Misty had never seen congratulated her and wished her the best. Most of the well wishes were fake but Misty loved the effort. A couple black girls got between her and Chop on the dance floor. Their small outfits made Misty feel like a nun. They looked like two strippers putting their legs and asses all over Chop. Chop kept dancing and smiling. Misty didn't hesitate. She punched the girl blocking her way to Chop in the face. She pulled the girl grinding on Chop to the floor by her hair. Chop kept dancing. The bouncers rushed to the dance floor and carried the girls out the back. Chop doubled over in laughter. He took his gold and diamond chain with the huge butcher charm and put it around Misty's neck. It was the best night of her life.**

That was three months ago, almost to the day. Misty sat in her car in front of the crime scene tape at the Long asphalt plant. She'd been avoiding the place. She kept saying to herself that Chop didn't deserve to die but she really felt that she didn't deserve to lose the love of her life. Maybe Chop was a drug dealer, maybe even a thug but what the hell did she do to deserve this agony? She was alone. Marie was losing her graciousness by the hour. Misty was no longer her grandson's fiancée and wouldn't be family anytime soon. Billy was really nice but so what. Nothing connected them anymore. Her mom could only offer an 'I told ya so'. Diana couldn't help who she was. The world had become exceptionally cruel.

The night Chop got killed Misty called Blake. He was a good little brother, too smart for his own good sometimes but good to talk to. She called him to discuss something that had been on her mind for a long time. One of Misty's co-workers at Autumn Care told her that she heard that Chop had been sleeping around on

Misty for months. She said he creeping with Kiana. The co-worker made Misty promise not to tell Chop before she said it. Misty dismissed it. She never asked Chop where he was going when he stayed out all night, she just didn't. She let the rumor invade her every thought for weeks. One night, when Chop was out, images of the two of them played in Misty's mind. The idea of Kiana being with Chop and then smiling in her face made Misty physically sick. Kiana was so gorgeous. She was beautiful with the smoothest honey brown skin, courteous and generous to a fault.  Misty used to wonder how she and Chop got so close. What did he say to her that made her be a pen pal to Pound in prison for Chop?

She called Kiana one night when Chop was gone. Kiana didn't pick up. She picked up the next day and the following nights when Chop was home. *Were they fucking that much or was it a coincidence?* she thought.

Misty couldn't let go of her denial of being intimidated by black women. Every black girl gave her a pang of worry. She couldn't be black for Chop. He never asked her to but it seemed like that's what everybody thought he needed. Her greatest fear remained that he needed to have a black girl so bad that one day he would leave her because of one. But *Kiana*, his brothers girlfriend? If it were true, could it be love or just lust? She called Blake to ask his thoughts. The night Chop died, Blake didn't answer his phone.

When Chop cut Blake off, he didn't tell Misty where he got his drugs from. Outside of Blake, he never let her in on any of his dealings. The only reason she got involved initially was because Chop let it slip that his supplier wouldn't be able sell anything for a while, something about a drought. Blake had been begging Misty for months to talk to Chop about doing business with him.

Misty was aware of her dad's questionable activities. Growing up, she'd hear the sheriff, after he had a few whiskeys, joke about the characters he encountered on a daily basis. Misty was always daddy's little girl but when the sheriff condoned her relationship with Chop she knew it wasn't because of their closeness. Blake informed her that Chop and the sheriff already had a working relationship. Chop would make certain considerations for the sheriff for relief of pressure from the sheriff's office. One of those considerations was a brand new fifteen foot motor boat sitting on a Southport dock.

To Misty and Blake's mutual surprise, Chop chose to do business. This was just after New Years Day. The sheriff acquired drugs and money from various busts he chose not to report. He had a time proven system that assured a steady supply of heroine. People would always sell it so after they bring to the state, rob them for it. If you wanted to sell drugs in Brunswick County you had to kick in or go to jail for a long time. Jail was for the poor.

Having Chop as a customer made Blake legitimate, he was so grateful to Misty. Misty tried to placate her brother after Chop cut him off and it was impossible. Blake kept telling her to leave Chop, she deserved better. The beef between him and the Long's could boil over and he didn't want her to get hurt because of it. Misty knew that Chop paid the sheriff well and continued to do so, Blake was feeling left out. She told him that Chop planned to stop selling drugs altogether and they planned to move to Lockwood Folly, an upper middle class suburban golf community.

Blake called the night of the day Chop was discovered. He gave his condolences and offered advice. It was time to come home, at least leave Cedar Grove. She wouldn't do anything immediately, he figured, but asked her to start preparing for the inevitable exit. Diana offered that advice in the driveway. Marie echoed those opinions on the way to the funeral home. Misty planned to be in her new home in the Lockwood Folly community in three days. New furniture had been ordered and schedule for delivery.

Billy called and met her at the new house. Misty never saw Billy so nervous, limping and on the verge of crying. She reconsidered her connection with him. They would always be friends because they saw the best in other. He shared the news about Treasure, Tremaine and Pound. Misty was alarmed but not devastated, the only way for someone to accomplish that would be to bring Chop back to life and kill him again. Billy didn't want her alone. He wanted her to go to her mom's but that was the last place she'd go willingly. Even the sheriff hadn't called to see his girl was okay. How could he not know she was hurting? She hugged Billy in her new driveway then left for the Long Asphalt Plant. She'd been at the asphalt plant for hours. The sun had set an hour ago. How did Chop end up here? Who was he with that night? Did it even matter now? What was she to make of her life?

The worry and grief made her weak, turning the ignition was a chore. Her

Lexus crawled down the long gravel driveway. She looked right and then left. She turned left on the highway while still looking right. The blaring horn never registered. She accelerated as a Buick Regal fishtailed toward her. The left side of her front bumper collided with the Buick's bumper. The air bag exploded as she flew from her seat and through the wind shield. Oncoming cars veered away from her as she fell face first in the median.

## Chapter 22

*TV-"We'll show you live footage of Holden Beach fire fighters putting out a raging fire in the home of Ike Long, owner of Long Landscaping, Long heating and Air and Long trucking. Ike Long's car was also set on fire and burned beyond recognition. The house belongs to Ike Long but it isn't where he lives I'm told. He is beleived to be in the burning house. We'll keep you posted on future developments.*

*Right now there's an Amber alert out for Heather and Cassandra McKinley. Heather and Cassandra are cousins and are of the Sunset Beach community. They were last seen June 30$^{th}$ at the Oceanside Ice Cream parlor in Sunset Beach. Both girls work at the ice cream parlor. Heather is fifteen, five three, slim build, blond hair and blue eyes. Cassandra is seventeen, five six, medium build, brown hair and brown eyes. If you have any information on the girls or know their whereabouts call 910-"*

*8:30pm*

"Fred!" called Linda from upstairs in the bedroom. The reverend sat downstairs in the den with a bowl of pistachios.

"What!"

"Get the door please." The reverend put the bowl on the coffee table and turned off the TV. He put his sneakers back on and buttoned his shirt. He tucked it in, grabbed his keys and approached the door. If he didn't want to talk to the person he'd tell them he was just heading out and drive the opposite direction of the visitor until he/she was out of sight.

"Billy? Hey man." They shook hands. Billy smiled.

"Hey Rev. I didn't mean to bother I just-" The reverend stepped back and opened the door.

"No no no. Come in, please." Billy grimaced as he limped inside.

Reverend Greene lived just in Calabash North Carolina, a beach town near the state line. A retired educator, the reverend started as an elementary school teacher and retired as principle of Shallotte Middle School. His smile was his ID. People knew the reverend by his smile if not his name. Even twenty five years ago when he used to spank kids in school, he did it with a smile. The reverend wasn't a Cedar Grove native, he was from Goldsboro. He used to visit his uncle in Supply who was a deacon at Cedar Grove Missionary Baptist Church.

As a teenager Freddie's only interests were the girls and the girls were mutually interested. Freddie, a high yellow kid with a huge afro, straight teeth and full beard was a chick magnet. He learned to fight by defending himself from angry boyfriends. He was a big and beefy kid who was unusually strong but never played sports. For money during the summer, he'd mow lawns with his uncle's lawn mower and pull weeds from flowerbeds. After driving to somebody's house, he'd hop on the back of the truck, stand the riding lawn mower up grab it and lift it with his legs. He'd casually walk it off the back, sit it down and cut the grass. He moved in with his uncle and got a custodian job in the Brunswick County School system when Billy started seeing Angela. Freddie had eyes for Angela but she was too wholesome for his tastes. Freddie preferred super freaks.

UNC Wilmington granted Freddie a minority scholarship. He almost flunked out of college because he kept skipping classes. Whenever a girl called for sex, regardless of her appearance, Freddie was too ready. It took his parents paying him a surprise visit (and his dad giving him a surprise beating) to straighten him out. After graduation, he became an elementary school teacher in Brunswick County and moved back with his uncle in Supply. He bought an orange Plymouth Duster and chased the girls harder than before.

Somebody, a jilted lover of one of Freddie's girls, riddled the left side of the car with bullets. The car was on the lot just four months prior. Billy talked to the man who did it and got him to leave Freddie alone. Billy was from Raeford, a small town in Hoke County. He and Freddie were friends because they were considered outsiders to many in the county.

Painful STDs couldn't deter Freddie's hunger. He'd be back at it before whatever illness he had cleared up. At a Lake Waccamaw cook-out, he punched a man over a girl and almost killed him. Freddie and the girl weren't an item but she brought a date to the cook-out and Freddie didn't like it. One day he woke up in Anita's house with her husband Arthur standing over him with a gun. It took a whole day of begging and praying to get out of the house alive.

He found his calling to preach soon after he proposed to Linda Hankins. She was from a good family like Angela's, just not as religious. Linda was pregnant by Freddie and so was another woman. The other woman was a one night stand. Linda was his woman though he wasn't truly in love with her. After a few months apart, he decided he did love Linda and with the help of his family, bought a house and convinced her to marry him. The other woman moved away and didn't introduce her child to Freddie until the child, a girl, was twelve. By then Reverend Greene was an assistant principle and the pastor of Cedar Grove Missionary Baptist Church. He took her in with his other daughter. The girls went to college and started families. Linda's daughter lived in Raleigh and the other daughter lived in Wilmington.

Billy left his sneakers at the door, lush beige carpet welcomed him. His thick cigarette odor harassed the peach air freshener Linda bombed the house with. The reverend gave Billy his seat on the couch and sat on the sofa after putting his keys on the table.

"You're just coming in?" Billy asked.

"No man, I've been here all day getting ready for the service tomorrow. I gotta tell you, I ain't never had a funeral this soon after the death but if that's what Marie wants then hey. You doing alright?" Billy nodded but his eyes and slumped shoulders betrayed him. "You sure brother?" Billy looked exhausted and as if he'd seen a ghost. Behind his clean dress shirt sleeves his wrists were heavily wrapped. Billy limped heavily and his right leg seemed swollen. The reverend didn't want to know if he had to ask. "Well how's Marie doing? They say she's cooking up a storm."

"Is she? She's been wearing me out. The spread tomorrow could feed a thousand people." The reverend couldn't wait. He leaned back and put his keys on the sofa beside him.

"Do you have anything you'd like to say at the service?" Billy closed his eyes and shook his head. "Do you know how your son got the name Chop?" he asked. Billy shrugged.

"I never even asked him. I remember when he would come and see me. I'd be calling him Erving but Angela and Marie was calling him Chop. So I called him Chop." The reverend smiled.

"Well, Erving was in the fourth grade-"

"Yeah, he was around the fourth grade then," Billy said. The reverend nodded.

"He'd gotten into it with one of his classmates, just some pushing and shoving, nothing too bad. I gave both of them a warning and sent'em back to class. The other boy's big brother was in the seventh or eight grade. When school let out that day they cornered Erving in front of the buses. I guess the biggest boy thought Erving was a easy way because he took two big handfuls of his shirt and slammed him up against the bus. Erving kicked that boy square in his little nuts." Billy laughed and sat back, giving the reverend that smile he was looking for. "The boy fell back on his back pack, holding his mess and whimpering like a kitten. The little brother tried to rush Erving and Billy I'm telling ya. Erving hit him with a karate chop across the neck. You could see the effects of the chop ripple down the boy's body. He just fell out like in the movies, twitching like he was in a seizure. Scared me to death. We thought your son sho'nuff knew some shit. Erving got in a Bruce Lee stance, pulling his dungarees up like he fitna kick somebody 'cross the head or something." The reverend picked up the bowl pistachios from the table. He offered Billy some, he declined. "So I snatched his little behind up and took him back to my office. Angela was at work. Marie told me to tear his ass up. Told me to whoop him with my belt until she got to us. When she got there she took my belt and whooped him some more. She looked more like Bruce Lee than him." They laughed. Billy took some Pistachios sat back. "The next day and everyday afterward, the kids called him Chop. Then when he got to playing football, people cheered for Chop."

"I swear I never heard that," Billy said between giggles.

Behind his smile, the reverend studied Billy. Whatever funk he came through the door with soon returned. Losing loved ones took the worse toll on people. They were easy to amuse because they were desperate for a laugh. Laughter couldn't cure but it could heal.

"You know what I was thinking before you come in?" the reverend asked.

"One more person drop in on me unannounced and I'm moving."

"No," the reverend said laughing. "I was thinking about how blessed I am. I worked hard for what I have but I've been give so much more. Even the chance to work for what I wanted was a blessing, ya know." Billy nodded. "My biggest blessing in life is knowing the joy of giving. I mean, somebody is in crisis and I can help them out of it. Outside of children, it's the greatest joy. I pray the most for folks who can't stand to give their time or help to somebody. That's why God got us here now." The reverend put the bowl down on the end table. "People can say what they want about your son but I knew him, you hear me. His heart and his good deeds far outweighed whatever shortcomings he had. He's brought so many folks up out of terrible situations. His only condition was to not be praised for it. I'm gonna praise him at the service though. I'm gonna shout about the kids he educated, people he employed, the sick he cared for and the lives he saved. This is a big deal Billy. See, people don't know that a lot of the things the church does is largely financed by a precious few members." The reverend took the black side on his left hand and hit his right palm. "Chop paid house notes, medical bills, scholarships, he paid for whole food drives. Very few of those gestures were asked of him. He gave willingly Billy. His sins made him human but his joy of giving made him worthy of the kingdom of God." Billy nodded. The reverend had a talent of stirring his audience, no matter how big or small. Billy had a talent of holding his stirred spirit inside. "Marie and Angela did a good job with him but his need to give was hereditary."

"Oh yeah," Billy said.

"Come on now. You remember when them boys was gonna shoot me and you stuck your neck out for me?"

"Yeah, I remember. I figured if I saved your life you'd let me keep my girl." The reverend doubled over in laughter. He sat up and wiped a tear from his eyes.

"I wasn't shit back then man. Being away from my daddy and mama, I thought I was entitled to be crazy. My uncle kept telling me that God had a purpose for me. I thought I was serving my purpose with them women but I wasn't. God put me around people like you to keep me until I came to my senses." Billy shook his head. "No no, come on now. I ain't shooting you no mess. That's why Angela chose you. She wanted a man with sense that wasn't trying to prove nothing out the way of himself. And you was kind. You went to see about people who couldn't give you nothing for it."

"And you was so broke back then," Billy said with a chuckle.

"Man that grass couldn't grow fast enough. Didn't have the sense to find a woman with money. It worked it out though. I found something special, something Erving had. Something he got from you." Billy and the reverend sat in silence for a minute. "Billy, going forward you gotta know your fulfilling God's purpose not the world's. The world don't reward you all the time for doing God's work. That's why you did all that time and Erving's no longer with us. Don't second guess yourself. God made giving and caring a joy for you so do what makes you feel good. It'll ease whatever worry you got."

Billy just had called Andy Stahl while sitting in his truck in Reverend Greene's driveway. Andy got the safe opened. It contained jewelry, flash drives and documents, looked to be contracts. Billy asked Andy to put the contents of the safe in a bag and take it to Marie, only Marie. Billy called Marie and told her to be on the look out for a skinny red haired white man with a baseball cap. Marie sent Billy a text while he sat the reverend thanking him and saying she got everything. Carol texted him too, she was home and needed a partner in the shower. Billy stood.

"Thanks Rev," The reverend stood and hugged Billy.

"Anytime brother."

"Listen Rev, I wanna talk to you about something. I was wanting to help with giving-"

"Hold up Billy," the reverend turning the TV up. "Look at that, they showing Ike Long's house in Cedar grove."

*TV-"We have breaking news. Ike Long of Long Landscaping and Long Heating and Air was found dead in his burning house in the Cedar Grove community. The house I a total loss, the fire chief suspects arson. A driver dialed 911 after seeing huge billows of smoke come from over the trees. In related news, the Brunswick County Sheriff's Office released a statement saying Ike Long was a person of interest in the murder of Erving "Chop" Belle. Ike Long's brother, Early Long was found dead in his home in Phoenix two nights ago. Sheriff Helms told the Brunswick Beacon that Early Long, 48, had connections to Heather and Cassandra McKinley, the two missing girls from Sunset Beach. This is a bizarre story. We'll keep you updated as it develops here on"-*

The reverend shook his head. He reached for the house phone.

"Lord have mercy. Ike Long is...he just called me this morning."

"Is that right?" said Billy. The reverend nodded, he put the phone down.

"Man he called and told me to pray for him. We prayed for thirty minutes. He said he felt better. Excuse me." The reverend left Billy in the living room as he gave Linda the bad news.

## Chapter 23

*Bucc's Home*

Neal went in and out of consciousness. Thick yellow rope squeezed his arms to his body. The ropes went through sheetrock and were fastened on studs in the kitchen wall. Neal sat in a wooden chair. Laces from his sneakers tied his feet to the chair at the ankle. He went to Bucc's like Mack T instructed him to. Bucc's doublewide trailer sat on Mt Pisgah across from Cedar Grove Road. Bucc was an original DBG. He started hustling for Ike Long the same time Pound did. When Pound got of prison Bucc had cut ties with Ike because his suspicion that Ike set him up along with other small time dealers. He knew everybody and what everybody wanted. He had two homes like Mack T, one near Cedar Grove and one away. His home near Cedar Grove was a DGB hang out. Guys smoked weed and drank liquor in the yard and in the living room while waiting for their phones to ring.

Neal's baby's mother, one of them, dropped him off at Treasure's where his Kawasaki Ninja waited. He drove straight to Bucc's. Bucc waved him to the back of the house. The place was deserted. Sheriff Deputy cars whizzed by every minute to and from Ike Long's burning house.

Neal and Bucc had a nice conversation about bitches. Bucc knew almost every woman in the county, if not them then their mothers or aunts or cousins. Neal rolled a blunt and Bucc poured him some Ciroc vodka. For twenty minutes they joked and laughed. They kept speaking when Pound and Mack T came through the back door. Pound gave Bucc a dap and punched Neal in the face. Immediately they grabbed him, put him in the kitchen and tied him up. Pound slapped him across the face repeatedly.

"Where it at homeboy?" Pound asked an inch away from Neal face. "Where all this work at you 'sposed to have?" Neal looked to Mack T. Mack stood against the wall with his arms crossed.

"He asked you a question little cousin," he said.

"Man, I come here see if y'all needed some-"

Pound slapped slobber and blood from Neal's mouth. Snot ran from his nose. Neal seemed to be in shock. Someone pulled up in the front yard. Bucc went to check on it.

"Who you think you playing with?" asked Pound. "Where the fuck is the shit at?"

"Tell him Neal," said Mack T calmly.

"Nigga how you gonna do your own family like this?" Neal cried to Mack T. Neal's dad and Neal's mother were siblings. "All I'm trying to do is-" Pound slapped him three especially hard times. Neal slipped in and out of consciousness.

"If I ball my fist, you're gonna lose teeth and your jaw is getting knocked out the socket. Where is the shit boy?" Neal looked to Pound then again behind him to Mack T. "Mack, he think you fitna save him from me. He think if he keeps his mouth shut he'll be alright." Pound walked to the sink. Mack T lifted Neal head up and checked his bruises.

"Mack, you said if you liked my shit you'd cop and put me on with-" Mack T slapped Neal across the head and almost snapped his neck. Neal's eyes bulged, he saw stars. The stars put a strong glare on something, Neal couldn't think of what it was.

"Tell me where the work is and I won't let nothing else happen to you. Tell me right now so I can get it and we can be done with this." Neal never felt so much hate for a relative than he did right then. He looked up to Mack T, the motorcycles, the clothes and the trucks, all the dope boys loved him and he didn't even sell dope. Neal thought Mack T was new to the drug game and that he could run Cedar Grove through him and Pound. Pound turned every spider of the stove on high. He filled four pots with water.

"My half is at Grandma's," Neal said.

"You got bricks at Grandmama's house?" Mack T asked.

"Who grandma?" Pound said over his shoulder.

"Grandma Sherry," Neal said looking at Mack T.

"Okay family," Mack T said pulling his keys from his pocket. "I'm a go get it. Where is it in the house?"

"Hold up Mack," Pound said walking back to Neal. "Your half? Who got the other half family?" Neal rolled his eyes and turned his attention to Mack T.

"In your old room, under the bed."

Pound slapped the feeling out of the left side of Neal's face. Mack T held Pound back. "You think I won't fuck you up nigga! You don't think I know where that shit come from? This a game to you?" Bucc came back, smoking a blunt. He sat at dinner table across the kitchen from Neal, as calm as you please.

"He just told us where the shit is at, ain't that what we wanted? Let's go get it," Mack T said.

"Fuck that, you go get it." Neal never saw Mack T let anyone talk to him like Pound. Pound wasn't a big hustler, he was just Chop's brother, that's all. He wasn't making any money, Neal reasoned. Neal couldn't wait to ask the sheriff to set Pound up. He would gladly sign any statement putting Pound under a prison.

Mack T must have been letting him blow off steam since his brother came up dead, Neal figured. Mack T rubbed his bald head and strolled out the back door. Pound sat a pot holder at Neal's feet. Neal watched the boiling pot of water leave the stove and approach him. The buzz of marijuana and alcohol he received from Bucc had been slapped out of him. Looking at the boiling water made his nerves become sensitive. Pound sat the pot on the pot holder with a small measuring cup beside it. "Don't be scared little nigga, be honest. Let me tell you what I know first. The dope you got belong to the sheriff. Him and his son Blake got you out here peddling they shit." Neal was silent. Pound, squatting in front of him, chuckled and dipped the measuring cup in the pot. Neal shook his head.

"No no no my boy Blake-" Pound let a few drops hit his bare foot. Neal tried to jump through the rope. He was going nowhere. Piss rushed out of him, running down his leg.

"What you just say?"

"Blake," Neal blurted like he just came up from being under water.

"Blake? Blake what?" Pound asked. Neal tried to lessen the pain of his foot with deep breathes. Pound dipped the cup in the water.

"Blake Helms, the sheriff's son. He got other half." Neal stared at cup. Pound put the cup down and stared at Neal. He stood and walked to the sink. Bucc offered him the blunt, he turned it down. He stared out of the window over the sink as a picture formed in his head. Mack T told him about every customer Neal approached the day before. None of those guys were caught in the sweep with Treasure and Lavelle and Syncere. They refused Neal's business and got busted. Pound took another pot and squatted in front of Neal.

"No Pound, I just told you where I got the shit fro-" Pound poured the whole pot on Neal's feet. Neal screamed and pissed himself again. Pound got another boiling pot from the stove. The skin tried to run from his legs. The nerves momentarily went numb. Neal shook, screamed and cried. He screamed and quickly sucked in enough breath scream again. Bucc sat up, balled his face, smoked his blunt and turned his head. He turned back, he didn't see this everyday.

"Look at me, look at me," Pound said calmly. He took some paper towels off a roll on the counter. He wiped Neal's eyes. "Look at me. Are you looking at me?" Neal gritted his teeth and nodded. "I did that because this is important and I don't need no more bullshit." Pound squatted down and sat the fresh pot down. "Who else is gonna be swept up by the task force?" The anguish on Neal's face was briefly replaced with worry. He looked away. Pound grabbed the pot.

"Okay okay okay," Neal snapped. "I'm supposed to come here and put y'all on. If y'all ddn't wanna be down then they was coming through here scooping everybody." Pound stood and let the information spin in his head.

"So...when did they decide this, when Chop died?" he asked. Neal shook his head.

"No," Neal said looking Pound in the eyes. "They planned this when Chop cut Blake off. They got me to help organize the sweeps after they killed Chop."

"What!" Bucc said, he stood and approached Neal.

Neal's burned up feet made him realize that he was only a pawn in Blake's chess game. He didn't sign up to be tortured. Pound was obliviously a more significant figure than Blake and the sheriff gave him credit for being. Neal felt that his life was in danger, he gave up the goods.

"Blake and his dad didn't kill Chop but they were their when he was killed."

Pound and Bucc listened as Neal spilled the details behind Chop's murder. It was the most sickening thing Pound had ever heard. He went outside to the back yard and snorted seven nail fulls of coke. He squatted down and cried in his hands.

## Chapter 24

*9:15pm*

"Oh Lord no," Diana muttered as her Expedition sped out of the driveway. "I'm coming baby, just hang on." She flew through downtown Southport and west on 211. Red lights and pedestrians were equally ignored. Sam told her not to rush. Misty was rattled but she wasn't too bad, just a fender bender he said. The news said other wise. Broken spine, dozens of bones broken, emergency surgery, chances of survival slim to none. Why did they have to mention Chop of all people? Would her daughter be forever associated with him?

Diana's phone rang, she didn't answer. She reached the twenty minute destination in eight minutes.

"Honey," he said rushing out of the emergency room double doors. "They're working on her so we can't see her." Diana tried to march by him and into the emergency room. Sam wrapped his arms around her. She swung at him, hitting his cheek and collarbone. "Diana, wha...what's your damn problem!"

"You're my problem you son of a bitch!" she screamed, her face turned beet red. "It's all because of you!"

"Honey, I wasn't even there. And if I was, you know it would've been me in there instead of-"

"This is all you Sam. All the dirty money, the messing over people. It's come back through our baby!" Sam rolled his eyes upward then looked to the highway. The two deputies with him went back inside.

"You really wanna go there right now when our child is in the hospital fighting for her life!" Sam screamed. Diana stared at her husband with eyes of pure hatred.

"I thought I was getting punished for condoning your bullshit when she got serious with that boy but no. We're paying the price now. You, for *all* the crooked shit you got going and me for not taking my children away from you." Over the years, Sam had given his wife few reasons to be so dramatic. Even when she found money and drugs in the house he'd spend a good deal of it on her.

"Misty had an accident today," the sheriff said stepping toward Diana, she backed up. "She's in a bad way Honey. I'm talking lacerations, fractured bones, spine trauma and brain injury. We, you *and* I, need to be here for her when she wakes up." Sam checked his watch. "They ain't gonna be done with her any time soon." Diana let Sam put his arms around her. She prayed silently as they entered the emergency room.

"My baby," she cried into the sheriff's chest. "The news, they said it was so bad. They said she was thrown-"

"Forget what they said." The sheriff squeezed his wife. "Our girl will be fine. She'll come through this because she has us, right?" she nodded as she held the sheriff.

Diana had her yard just she way wanted for the party tomorrow. Flags lined her driveway and decorated the big red oak in the front. She brought a store full of wicker sofas and chairs and spread them out at the foot of the yard facing the Intercoastal Waterway. Her guests would enjoy punch and beer on the furniture as they watched the annual Southport Fireworks Show. A round of apologizing and making up to Misty was scheduled for the morning. Guess it wasn't meant to be. Diana wanted to wring Misty's neck. Now she wanted to be the one near death if it meant her girl could be out of this predicament.

"Well," she said. "Let's sit and pray until their done with her. I'm gonna be the first thing she sees when she gets up."

"You sure are Honey. I guess we can sit over here and-" The sheriff stopped talking at the sight of Neal. He was being carried into the emergency room by Mack T. Marcus Tate, drug dealer, 1996 West Brunswick High Wrestling State Champ, suspected post-Chop DBG leader. Neal guaranteed Blake and the sheriff that Mack T, supposedly hoping to help fill the drug dealing void Chop left, would get on board because they were related. Mack T screamed on the receptionist and she let them into the emergency room.

"What Sam?" asked Diana, wiping her cheeks. "What's going on?"

"Sit." The sheriff took Diana by the hand and led her to the chairs. Diana sat and the sheriff waited for his moment. A nurse came out of the emergency room. Then Mack T rushed out the door. The sheriff caught the door before it closed.

There was only one available seat in the waiting room. It was next the man who praised his son Chop on TV during the trial for giving him a job and a house and a truck with drug money. He looked tired. He grimaced pulling in his outstretched leg for Diana to get by. She sat and looked toward the entrance.

"Misty's gonna make it," Billy said, nodding to his own statement. "So many people are praying for her." Diana took a deep breath and nodded and turned the back of her head to Billy. "I was just with her before the accident happened. She and Marie have been going at a hundred miles per hour lately."

Diana turned around. Misty lived in Cedar Grove for three years. Diana never thought she spoke to anybody but Chop and Marie. As she understood it, this man was in prison for murder. It was unsettling to know that her daughter was so close with such people.

"Misty is a strong willed girl," Diana said with an insincere smile, clenching her purse. Billy smiled sincerely and uncrossed his arms.

"Yeah," he said, nodding. "She's really special. You wanna know what I had to nerve to say to my son after he brought her to visit me for first time in prison?"

"She did what?" Diana asked.

"She visited me when I was in prison. She was so excited to see me. I was really surprised to see her." Billy sat up and turned to Diana. "My son didn't tell me she was white though. I ain't racist or nothing. It's just that he introduced her as the girl living with him in the house in Cedar Grove and all and-"

"Uh huh," Diana said. "So what did you say?"

"I told him she was nice and all but maybe he should rethink being serious with a white girl ya know." Billy shook his head. "She's beautiful, you know that. I was just afraid that they'd be in for more trouble than their relationship was worth."

"Did they see a lot of trouble as far as you could tell?" Diana asked. The nurse called two and three patients at a time from the waiting area.

"Chop acts like don't nothing bother him. Well, he was how he used to act. Misty bottles stuff up. A lot people, I don't know why, thought and hoped Misty wasn't genuine. Thought at the first sign of trouble she'd bail on Chop." Billy shook his head studying the floor. "She loved my son more than anybody. All she wanted was for people to stop giving her hell about it. She holds too much in, always trying to please everybody. I was the only one she could vent to. Everybody else wanted to tell her what she was *supposed* to do."

"Again, she's strong willed," Diana said.

"Maybe so but...she was the best decision my son ever made. He strived to be better than himself for her. Only a good woman makes a man do that. She's the last person should be laid up in here under the knife." Diana studied Billy. He was worried about her daughter. He was her friend, soft spoken convicted murderer. Diana's friends called and told her that Misty got into a terrible accident. None of them volunteered to come and see about her. They watched Misty grow from a baby to a woman and then washed their hands with her.

"Mr. Belle, I wanna say thank you for being there for Misty. If I can be honest, I haven't been the best-"

"Diana!" the sheriff called marching down the hall. "Diana, whatever you do, don't leave this hospital. I'm giving the two deputies here orders to protect you okay," he kissed Diana on the forehead, looked at Billy for a second and rushed out the entrance. "Don't leave this hospital." Diana and Billy looked at other.

## Chapter 25

*January 10th, a year and a half ago*

**Announcer 1: "Marshall Hamilton, the sophomore sensation for the West Brunswick Trojans pushes the ball up. Marshall has been the only one to do it for the Trojans tonight. Despite the constant double team from North Brunswick, Marshall has produced from the field."**

**Announcer 2: "The kid's fifteen years old with a shot as sweet as I've ever seen anywhere."**

**Announcer 1: "Roy Williams and Coach K didn't visit our fair county for nothing. The Scorpions press Marshall, he passes to the top of the key. He gets it back for a fade away behind the arc,"**

**Announcer 1 and 2: "Ohh!"**

**Announcer 2: "Nothing but net! Oh my goodness this kid is magical. The Trojans trail by five with twenty seconds left. The Scorpions-"**

**Announcer 1: "Trojans steal! Trojans steal and find Marshall Hamilton in the deep corner."**

Announcer 1 and 2: "Ohh!"

Announcer 2: "Oh my! This Shallotte crowd is rabid. An eight point Scorpion lead cut to two in two quick possessions. The Scorpions throw it in and are immediately fouled."

Announcer 1: "Tyree Taylor the Scorpions' center lines up for a one and one. Tyree Taylor, the six eight senior phenom of Leland has committed to UNCW for a full ride and-"

Announcer 2: "He missed, he missed! Trojans rebound, Marshall pushes the ball!"

Announcer 1: "And the crowd is on their feet to see Marshall do it again. Nine seconds and Marshall's trapped in the corner. He passes down the right."

Announcer 2: "Marshall races to the top of the key. He get's the ball as the crowd screams that he's open. Set three pointer for the win."

Announcer 1 and 2: "Ohh!"

Announcer 1: "He did it! He did it! He did it!"

Announcer 2: "81 to 80, another close one for the Trojans. Marshall Hamilton with another thirty point game! Oh my goodness, he's just too good."

Announcer 1: "Marshall celebrates with his teammates. His dad, Don Marshall of Marshall Developers, lifts him up at half court with a bear hug. Easy Mr. Hamilton, we need him at a hundred percent if we're going to Chapel Hill for the championship."

Don Hamilton couldn't have been more proud. His only boy, a high school star on his way to play with the big boys at Duke, NC State, Maryland, Kansas or North Carolina. Don wanted Duke but Marshall had his own plans. The team enjoyed a dinner at Pizza Hut that night, courtesy of the Hamiltons. Don left Marshall that night to meet Chop and EJ at EJ's office.

"Don, your boy is on fire," EJ greeted as they shook hands. Don nodded.

"He's something."

"He's more than something," Chop said, slapping Don across the back before sitting on EJ's desk. Don Hamilton, forty eight years old, six two, two hundred forty pound well built Army veteran. "He's the future. Watch how all these kids from Leland and Myrtle Beach come this off season to play with Marshall." Don sighed.

He had been very chummy with these guys for better than a year. Don had sought advice from a number of players around the area including Sheriff Helms and they were right. These guys, Erving "Chop" Belle and Eric Johnson Jr were suckers. Two guys ,in over their heads, desperate to clean their drug money.

Don acquired ten acres of land on Shallotte's Main Street. He had designs put a one hundred unit apartment complex at the end of town, price tag of twenty two million dollars. To get a loan for that much money Don had to have atleast a forty million dollar multi-asset minimum, Don's assets totaled around sixteen five, enter Chop Belle. While they had a number of conversations over the course of three years, Don had accumulated several small partners who invested various small assets. Don had miraculously raised seventeen point five million dollars in assets, seven million of that from Chop Belle alone. Chop put up his diner, his house, his three dozen mobile homes and his stake in a number of businesses he co-owned like Bryant Auto of Shallotte. Don recruited Chop to help him find that last six million and together they did. Chop found a Myrtle Beach investor who offered the last six Don needed. When he saw the list of investors the man withdrew his six million.

The name Erving "Chop" Belle meant bad business to him. Brunswick and Horry Counties have a number of wealthy people but in their small communities Everybody knows everybody's business and this man knew Chop Belle to be a two-bit country drug dealer. He offered to invest thirteen million dollars in cash and assets if Don would remove Chop from the equation.

"Listen guys, I came down here tonight to tell you to your face and not over the phone. The Hamilton Grove Apartments is a no go." EJ and Chop looked at each other.

“And why isn’t it a go Mr. Hamilton?” EJ asked.

“EJ, it’s still Don.” Don shrugged and sighed again.

“The zoning’s there. We already have all the contractor’s to build it. The mayor himself is already praising this as one of his accomplishments. What happened?”

“Well...the Hamilton Grove Apartments will be built. You two won’t have a part in it, that’s all.” Chop stood and strolled to the door.

“How the hell did we lose our part in it?” he asked. EJ looked at him with pleading eyes. He didn’t want Chop flying off the handle, even if it was justified.

“Guys, you’ve been great. I don’t want any hard feelings,” Don said. He walked to the door. As he reached for the knob Chop pushed him to the ground.

“Are you stupid or something?” he said standing over Don. “We invested a lot to make this project a reality. Now you’re gonna shit on us and these local companies who think their fitna build a hundred unit apartment complex?”

“I would never shit them Erving, just you.” EJ jumped over his desk and put some distance between Chop and Don.

“Why just him Don?” he asked. EJ allowed Don to get up. Chop almost flew off the handle at EJ.

“Listen, this arrangement we had felt good at first. Now, since everything’s in place I’ve been enlightened to a few things. Erving, I’m sorry but in the business you’re an undesirable dude. You’re on the wrong side of the law and I can’t have my company’s name and integrity compromised by such types.” Chop and EJ looked at each other.

“First off, you don’t know what I do. Second,” Chop put his face in front Don’s. “Newton Grove better not see the light of day if I’m out of the deal. I’ll rip your ass limb from limb.”

“Listen guy, after we fill the units maybe, and this is a big maybe, I’ll try and help you with a smaller project but right now-”

“Fuck you and that small project!” Chop barked. “If Newton Grove goes up without us you won't be alive to enjoy it bitch."

"Erving, EJ, Newton Grove is part of Shallotte's future. I'm a part of that and want you to be part of that. However, my development company doesn't front drug dealers okay." Don walked back the door. "Maybe in the future we do something else. Thanks for your interest but you can't be a part of this."

"We can't be a part of this? We help put this thing together!" EJ shouted as Don walked out. "Can you believe this dude?"

"I'm a kill that nigga," Chop said marching out the door.

"Chop no!" EJ said out the door behind him.

Chop caught Don at his car. He hit him with an over hand right across his face. Don shook it off and grabbed Chop's arm. Before he knew it, Chop's face was down on the pavement with his arm an inch from being twisted off and a heavy knee planted between his shoulder blades.

"I told you once, you can't get in on this, it's out of my hands," Don growled, his lungs ached as he sucked in the winter air. He twisted Chop's arm as he squirmed. "so let it go alright. Tell the folks you brought in on this, it's still a go for them. You don't wanna tussle with me son."

A month later

"I want to thank the Mayor of Shallotte and all of you here at this groundbreaking ceremony of Newton Grove Apartments," Don announced to cheers. "To all the local contractors involved with this project and businesses that will benefit from this influx of families, this is only the beginning. Shallotte is on its way and together, we'll make this town a city to be reckoned with."

The people applauded as the mayor stomped the spade shovel into the ground. Don took pictures for the press and praised the mayor's bravery for getting this done. He felt like Marshall Hamilton after a big game. His secretary called after the ceremony.

"Yeah Clara," he answered.

"You have a lot of messages. Are you coming back to Wilmington today?"
"Hell no, I'm heading in. I'll see you tomorrow."

"Hold on Don." He heard Clara shuffling papers. "This one message, I don't know who he was but he said to make sure you got it today. 'You took my future so I'm taking yours,' that's the message."

Don looked at the phone quizzically.

"Who sent that again?"

"I told you, I don't know. It sounded like a kid, a boy."

"Ah screw'em, I'll see you in the morning okay." It was two o'clock. Don was on his away to a late lunch with some colleagues when the phone rang again. It was a Shallotte Police Officer. He was at West Brunswick High School and had some bad news about Marshall.

Don frantically made a u-turn in the middle of Main Street and rushed to the high school. The damn car couldn't go fast enough. As he drove on the overpass he saw an ambulance turn north on Highway 17 toward the hospital. At the school, the principle let him know that Marshall was in that ambulance. They were pumping his stomach when Don got there. After twenty minutes, Marshall Hamilton was pronounced dead.

Don's eyes failed to register color. A warm pressure grew inside his skull. Every breath served as a device of torture giving him life to suffer this unimaginable loss. The doctors didn't tell him what happened because Don didn't ask. Mrs. Hamilton got to the hospital a half an hour later. The doctor informed her that Marshall was poisoned. Nurses and other hospital personnel had to pull Mrs. Hamilton off of the doctor.

Marshall's best friend, Scotty told the cops that Emmanuel Cook sold the ecstasy that killed Marshall. The cops found more drugs in Emmanuel's locker before bringing him to the principal's office. Through tears ad sobs, Emmanuel implicated Ervin 'Chop' Belle as his supplier. Don heard that at his home the next day and lost his footing. This one message, I don't know who he was but he said to make sure you got it today. 'You took my future so I'm taking yours,' that's the message.

*July 1st*

"Chop!" Anita hollered over her shoulder with the front door. "Hold on." She marched down the hallway and opened the door. The music cut into her ears. Chop and Kiana were in bed. They spooned violently, facing the window. Anita stomped in and slapped Chop across the head.

"What the fuck?" he said. He didn't stop screwing.

"Excuse me, but can you get outta my daughter for a minute and go outside, you got company." Kiana's face balled up in disappointment. Chop pulled out of Kiana and put on his jeans t shirt and new sneakers. Kiana looked out of the window.

"And tell them pigs not to come to my fucking house no more!" Anita said. Chop took his jeans to put on his boxers.

"I'll bring the feds over here. You slap me 'cross my head again I'm a get one of'em to whoop your ass." Anita rolled her eyes as he strutted into the hallway. The lights from Diana's Expedition blinded Chop as the strolled to the sheriff.

"Sam? What the fuck is you doing here?" he asked. The sheriff got off of the hood and walked back the driver's side.

"Get in, I got something you gotta see."

"It's in the car?" Chop asked, opening the passenger side door.

"No, it's up the road a little. I need five minutes." Chop shook his head and got in.

Up the road turned out to be Holden Beach Road. The sheriff pulled in to paved driveway five minutes outside of Shallotte. Cobblestone and surrounded by marsh, the house sat on Shallotte River. Chop had visited Don Hamilton and his wife there a lot over the last three year. He followed the sheriff around the huge garage doors to a wooden patio deck in the back. Only crickets could be heard this moonlit night. The lights from the house behind the patio came on. Don Hamilton, followed by his wife, appeared from the light sending a chill through Chop. They marched out of the house onto the patio. Mrs. Hamilton was crying and grimacing at Chop, so was Don.

"Sam, what you got going on?" he asked.

"We gotta talk to Don. He still thinks you had a hand his boy dying." Chop shrugged.

"Wasn't he in the courtroom when they I ain't do nothing?"

"Yeah but he doesn't want to believe it. I know it's ridiculous but you need to clear the air him before you have to start looking over your shoulder." Chop shook his head and got out of the SUV. He walked over to the garage door and leaned against it. The sheriff moseyed over to the patio where the Hamiltons stood.

"You think you can take our child from us and get away with it?" Don asked calmly, his body shook. Chop crossed his arms.

"What am I doing here again Sam?" Don pulled a .38 snub nose revolver from his pocket. He aimed it at Chop's face and pulled the trigger. Chop's shoulder exploded. He spun twice before falling on his back. He scrambled to get on his feet.

"Oh no," the sheriff said, slamming him down when he was half way up. Blake turned into the driveway. "It's okay, it's my son. We're going to get him out of here."

Chop roared, writhing left and right. Don handed his wife the gun and guided her to Chop.

"Okay hon', it's just like we practice, point and shoot, that's all." Slim and just under six feet, she got a hold of her breathing and braced herself.

"Where should I shoot him?" she asked.

"Who cares," Don said holding her shooting hand up.

"Actually," the sheriff said. "Try for the chest or the stomach. A head shot would be too much of a mess to clean up from this cement." Don looked at the sheriff and nodded. He lowered Mrs. Hamilton's hand.

"Why?" she asked, pointing the gun at Chop's chest. "Why did you take my son from me?"

Chop, with his hand holding his gushing shoulder, looked at her and smiled. "Answer me you animal!" she shouted. Chop turned to the sheriff.

"Yo Sam, you think you're slick. I got your ass though. If I die, all you muthafuckas gonna-"

The bullet hit him in the middle of the chest. His body instantly relaxed as his ghost rushed from him. The sheriff stood over Chop. Don took the gun from Mrs. Hamilton and she cried into Don's chest.

"Get this piece of shit off my property," Don said. Blake pulled out a wide sheet of plastic and a blanket from his mom's Expedition.

"Hold on," the sheriff said walking to Chop. "Don, could you help me. I need him stood up against that tree back there." The sheriff spread his feet and bent his legs. "Blake, get my rifle and rope son." Don kissed his wife. She took the gun and went inside. The sheriff grabbed Chop by the bloody end and Don grabbed him by the legs. "We gotta decorate the body," the sheriff said with a chuckle. The atmosphere was a little too heavy for him.

A pine tree, two feet in diameter, stood just inside the woods to the left of Hamilton's home. As the sheriff held him up Don tied Chop tight around the tree by his neck and waist. Don walked to the patio to get the pressure washer for the blood on the pavement.

"Go 'head son," said the sheriff. Blake held the AK-47. The assault rifle carried a hundred rounds. Blake took aim. "Well, go 'head. He's already dead." Blake seemed to put on his best sniper routine. Misty had called him ten times that night. He didn't want to hear about Chop tonight. He wanted to gets high but the sheriff didn't want him under any influence while working with him.

**Blake lowered the rifle and the sheriff snatched it from him. Damn thing wasn't even cocked. He started with the legs and started his way up. Pieces of flesh ripped away from Chop as his body clung to the ropes. After forty or so rounds the sheriff stopped shooting. He turned to his soft son. "Get the plastic and blanket."**

**Blake laid the plastic it at Chop's dangling feet. After cutting him from the tree, they rolled Chop in the plastic and then rolled him up again in the blanket.**

**Don was inside with his wife. Mrs. Hamilton sat on the floor of the master bathroom. Her head rested on the side of the toilet bowl as she waited for the fourth retch. The sheriff elected to call him sometime later in the day and get his money. The sheriff left his car with the Hamiltons. They went to Anita's. One car had gone for the night. He wedged the door open with his knife and went into her bedroom. He grabbed her by the throat.**

**"We're taking Chop's truck. We weren't here and he wasn't here, got it?" Anita nodded showing the sheriff pure terror through her eyes. He slammed her to the mattress and left.**

## Chapter 26

*July 4th Midnight*

Mrs. Hamilton sat at the end of the dock behind her home, her toes grazed the Shallotte River. She knew to bring three bottles of merlot with her this time. Last night she had to get up and get another bottle from the house. She had a framed picture of Marshall from ten years ago. He smiled and hugged his mom all day that day. He was four then, not yet a basketball star, just a happy momma's boy. He loved to put a pillow in his mom's lap and rest his head while they watched Shrek. Mrs. Hamilton would run her fingers in the boy's brown hair, not a care in the world. He couldn't stop smiling and laughing back then, his laugh haunted Mrs. Hamilton. It only got louder after she murdered Chop. The idea of vengeance sounded so good, especially after Chop paraded out of that courtroom. It became an obsession. She had suffered ever since that night. Rarely sleeping, deep depression. She was never a big woman, she looked emaciated.

The dock was a two hundred and fifty feet from Holden Beach Road. People whizzed by getting their final preparations together for the fourth. It was as if everyone driving by knew her and knew what she was going through but couldn't be bothered to offer any comfort. Mrs. Hamilton had plans to guzzle tequila and pass out if she couldn't sleep. Due to traffic, cars slowed and traffic became congested.

A black Chevelle pulled in to the Hamilton driveway. Two car doors opened and slammed. Guns were loaded. Motion lights came to life as Mack T marched to the front door. He kicked it in and marched up stairs.

Mrs. Hamilton turned and looked to the second story window of the bedroom she shared with Don. She slanted her head as Don hollered. Gun shots interrupted the chirping of crickets and the collective hum from the road as Don jumped out of the window. The uncompromising Earth received Don on his back. Mrs. Hamilton didn't turn away but she wasn't alarmed, things weren't registering properly. Pound, marching toward the dock, cocked his Desert Eagle. His teary eyes met Mrs. Hamilton's. She grew concerned. He stopped half way down the dock.

"Who are you?" Mrs. Hamilton asked. Pound raised his gun. Mrs. Hamilton looked confused.

One bullet hit her chin jerking her into the river. Pound walked down to the edge of the dock. He shot her breasts, stomach, ribs and head until the clip ran out. He kicked the bottles of merlot and framed picture of Marshall into the river behind her.

Mack T joined Pound on the dock. "Let's roll homie."

After finally getting the girls to sleep, Treasure headed for Oak Island. She pulled into the parking lot across the street from the address Neal gave Mack T and Pound. She had two 9mm glocks carrying thirty round clips. She watched the house through her rear view mirror. People were leaving and going constantly. It would be impossible to go inside, kill Blake Helms and walk out unnoticed. Her luck wasn't good enough for him to leave the house alone and drive somewhere secluded for her. She shook it out of her head contemplated all options.

"He's gotta die tonight," she said. It was two cars in the yard, probably six people inside at the most, not counting the frequent traffic. Treasure was stone sober. She felt like smoking a pound of bud to the head but she had watch over the girls. Tremaine was dead. How could that happen? Whatever nerves she had were numbed by sorrow. "Fuck it," she said shedding tears. She held both glock. "Chest shots only. Heads if I can get'em. Can't nobody live."

Treasure cocked the guns, wiped her nose with her forearm and got out of the car. Rap music blared from the house. She started with an unsuspecting couple who pulled when she got out the car, one in the back of each head. Somebody opened the door as she approached it and received four shout in the chest. The music, weed odor and commotion came from the living room. An tall older white fellow sat at the at in the kitchen. As soon as he turned his head Treasure blew his face off with a double tap from the 9mm on her left.

Three guys, two wearing gas mask bongs and a naked black girl Treasure knew were in the living room. They seemed confused. Treasure shot the real fat guy in the stomach five times and the girl started screaming. It was Clarissa James, she used to be with Treasure's cousin Lucas. Treasure put a bullet in her neck while the other two begged for mercy. Blake was the one with the gold chain and diamond encrusted biohazard charm. He unbuckled his mask and let it fall to the floor.

"Please," he said. "I got a lot of upstairs just-"

Treasure shot Blake between the eyes and then in the chest. She stood over him and shot five more round into him for good measure. She didn't wait for the other guy to take his mask off before she shot him.

Sheriff Helms was too late. Neal told him everything he told Mack T and Pound. He sent the Shallotte police ahead of him and all available Sheriff's deputies but they were too late. Some officers shuddered at the sight of Don.

They could have sworn he was dead. He coughed up blood and a dozen cops jumped. The paramedics put him on a stretcher and rushed him to the emergency room as the sheriff and his deputies searched for Mrs. Hamilton.

These scenes were especially rare in Brunswick County. Folks like the Hamiltons seldom came to such a end. Now the county would be the talk of the state. The sheriff called Mrs. Hamilton's cell phone, it rang on the kitchen counter. A deputy brought him to the dock where a unopened bottle of Merlot and blood splatter awaited him. A picture frame, stained with blood, sat still on the river surface. The sheriff tried not to imagine that lovely woman.

"We gotta comb the river," he said turning to Deputy Terry Long.

"What about Julius and Billy Belle? And Marcus Tate?"

"I got something special for them, come one. Shallotte'll take care of this." Terry kept the gas pedal to the floor all the way to the sheriff's home in Southport. "These animals have gone too far." The sheriff could foresee his grip on the county slipping because of the violence. Forget the criminals. The public couldn't stomach two teenage girls gone missing and a respectable couple who watched their only child's killer walk free being murdered themselves. The SBI and FBI would descend on Brunswick County and investigate everything. Deputy Long, police lights flashing, floored it to the Helms residence in Southport.

The back door was wide open. Diana couldn't be bothered with it after hearing about Misty. The phone in the kitchen was on the floor whining to be put back on the hook. The sheriff left it there and headed upstairs. He had a compartment behind his wife's closet and another inside the floor that held money and drugs. Deputy Long's mother had a storage unit in Winnabow that the sheriff considered safe.

The key sat in the drawer of his nightstand. The gunmen stepped out of Diana's closet. Bucc trained his Desert Eagles sideways on the sheriff, he chuckled.

"Y'all crackas thought y'all was slick. Can't stretch my homeboy out and-" The sheriff's left hand rested on his .40 cal service weapon in the drawer. He slowly gripped it and pushed the slide against the top of the drawer. "think you fitna live. We gonna kill ya whole family goddamn devil." The sheriff stood straight.

"Listen sir," he said. His hands were on his chest. He ever so slowly spread his elbows from his body. "You got some bad info from somebody and I mean bad. I, nor has my family, ever had anything to-" The barrel the .40 cal pointed at Bucc's center mass from behind the sheriff's loose buttoned shirt. He held it under his right arm and pulled the trigger. He kept pulling the trigger while sweeping his feet away from the bed while turning to face his target. In a second, he and Bucc hit the floor,

Sheriff Helms stood.

"Terry!" he called. He kicked Bucc's leg, nothing. "Terry watch out, their in the house!" With two hands on his gun, the sheriff crept down the steps. Blood slowly enveloped the hardwood floor. Terry was on his back with his throat cut. The telephone still whined.

Outside he checked the patio and bushes with every step. He tried spot any sound that wasn't the Intercoastal Coastal Waterway brushing against the bank.

The Parkers were an elderly couple who lived three houses down. They weren't having guests for the holiday but a rented Ford Escape sat at their mailbox. *That's their car* thought the sheriff. All the residents on the sheriff's street were older people. They were all asleep and all the lights were off. Moonlight gave the sheriff guidance where the streetlights wouldn't. When he approached the seagulls they didn't fly away, they just stepped to the side. He felt the vibration from the bass of the music coming from the SUV. There were at least two of them inside. He hoped Julius "Pound" Belle was in the car.

A bullet hit the sheriff in his right arm, knocking him on his left side. He raised his gun the direction of the shot then dropped it. The sheriff had never been shot before and the bullet shattered his humerus bone before settling in his lung. The music from the SUV disappeared. The sheriff, laying on his back, watched to the Swain house. The wooden egg shell colored house seemed uninhabited.

The kid stepped from behind the Swains garbage can. Short skinny body, big sneakers, big shorts and t-shirt, the 44 magnum seemed bigger than him. His name was Cola, a junior DBG who never killed anyone before. His nerves settled as two young men, holding guns and their sagging pants exited the SUV and walked with him to the half dead sheriff.

"You killed my big homie?" Cola asked, making his voice extra deep. The sheriff tried to grabbed his weapon. Two shots from a 9mm pistol charged into his stomach. Cola bent his knees and flexed his shooting arm as he aimed at Sheriff Sam Helms. The sheriff turned away from the kids before his got blown away.

The boys stepped closer to the sheriff. Sam Helms was no longer recognizable. His head was I shreds. Blood and brain matter seemed to shoot from the sheriff's neck. A porch light across the street from the Swains came on and the front door opened.

"Hey!" shouted old man Herman Parker from his porch. He wore a grey onesie and held a .22 caliber rifle. "Why the hell'er y'all round my house?" The three kids looked at each other. They shot the front of Mr. Parker's home to hell. The windows, gable and the flowers succumbed to destruction. Herman fell back on his ass, turned on his stomach and crawled with his elbows like he did in the war.

"Yo," said one the guys, "why did Bucc let this cracker walk out the house?" Cola ran his gloved hand over the waves on his head in frustration.

"Man this pig ass muthafucka killed Bucc man. After we stabbed the shit out of the other cop, I waited in the kitchen. I heard the gunshots and heard this dude mumbling down the stairs. Bucc up there dead now."

Cola pulled Deputy Long's vibrating phone from his shorts. It was text from a fellow deputy. There was an Oak Island massacre at the Blake Helms residence. Blake Helms is deceased, no witnesses.

*2:00 am*

"Are you sure," Marie said. Kiana nodded furiously.

"They came and got him from Momma's house. They came back without him and got took truck. They told Mama they'd kill her if she said something Marie."

"Oh my," Marie said. Kiana sat across from Marie at her dining room table. Don't worry, they ain't gonna get away with it. No sirree." Marie couldn't remember the last time she was up this late. Six hours ago a white man named

Andy Stahl handed her bag of Chop's belongings. She put away the gaudy jewelry and began reading the documents. Her anger wouldn't let her sleep.

There were people close to Chop who were conspiring against him. He entered, only verbally, into an agreement with Hamilton Developers to contribute assets to a loan application for Newton Grove Apartments. Apparently the development company turned their back on Chop and Chop intended to sue. While bringing his own assets with Hamilton Development, helped Don Hamilton sell the Newton grove Apartments to potential investors. When Hamilton voided his business relationship Chop he didn't do so with investors Chop brought to him.

These investors were mainly retirees with surprising number of assets. They weren't keen on how to fully exploit their possessions, their number of financial woes were a testament to that. Chop paid a lot of these guys to invest in the Hamilton Development venture knowing they would have done it anyway if it wasn't Chop (young black kid) asking them to do it.

Newton Grove Apartments was a reality and at full capacity. These investors had in Newton Grove a great monthly cash flow and saw Chop as a threat to it. They were willing to testify along side Don Hamilton the Erving "Chop" Belle never had a part making Newton Grove Apartments a reality. A lie they felt couldn't be proven wrong. They didn't know Chop covered his ass.

Andy Stahl handed Marie physical proof of Chop's instrumental involvement in the Newton Grove Apartments, documents of private cash loans from Chop to various Newton Grove investors, taped conversations discussing the money they were set to earn. Chop was suing for thirty percent ownership of Newton Grove Apartments. That would bring Chop seven hundred eighty thousand dollars a year from a rental property he wasn't aloud to invest a penny in. If he were to be rewarded what he asked, a number of investors would lose their piece of the Newton Grove pie. They found out about Chop cache evidence and had him killed.

Marie's blood boiled as she skimmed through the evidence. Then at midnight Kiana came through the door with Jared. She told Marie the truth about her pregnancy for the first time and told her about the night of the murder.

"Put Lil J to bed and come back out here" Marie said. She shared what she discovered with Kiana.

*2:30 am*

The police said they want to talk, just talk. Bullshit. They wanted to bust him. His lawyer called him and told him that the FBI wanted to ask him questions. Bullshit. They wanted to hang those two missing sluts on him. The only joy Andre Long could feel was the prospect of those girls really being dead. He hoped they were discovered in the ground decayed but not so much that their retarded mothers couldn't recognize them. He wanted to see them doubled over in grief, screaming for their sweet little whores to get up. It would serve them right for putting his name in shit that he had nothing to do with.

He watched the smoke billow from his old home all day. His dad was burned to ashes. Driving around in a friends car, he cruised Cedar Grove up and down as the police and fire department scrambled back and forth. He watched the breaking news from the TV in the car. The whole time Ike told Andre to keep his distance from Cedar Grove, really Brunswick County, and now he managed to get killed himself. It didn't have to be like this. They could have left together. They could have killed Pound, Mack T and the rest of them together. They could have killed Chop before someone else did it and disposed of him the right way, together.

Andre graduated from woos to stems. He parked his friend's Honda Accord in an open field in Ash North Carolina where he cried and got high. His mother kept calling but he never answered. The police were hunting him. As the news stations broke story after story about the three massacres of the night, the police named Andre Long as their one and only suspect in the disappearance of Cassandra and Heather McKinely, the murder of Tremaine Gore and the murder of Early Long. Ike wouldn't be around to hold his hand for this.

Atleast fifty people were searching for Andre for killing Tremaine. He couldn't visit his children or any of his girlfriends and black neighborhoods because somebody was watching. If Andre didn't leave the area soon he wouldn't be alive.

Andre wanted to run and would if he could get to his dad's money. Ike Long never officially divorced Andre's mother. Those businesses and there accounts should go to her. She would surely liquidate some of it and send Andre whatever he needed to survive. Where could he hide until then? And how could he hide from everybody else?

Four pairs of headlights crawl from the road into the field toward Andre. They were in no rush. Andre saw them through his rearview mirror. He wasn't alarmed. His AK-47 sat on the back seat a 9mm glock sat on the passenger seat. He put the crack stem on the floorboard and picked up the 9mm. Fourteen car doors opened and shut. Shotguns, AK-47s, AR-15s and M1s were cocked as the men approached the Honda. Andre grabbed the 9mm and cocked it. The Ak-47s, AR-15s, shotguns and M1s were ten feet away when the 9mm sounded. Patrick, Sean Gore's oldest son and the late Tremaine Gore's uncle ran to the driver side of the car with his shotgun. He turned his head, looked to his company and motioned his thumb across his neck. They turned around and went back to their cars.

## Chapter 27

*Independence Day 12:00pm*

"Carol baby, wake up. Carol!" Billy shook his woman's shoulder like he was making a cocktail. She turned over and swung at him. "We need to get ready come now."

"It's eight o'clock, the service ain't until eleven."

"We the family babe. We gotta be their extra early." Billy tied his tie as he spoke. "We gotta get all of Marie's cakes and stuff to the church too."

"No, *you* gotta get Marie's cakes to the church. And I'm not gonna be seated with the family Billy. It needs to be just y'all okay."

Marie was oddly serene. The house was filled with talk of murder and tragedy. So and so was killed last night. Such and such happened in Oak Island and even on Holden Beach Road. The Sheriff was murdered at his home. Misty's near fatal accident was spoken freely in jest, out of earshot of Marie and Billy. Nobody knew where Pound was and like the Candyman, they were wary to speak his name.

"Mama, I don't know why you doing this today, it's too soon," Nathaniel said, after taking a ham out of the fridge and into a cooler headed to church for the after-service meal. Harriet placed various sweets in plastic carriers spread around the kitchen counter. He stood over Marie in the dining room. "It's just too much going on now." Marie sat at her dining room table where she had been less than five hours ago. She wasn't tired, she was restless and anxious. The day was going to be more significant than she thought thirteen hours ago.

"I'm fine son, okay. We're going to celebrate the life of my grandson today. So make sure you don't smash anything in them coolers." Marie got up so she better direct the activity in the kitchen. EJ and his beautiful wife Dion entered the front door and gave everybody hugs and hi's on the way to Marie.

"Ms. Lance," EJ greeted. *So bright and helpful* Marie thought.

"Hey baby, you looking handsome as usual. Dion, girl you look ravishing." She and Dion kissed each other's cheeks.

"So do you Ms. Lance and I know you know it," Dion said. Her smile was made for magazines and commercials.

"Well," Marie said smoothing out her dress. "I do alright." They laughed and greeted other visitors as they entered the home.

"I'm glad to see deputy cars in your yard," EJ said, Dion nodded. It's cars up and down Cedar Grove. They got two big tents set up in the church parking lot from the church with TVs in'em. That might not be enough."

"Yeah," said Dion walking behind Marie and putting her hands on her shoulders. "And to have the forethought to have the service while everybody's home was just brilliant." Marie turned around and put her hands on her hips.

"I wasn't say nothing. Ain't nobody figure it out but you." Everybody laughed, everyone but Nathaniel. Marie said rubbed EJ's back. "It's been a lot going on and I hope after today everything can be peaceful,"

"Yeah," Nathaniel said from the other side of the counter. He looked around for Kiana. She was in the bathroom getting Jared ready for the funeral. His fear was she would activate a Pound signal to summon him if he dared speak of him. "You see who ain't here don't you? Billy's last boy. He's in hiding cause he was in some of that mess that went down last night."

Marie marched around the counter and slapped Nathaniel across the face. The kitchen went silent.

"Don't ever speak about Julius or Billy like that again," pointing her finger between Nathaniel's eyes. Nathaniel looked around the kitchen and back at his mother. He went about his work of packing food.

"Mama," Cedric said entering the kitchen. The reverend is ready.

The family went outside the front yard where Reverend Greene and Billy Belle stood, ninety nine degrees already. They made a circle and the reverend lead them in prayer.

"Why Anita?" Pound cried, standing over Anita. She was on the floor in the corner of her master bedroom. Pound had disfigured her face by hitting her with the butt of his Desert Eagle. Pound wore a long white t-shirt with a picture of Chop on it. Anita kept staring at the t-shirt through swollen eyes.

"I swear Pound, they said if I said something they was gonna kill me. The sheriff himself told me not to say nothing. I didn't even say shit to Kiana. I didn't know Chop was, that they killed Chop til the next day, and it all came together. You know I couldn't say nothing after they-" Pound hit her again.

The family left Marie's in two limos and they crawled to the church. Cars lined the road well past the curves. People Marie had never seen before walked merrily from past her and along side the limos in the oppressive heat. Excitement seemed to germinate from the cedar trees towering over the road. Two deputy cars pulled in behind the limos. Two deputies got out of the cars and flanked the limos by foot. Given the recent violent activity in the county, they weren't going to allow it at Chop's service. Marie, Nathaniel, Harriett, EJ and Dion sat in the front car. Billy, Kiana, Jared and Cedric and his wife sat in the second limo. The church was a mile away.

The closer they got the thicker the crowd on the road got. People covered the road, the deputies had to make a path. The festive mood couldn't denied. DBGz dotted the crowd with long airbrushed t-shirts of Chop. Some carried back packs and handed out bottled waters. One of the walking deputies asked for a bottle and was ignored.

"Look at all these people," EJ said. "Chop was really loved wasn't he?" Children, drinking sodas and bottled water pressed their hands on the windows and waved to the shiny tent.

"Oh look, theirs Carmen from work," Dion said. Carmen was a fellow teacher at Cedar Grove Elementary. She was the first of the few folks, precious few white folks, who said Chop was innocent before his jury reached a verdict in his trial. "She brought her husband and the kids."

"Rev. Greene's gonna get his preach *on* today," Harriett proclaimed. "He's gonna give us a good one for Chop's home going." Nathaniel nodded. He looked away from his wife to hide his disdain.

"Yeah, Rev. Greene'll do right by Chop," Marie said. "So," she said patting EJ on the leg. "This may not be the right time but it just happens to be on my mind. Have you given any thought to Chop's estate?" Nathaniel's ears perked up. He struggled mightily to keep his eyes looking out the window.

"No not really. I planned to get to it at the beginning of next week."

"Yeah, that'll be good for everybody," Marie said. Everyone nodded, even Nathaniel. "Just remember, Billy gets the house and the restaurant is his too."

"Oh hell no!" Nathaniel said. Eight eyes stared at him in disbelief. "Mama, doesn't Billy have a home? You could rent the house out, make some money and sell that restuarant." Marie pulled her back off the lush black leather seats.

"Nathaniel Hill, Chop wanted his daddy to have that house back and to have his restaurant. And I'm going to carry out those wishes." She relaxed. "You act like *you're* about bury your child. Let me tell you something boy, you don't wanna know what that feels like!" Nathaniel wanted to cuss the whole limo, but he was outgunned.

Reverend Greene, in a forest green robe, greeted the family with a smile at the church steps as the deputy cars directed the limos. Green indoor/outdoor carpets lead folks from the sidewalk to two huge white tents in the parking lot flanking the church's left side. The tents were air conditioned and already filled to capacity. Two sixty inch flat screen TVs and twelve inch speakers would feed the occupants the funeral from the view of the balcony. News vans were set up on the right side of the church The cameramen weren't aloud n the church so they filmed the crowd outside.

Flowers invaded the foyer area. They encircled the choir stand behind the pulpit as the choir "Marching Upward to Zion". The floor in the wings of the church couldn't be seen for the flowers. Chop rested at the altar. The closed casket was mahogany and gold handles. Leonard Hope, People's Funeral Home owner, gave Marie the coffin. Chop had given him so much in the way of loans and other financial help for loved ones. It didn't feel right to charge he said.

Nathaniel held Marie as they sat on the front pew. Marie had gone to so many of these things and never got used to it. Chop truly looked to be sleeping. His reddish brown skin was radiant. His expression was the same one he wore the most in life. One of confidence, one that signified the subtle delight of a mind knowing he could have anything he wanted and most folks just weren't as a capable. Harriet said a prayer over his body.

Kiana went into convulsion at glance. A deacon held her as Jared stood on his tippy toes attempting fan her. Billy got her settled beside Marie.

Billy didn't go back to the coffin, nor did he go back to his seat. He walked to the bathroom while folks were still being seated. Spirits stirred as they found their seats. Reverend Greene had to stop and think how he'd get by all the flowers around Chop and in the pulpit. He sat as Billy left the front pew. When everyone was settled he started the service with a prayer. After the prayer he went to the bathroom.

Billy vomited in the toilet between sucking a Newport. His forehead soaked in sweat. Sunlight warmed the back of his head as his back leaned on the toilet. A five year old Chop kept running through his mind laughing, smiling and jumping into his dad's arms. He kept getting on the lawnmower with Billy, unwrapping Christmas gifts, playing video games, on his knees saying his prayers at the end of the bed with his dad and mother. Billy's gut turned.

"Man," the reverend said, "Get up from that floor and come on." Billy couldn't look up. Shame and sorrow was an arresting mix. "Come on." The reverend grabbed Billy by the arm. Billy tried to snatch his arm away. Freddie Greene was still a giant of a man with superhuman strength. He lifted Billy with one arm like a toddler. Billy stood as if it was his idea. He and the reverend hugged. "We gonna get through this today Brother Belle. All that running around for everybody else, I'm gonna watch after you today, alright?" Billy chuckled behind tears, he nodded. "Come on now, you hear the choir singing, this thing is happening now. We got two hundred people outside in tents and the church is filled up, Chop ain't been gone but four days, that ain't nothing but love man." Billy rinsed his mouth in the sink and walked out of the bathroom in front of the reverend.

Every selection from the choir prolonged the service and it was wonderful. Carol's Brother Deacon Harvey brought the house down when he sung "His Eyes Are on the Sparrow". People in the tents stood and sung and cried with the church. EJ went to the right podium with prepared remarks.

"Wow," he said as took in the enormous crowd. Easter Sunday didn't bring this kind of crowd. "If I didn't know before standing here today I could gather that my friend and brother was loved." People seconded his words. "Erving Belle. Chop. Our friend, our brother, our son, our cousin, our nephew, our neighbor, all in Christ. I can't um...I can't believe that...this man was such a good human being. Such a gift, he gave so much joy only by being, existing. I mean um...-" EJ glanced at the casket and took a deep breath, tears ran down his cheek.

"It's alright, tell it son!" someone shouted.

"A lot has been said and written about *our* brother. A lot has been done to sully his name and somewhere somebody's probably happy that he's no longer with us." The congregation responded with deep oohs. "That's fine, you know why? Cause you and I know who he was, you and I knew this man's heart, how he gave, loved and cherished us. There isn't a man who's lived that has given so much, done so much and suffered so much without being derided and cast aside, so here we are. It's seems to be the fate of such men, the fate of God's favored." Marie nodded and moved side to side as EJ's words swam around in her head. Hearing that voice speak so powerfully affected her. She often said those things in Chop's defense but they didn't ring as true as they did today. "I just want to say to y'all, thanks for paying your respects and showing your love today. Our community will press on because we know Chop wouldn't have wanted us to sulk too much. He would've wanted us to go on with the spirit of giving that made this community and still strengthens this community! We need to watch out for each other, bring each other up! That's what Marie taught Chop! That's what we taught Chop! Those are the examples that he set forth that we'll remember when our brother's sick, when our neighbor's in need, when a child in the community needs to get to school. Cedar Grove'll be alright because the things that we love and miss about Chop still lives in us." The congregation resounded in amens and hallelujahs. "Lord knows I miss my brother. His number one goal was to enrich this community at any cost. Don't worry about it brother, all of us in here are gonna pick up where you left off. We, us, we gonna keep improving this community! Your work won't go in vain, it'll go full steam ahead! We love and will always miss you. Save a place for us!" People cheered EJ as he went back to the front pew.

As the service drew to a close, they rolled Chop into the foyer. Reverend Greene stood at his feet and shook hands with the congregation as they viewed Chop for the last time. Marie gave Chop some last instructions. Tell Angela she said hi, watch over the family, enjoy your peace. Nathaniel stood over the coffin and held the rail. He shook his head slowly and bit his lip. He had written Chop off a long time ago, blamed him for his sister's mistakes. Chop looked too much like Billy. Just a few days ago, he tried to remember all the times Chop would come to him for help and advice. He shuddered remembering his past rejections of Chop and Pound. They were his family, blood. They desperately needed a man in their lives and we Nathaniel didn't step all the undesirables did. Chop could've been a different person.

If Angela was looking down from heaven like Nathaniel thought he hoped, what would she think of watching Nathaniel work like a dog to help the state put away her son? How would she feel about her big brother? Hatred of Billy deprived him of good sense when it came to Angela's boys. He forgot that he loved the boys and if something were to happen to them he would feel deep remorse like family feels when one falls too tragedy.

"I'm sorry nephew," he said and stumbled off.

The reverend held Billy as he approached the casket. He was looking in the mirror twenty five years ago. Chop looked peaceful. He never seemed rattled in life, always had some measure of control. He became a very capable young man despite the odds. Reverend Greene's words about Chop's goodness being traits of his father sounded so good. Billy had been trained by his hard earned wisdom to look for the other sides of a story. If Chop is good traits from Billy where did the bad come from? Certainly not Angela. Billy put his forearms on the side of the coffin and studied his son.

Somebody hated his flesh and blood enough to kill him. Billy had no illusions about his son. Their conversations were always frank. Chop was capable but also brutal. His ultimate goal in life was to make things better for those closest to him. *Good Intentions*. That's how the road to hell was paved and the world only showed him drastic ways to get what he wanted. Billy could have showed him a better way to live. He could have strived for something better in his family and Chop would have learned from that example. Ambition was great as long as the things you were after were of true value. Angela was priceless. She was worth moving heaven and earth for. Billy saw that and pursued her and they made Chop, one of the most benevolent souls Cedar Grove ever had .Billy's absence gave the worst of Chop a chance to flourish along with the good. Letting the guilt go would be no easy task.

Members of the Cedar Grove Missionary Baptist Church were buried at the Riley Brown Cemetery two miles north of the Church. Kiana hollered and cried when they lowered him in the ground. She buried her head in Billy's chest. The burial ceremony was rushed a bit because of the searing sun. The family went back to the church to have supper.

At the church dining hall the left wall was lined with food, fried turkey, chicken, fish, glazed ham, macaroni and cheese, collard greens, rice, bread rolls, punch, potato salad. The other half of the wall was desserts, pies, cakes, puddings and cobblers. Billy ate first and joined the ladies in the kitchen serving and cleaning. Reverend Greene and his wife ate with the family. The laughed about the good times. Marie and the Reverend did what they could to keep Chop alive and free. He was in a better place and everybody would make it through this.

"Marie, I gotta do something," EJ said checking his phone. "The food's so good. Dion, make me a plate."

"Where are you going?" Dion asked. "The car's at Marie's."

"I'm going back to get it. You can find a ride home can't you," he kissed his wife and took off. She looked at Marie and shook her head.

"That's a good man," Reverend Greene said. "Chop had a good friend in him."

He sure did," Marie said. "Dion, help me up baby." Marie stood and headed to the kitchen. It took her fifteen minutes. People went out of their way to pay their respects again and again.

"Billy," she called like a drill sergeant. Billy bent over the sink wearing an apron and rubber gloves stood straight. "What the hell are you doing?"

"I'm getting a head start on the pans so I don't have to look at'em tonight."

"Don't worry about that baby, these ladies'll scrub everything clean. You remember those papers you gave me yesterday?"

"Yes ma'am," Billy said scrubbing the inside of a pot. "You think something missing?" Marie shook his head.

"Something's up," Marie took the pot out of Billy's hand and sat it down. "Come on we gotta go." She headed to the door behind the kitchen.

"Where we going?" Marie put her hands on her hips.

"Boy, take that apron off and bring your ass!"

Chapter 28

*Twenty minutes ago*

Don Hamilton woke up with searing pain all over his body. The morphine helped but still. How he got to the hospital escaped his memory. His eyes scanned the room for Mrs. Hamilton. Trying to turn his head, his neck screamed in protest. His arms and legs hurt but couldn't obey his commands.

"Mr. Hamilton you're up," the nurse said cheerily walking in the room. She walked around his bed. "How do you feel? You need anything?"

"What am I doing here?" he whispered, his throat was dry. The nurse slowed her movements, she remembered that she was told to watch what she said around Mr. Hamilton.

"Mr. Hamilton you got shot. You were lucky No vital organs were harmed. Would you like some water?" Don nodded. "Okay, I'll be *right* back."

*Shot* Don thought. There was only one man that would purposely shoot him and Don took care of him a few days ago. The nurse came back with a cup of tepid water. Don gobbled it down.

"Excuse me nurse," he said. His voice was weak. His breathing was labored. "I need you to locate my wife, is she in the cafeteria or something?" The nurse looked as if she just spent money owed to Don before coming to pay him.

"Mr. Hamilton she's not here. I mean she's actually... it's just...I'll try to locate her."

"Thank you and I need you call someone for me. It's Sheriff Sam Helms his number is 910-"

"Mr. Hamilton, you weren't the only one who was shot last night. The sheriff was actually killed." Don's mouth dropped. The nurse nodded matter-of-factly.

"Oh my god, well I need to call Sheriff's Deputy Terry Long. His number is-"

"Mr. Hamilton, again there's a lot that's changed. Deputy Long was actually killed with the sheriff last night." Don began to dislike the nurse. She was only the messenger but her message was grave. She turned on her heels without a word.

"Nurse, I know this isn't your job but I have twenty dollars for you'd dial this number."

EJ entered the Brunswick County Hospital, the black polished leather of his briefcase glistened through the huge windows. Things were looking up. Everything he strived for was in reach. Just a few hours ago all seemed lost. With one phone call he was back in the money. He located Don's room. Don didn't seem to share his excitement.

"Mr. Hamilton, how are you?" he greeted. Don looked like shit warmed over. At least he was alive.

"How do I look?" Don growled. "What on earth happened? Did you know I'd be attacked?" Don asked. EJ sat and pulled the chair close to Don. He sat the briefcase in his lap.

"No sir I didn't. I don't know who did it but I have an idea who it was. If what I believe is true then that means one of us, me, you, the sheriff, the sheriff's son or your wife told somebody what happened to Chop. I know I didn't. I can't imagine who your wife knew who knew who I suspect attacked you. That leaves the sheriff, his son and yo-"

"What do mean *knew*?" Don asked. EJ was a mental stenographer. Don didn't know about is wife.

"Your wife *is* a wonderful and trustworthy woman. I'm not even gonna ask her if she told anybody once she gets here." EJ watched the worry erode from Don's eyes. This money wasn't gonna come easy.

"Did they hurt my wife? Tell me if they hurt my wife?" EJ didn't look away as he opened his briefcase.

"I heard you were almost killed Mr. Hamilton. The other casualties were the sheriff, his son and his friends and Deputy Long. They actually got killed though." EJ pitied the fool who finally told Don what happened to Mrs. Hamilton.

"So...who did it and why?"

"Again, I don't know. I believe it was the sheriff's son who brought this on. He and the sheriff had ulterior motives for wanting Chop dead. I fear he was on his way to glory without your input and the forty thousand dollars you pad him." Don sighed and stared at EJ. "I know involving the sheriff was my idea but I was against him involving his son from the beginning. Maybe he told somebody he considered a friend and that friend gave Chop's brother some sensitive info, maybe even sold it to him." Don tried to sit up, wasn't happening.

"Before you came in I entertained that same scenario. The problem is, out of everybody involved, you're the only one who remained untouched. Tell me how that works out of all of, you're the closest person to Chop him and his brother." EJ pulled a pen from the briefcase. He poked the pen's button a couple times.

"Mr. Hamilton, in case you forgot, I started this party. I brought Chop's money to you and you turned him down. Had I not come back to you and told you about the shit he had cooking for your ass. You'd be on you way to giving him thirty percent or more of Newton Grove Apartments. When he killed your son I gave the sheriff the contract to bring him to you and then dispose of him. There's was no benefit for me in you and the sheriff's death, especially not you. All I want is my ten percent Newton Grove like you promised." Don Hamilton stared a hole through EJ. EJ chuckled as he pulled out the Newton Grove contracts he waited so long to see signed. "Come on man. I'm trying to make a better life for my family."

"By killing mine?" Don Hamilton tried but couldn't see who it was inside the door. EJ's bladder almost forced itself out of his behind. His mouth was a desert. He stared at Don. EJ turned around and his eyes started to ache. "You don't think you could've given your family a better life without killing my grandson?" Marie's arms hung. She spoke as if she was trying to get a five year old to see the obvious error in his ways. Not really life or death but it could be in the future.

EJ poked the pen button violently. The cops would definitely know she died by a pen through the windpipe. He could take one of Don's pillows and suffocate her but the cops wouldn't believe she choked on thin air by the doorway.

"Marie why are we here again?" Billy asked as he approached the door. EJ was pale. "EJ what's going on man? Why are we in this man's room the same day we buried Chop?"

"Those papers you took out of that safe was proof of how a bunch individuals plotted to cheat Chop out of a piece of that apartment complex they got at the end of Shallotte. Chop was gonna sue and bleed that gentleman on the bed dry. Mr. EJ here, that man and the late sheriff got together and they killed Chop."

"Mrs. Lance I-"

"Shut up EJ!" she screamed. "You...you Judas." Marie turned to Billy. "Chop killed that man's son Billy. He did it and he was sorry. Sorry couldn't bring the boy back though. Ever since a child Chop felt that people came into his life only do him wrong. If somebody stopped short of what they promised they had a enemy in Chop. Because of that he did things I still have trouble believing." She turned back to EJ. "His best friend here delivered Chop to this man for a piece of what Chop was entitled to."

"Wait a minute Marie, wha...what are you saying? That EJ, *our* EJ killed my son?" Marie stepped aside and motioned her arms toward EJ as if presenting him to Billy.

"Tell him EJ. Tell him what you just told that man a minute ago." Billy was confused. EJ was the last person he suspected to kill Chop and he didn't intend to believe it now.

"She's got it all wrong, ain't that right EJ?" Billy asked. EJ nodded. His lips tried to make a sound. Don, despite the pain managed to sit up on his elbows.

"Your son was below scum," Don Hamilton said. "He killed my son for no reason and he got what he deserved. I only wish EJ was their when it happened. The shock of betrayal would've gone nicely with the bullets my wife and I put through him." Billy saw red, he pushed EJ aside. EJ fell to the floor. Billy choked Don Hamilton pulling him up by the throat. Pain shot through Don so bad he wanted to pass out.

EJ stood and ran out of the door. Marie stood in hallway holding up a small blac glock 40. She aimed for EJ's back.

## Epilogue

*"Hope you're enjoying your Forth of July Holiday. We have Breaking News from Supply, North Carolina. The family of Erving "Chop" Belle had his funeral*

*today, four days after his murder at Cedar Grove Missionary Church. It was a major turnout with more than two thousand people converging on the church. But trouble followed the service.*

*The Brunswick County Hospital was the scene of yet another murder in the county this week, rather in the past twenty four hours. Marie Lance, seventy five years old, is currently detained at Brunswick County Jail for the attempted murder of Eric Johnson Jr . The incident occurred at the Brunswick hospital near the room of Don Hamilton of Hamilton Developers. The disagreement between Mrs. Lance and Mr. Johnson allegedly started in Mr. Hamilton's room and ended in the hallway with fours shots into Mr. Johnson's back. Marie Lance is Erving "Chop" Belle's grandmother and Mr. Johnson was Belle's lawyer and best friend. This happened less than an hour after Eric Johnson Jr and Marie Lance stood side by side at Erving "Chop" Belle's burial site.*

*Also, Don Hamilton's wife was found dead in the Shallotte River bordering their home last night. Before the late Sheriff Helms and Deputy Long were murdered in Southport last night, my goodness, they were at the Hamilton residence investigating Mrs. Hamilton's murder and Don Hamilton's attempted murder. Very bizarre events in Brunswick County. We'll keep you posted on any further developments."*

The Cedar Grove community would learn of EJ's devious endeavors. He'd lose the love and support of those closest to him. Because of this, the community may have already lost Marie. Overwhelming would be understating the circumstances. Dion was still young and stunning to look at. She'd surely leave him and start over. Everything he worked for, honestly or otherwise, was crumbling.

Pound sat on the hood of Mack T's '78 Buick Electra. They didn't bring any weed with them. The fifth of liquor shared hours ago was wearing off fast. Eight o'clock at night on the Fourth July, they stood outside of the Brunswick County Sheriff's office. The madness seemed to know no end.

"That punk son of a bitch!" Mack T said slapping the top of the car. They still wore the t-shirts of Chop.

"I ought to snap his wife's fucking neck," Pound said popping his knuckles. "I ought to go to his daddy's house and just stab him in his fucking head!"

After being interviewed, EJ came outside rolling in a wheelchair. Marie shot him in the legs and butt. She walked up to him and the gun was already in her purse. His tie was gone and his suit was disheveled.

"They're going to let her go. I told them I'd sue them if they'd charged her," EJ said. Pound punched him with all his might in the stomach. EJ doubled over I the wheelchair. Mack T grabbed him put him in the back of the Buick.

"Pound I...I think she's confessed already. They're not gonna give her a bond until tomorrow." Pound rolled back on his backside.

Billy walked out of the station with Carol. His arm rested over her shoulders as Mack T pulled out of the Brunswick County Government Complex.

"This has been a crazy day," he said walking to the truck. "I can't believe Marie"

"If what she said about EJ was right then she should've killed him. He really had a part in killing our Chop?"

"I don't know baby." Billy got in the truck and turned the engine. "We gonna let the police handle it. I been too lucky, God is definitely looking over me." Billy and Carol left the complex and went home, They both had to be at Chop's Diner at 5am.

Mack T headed south on Highway 17 and turned right on 211. Pound sat in the back with EJ quietly.

"I'm sorry man. I don't know what I was doing. Chop was my brother man, I shouldn't of never-" A seven inch long two inch thick serrated blade slide under EJ's floating ribs and jabbed his vitals organs repeatedly. EJ couldn't speak or resist. Blood covered Pound's hand and soaked the suede seats. EJ's last sight was Pound shedding tears, grunting and rocking the whole car with each jab. His gritted his teeth and dug the blade deeper.

Authors Notes

Hope you enjoyed this book, I started it in 2010. Back then this story was something totally different but not better. It evolved with my writing skills. I'm more than s pleased with the characters in Chop Down. They don't represent any real person I know but I tried to make them as colorful as possible. Cedar Grove is the neighborhood I'm from in Brunswick County and where I reside today. I love it, Leland to Calabash. I ove my people. All the homeboys and homegirls who gave me a shot, much love. I'm keeping it hot so don't worry. We on!!!!

Shoutouts:

Isaiah Izzy Bellamy

Courtney

Mckenzie Neal

Courtney Williams

Becca Manle

Dean Lk Bryant

Matthew Hewett

G Dot Runna

Curtis And-Rayshieta Cole

Ashley Lauren Williams

Dedrick X-Two Barringer

Kristen Price

Sagela Caj' Hewett

Samantha Lovein Him Bryant

Jason Henry Bryant

AwaxThe GodKing

Tangela Mckenzie

Andre Davis

Me'shack Adams

Dominique Jacobs

Nicholas Devon Hewett

Nyce Guy

Crystal Hewett

Lorna Marlowe

James Fullwood

Brien Hewett

Marcus Gause

Shad Adams

Erik Bucc Gore

Kelly Hewett

Adam Rottin King

Michelle Green

Elise Fullwood

Tony Johnson

Robin Williams

Tanea Bernard

Robert Rah-Blo Lawson

Kyna Bryant-Hardy

Victoria Lyons

Victor Hewett

Samara Hewett

Darelya Leblanc

Erika Vaughn

Deonna Green

Wesley Bryant

Desmone Barringer (Hold ya Head)

Jason King

Rhonda Williams Barber

Brandon Ricardo Hill

Keisha Brown

Latasha Frink

Kelleigh Gamble

Bryan Bernard

Sh-Rhonda Turner

Andre Herring Jr

Mallen Marlowe

Gwen Hewett

Chanda Marlowe

Tj Johnson

Rodney McCray

Mashonda Gause

Mary M

Geff Gore

Art Gamble

Shanna Elliott

Lakeisha Gore

Rita Langford

Kevin Brown

Sharel Duverglas

Monica Renee

Jimmy Bryant

Jamieka Elliott

Kenya S. Hewett

Milton Williams

Kyseria Hewett

Anthony Montell Hewett

William Mckenzie (Hold ya Head)

Kim Grissett

Will Gore

Reeces Toocuteforthat

Precious Bernard

LaKedra Msldc Robinson

Tina L Bryant

Mook Hill

Lionel McNeil

Cathy Johnson

Emmett J. Grissett Jr

Denesia Brown

Barbie Matthews

Twan Tha Jugg Fullwood

BA Stanley

Corey Harris

Nakosha Gause

Tobais Fullwood

Kayla Morgan

April Evans

Jamar Fullwood

Cordell Bryant Boss

Travis Gause

Evelyn Johnson

Lonzie Bryant

Jè'rèmý Màrtìn

Gucci Montana

Anthony Bryant

Jessica Hewett

Stefche Stevoff

Tory Upchurch (Hold ya head)

Tiffany S. Grant

Lashana Ledbetter

Lottie Johnson

Tamara Stanley

Charmione Lance

Cleveland Troy Simmons

Anya Stevenson

Shannon Mitchell

Myra J. Meeks

Leslie Grissett

Stephanie James

Antwanette Tweet Mims

Sonja Lance

Juan Johnson

Renata Hankins

Deatrice Gore

'Ayoo Ty'

Dat Red Boy Johnson

Lynn Grissett Jr

Joslin Perry

Natia Brown

Lillian Jade Bryant

Unique Thangs

Marsha Bryant

Constance Bryant

Stacey Askew

Nicole Galloway

Stanley Mary

Kendrick Frink

Jarvis Herring

Brandice Jordan

Angèle Rodgers

Fortyone (Hold ya head)

D'Enriqua' Johnson

Reggie Burney

Wykila Unique Williams

Dino Daniels

Rodlyn Mccray

Tiffany SoFancy Hill

Justin Scott

Chrystal Johnson

Dennis Obrian Thomas

Marie Holmes

Rayj Johnson

Crystal Genter

Shawdii Redd

Kellen Djkelz Robbins

Clarence Preston

Harold Christopher Gamble

Likendreia Tate

Troy Bryant (Hold ya head)

Tiffaney Hill

Stephanie Hewett Bellamy

Julian Take-flight Wilson

Joshua Hewett

Ray “Digi” Bryant (RIP)

Mini Mo Betta

Shawnda Hewett

Clover Clicquot

Joseph Stanley

Delphia Daniels

Jamar Fullwood

Jomondre Frink

Reggie Frink

| | | |
|---|---|---|
| Shanta Vaught Johnson | Veronica Inoyumad Daniels | Michael Fauntleroy |
| Latoya-Blacbeauty King | Shameka Herring | Shanaya Hill Dewitt |
| Kindra Jenrette | Corey Hill | Lindsey Gore |
| Utrillia Bryant Fullwood | DeAnthony Hill | Mahogany Brown |
| Rody Frink | Yosha Tywonia Cortes | Tara Johnson |
| Samantha Bland | Penny Hill | Brian Charles |
| Tremayne Johnson | Deangela Robinson | Taja Soblessed Stewart |
| Jason Woodard | Brenda Johnson | Kaneka Grissett |
| Breana Le'nae Hewett | Alexis LeXy Green | Taneidra Hewett |
| Myron Grissett | Brittany Means | Rah Bryant |
| Jr Stanley | Darren Marlow | Nisson Odom |
| Elisha Bernard | Dujuan Marlowe | Roy Woods |
| Letitia A King-Bryant | Kiandria MadeforBoss Grissett | Brittney Gause |
| D'angelo Hill | Ny'Asia Rose | Tony R. Marlowe |
| Lisa Stanley | Tosha Barringer | Frederica Best |
| Chateka Hankins | Trazia Holmes | D Jay Grissett |
| Charity Birdie Bryant | Mark Jonathan Darby | Tasheka King Williams |
| | Trish Johnson | Shalamar Bulter |
| | | Lindsey Fury |

Taneisha Lashay
Morris Mitchell
Ashley Luedeke
Chris Lee
Arianna Wilson
Natalya R Massey
Tiffany Branch
Michael Bird Man Frink
Eddie Bails Jr
Dae Marlow
Tatyana R. Morgan
Lori Hewett
Lori Hewett Williams
Derwin Hewett
Megan Grissett
Erik Grissett
Megan Antoinette
Squirmaine Wigfall

Ashley Johnson
Calvin "Dutch Diamonds" Marlowe (RIP)
Santania Bland
Ashleigh ShostoppinErythang Williams
Courtney Danielle Grant
Temaine Black Gore
Mia Branch
Travis Johnson
Samantha Hewett
Gwenetia Hill
Freddie Hankins
Andrew Johnson
Regina Mullis
Tawanna White
Jamika Bland-williams
Candace Johnson Earl

JT Ledbetter
Venee Robinson
Letista Thompson Bessent
Tia Brenita Green
Katia Green
Tristan Johnson
Travis Gore
Nikki So Lovely Grady
Marcus Bernard
Tina LeGrande
NisaNay Sanders
Debra Stanley
Geraldine Hill Robinson
Kaleb Hewett
Talbert Fullwood
Samantha Watson
Khyne Daniels
Montoya Stevenson

CHOP DOWN By Floyd J Williams

cc

Lorene Hewett Williams

Chasey Carter Brown

Nicole McCracken

Ashanti Marlowe

Tiffany Bernard Sidberry

Elenora Green

Arial Fullwood

Alexis Overocker

Ricky Mcneil

Louvenia Cox

Azia Hill

Allison Washington Metts

FixitToriano Fullwood

Saketha Stevenson

Lawrence Smith

Patrick W Reed Guillory

Glenda Winborne

Chenita Grissett

Jerell Gore

Lashandra Humphrey

Spencer Fullwood

Veronica Tyler

Ravin Gore

Dewayne Lewis

Cindy Doingme Williams

La Tonya Johnson Payne

Ced Simmons

Cheintay Graham

Kurtis Cole

Missy King-Bates

Holly Bates

Shaquna Fauntleroy

Lamont Daniels

Stephanie McCray

Raquel Vereen

Shalonda Thomas

GraceLynette Mckenzie

Brittany Smith

Ebony Fullwood

Victoria Bland

Alonzo Hewett

Whitney Bland

Cyquainda Punkie Daily

KristenMoon'ique King

James Gore

Cynthia Vereen

Terrence Clarida

Lisa Gray

Patrice Shaw Stanley

Nicole Cobb

Raymond Marlowe (RIP)

Shaun Questsan Long

Michael Petey Powell

cci Williams

CHOP DOWN By Floyd J

| | | |
|---|---|---|
| Codella Sellers | Thalia Deanne Bellamy | Lionese Martin |
| Kevin Hankins | Angie Hill | Jason Jenrette |
| Lavonda Fullwood | Timohy Bryant | Shevonn Pigotte |
| Dana Taylor | Chris Wright | Ricka Miller |
| Matthew Bryant Darby | Pecola Holmes | Kourtney Johnson |
| Shakirah Ford | Rashame J. Gause | Carol Hewett Briggs |
| Quanita Berry | Kanika Simmons | Chase Jerard Leak |
| Ellen Marie Bryant | Sharyl Bellamy | Urshala Brooks |
| Ria Hewett | Alichia Hamilton | Tamarkus Fullwood |
| Eric Johnson | Felecia Hill | Gisella Grissett |
| Majid Powell | Tonya Stocks | Carneisha Blue |
| D'Atra Queen | Latasha Datrealbytch Bland | Amelia Martin |
| Jennifer Vereen | Kindral King | Makebasmom Bellamy |
| Tashika Robinson | Jacqueline Long | Charles Allston |
| Tiffany Marlow | Kareem Stevenson | Jennifer Daniels |
| LaTeisha Lawrence | Tarsha Griffin | Cindy Webb |
| Nicky Morgan | Sharonda Green | Xie Tracy |
| Marlena Gore | Shairan Taylor | Renee Darby |

| | | |
|---|---|---|
| Brenda Sue Hewett | Alorda Palmore Randolph | Lamar Bryant |
| Nick Bellamy | Fabrin Kiandra | Theresa Smith-Gadson |
| Zelphia Lynn | Ashley Mcneil | Adell Bernard |
| Mya Villacruz | Antionette Galloway | Yvonne Bryant |
| Yolanda Stanley Morgan | Nick Evans | Dwight A. Bryant |
| Brianna Nicole | Daryl McNeil | Cameron Bessent |
| Trina Hill | Itena Bland | Alonzo Frink |
| Monika Michelle | Aisheia Bryant | Keisha Davis |
| Jerrel Faruq Metts | Brandon Hill | Kwabena Green |
| Shelia Johnson Williams | Myron Hewett | Andrea Bernard |
| Ellis Hewett | Terry Williams | Hindu Kush |
| Milissa Johnson | Kwame Bernard | Jeremy LeMar Thomas |
| Nikolas Sloan | Carmin Leach | Latoya Mitchell |
| Jeremy Bryant (Hold ya head) | Nichosa Miller | Kaleena Green |
| Jerome Thomas | Donna McGhee | Washington Lisimore |
| Sheral Johnson | SrCedric Hewett | Len Gore |
| Tavon Grissett | Jaleesa Evans | Chowan Gail Simmons |
| Sherry Leatrice Bryant | Tonya Randolph | Megan Brockington |
| | Shonda Grissett | |
| | Terri Mitchell | |

Frostie Vereen

Marisa Gause

Jessica Khamari'smommy Hardy

Sade Marlowe

Lavar N. Marlow

Curtis A. Johnson

Cameron Jackson

Jeremy Bryant (Hold ya Head)

Cynthia Stevenson

Ramon Brewman Williams

Gucci Flyboi Hill

Motashi Lance

Jason Bryant

Crystal Bland

Lynette Reed

Aldwin Lance

Shannon Eaton

Darrian Taylor

Roshann Sincere Stanley

Jelta Levern Bryant

Felicia Woodard

Robert Collins

Flora Johnson

Deanna Roseboro

Michael T. Marlowe

Deanna Bellamy

Jamie A Pugh

Shanieka Thomas

William Gause

Tremayne Stanley

Andre Hill

Gloria Jenrette

Terrell Randall

Candra Green

Janice Best Vaught

Rodriques Best

Dora Vann Mcneill

Latasha Stanley

Curtis Marlowe

Britanie Walker

Vondean Smith

Steven Johnson

Oneshia Williams

Andre' Herring

Esterlane Gause Ballard

Antonio Ward

Felicia Stanley

Jon Daniels

Sandra Marlow

Headbuster Lewis

Shirelle Grissett

Nashon Platypus Perry

Robert Frink

Sabrina Smith

Marvin Sleepy Bryant

Whitney Pigotte

Deborah Simmons Wright

Nicole Baker

Waterfall Gemini Dreadz

Bryan Bernard

Bryan Lucas

Carmaine Anydaynow Williams

Anthony Stevenson

Karen Eldridge

John McNeil

Derek Frink

Saki (Hold Ya Head)

Teeka Grissett

Herbert Frink

Angela Gore

Nicole Martin

Porky Robinson

Cynthia Stanley

Daryl Hewett

Pip Hewett

Eric Hewett

Sam Mallard Hewett

Eric Leite (Hold ya Head)

Theatric Witherspoon (Hold ya Head)

Cortland Ocasio

Amelya Nydrill

Carl Williams Jr.

Craig Grissett

Marilda Kerlegan

Monty Bellamy

Woodie Brown

Wayne Johnson

Dominique Bell

Mark Epps

Felicia Stanley

Dorothy Watson

Freda Greene

Dexter Galloway

Lionel Mcneil

Margie T. McBride

Latoya Hill

Archie Bryant Jefferson

Michel Gore

RB Clague

Derrick Hewett

Vonnie Fulwood

Alfy Hill

John Bellamy

Kenneth Bryant

Saundra King

Kescia Williams

Shawnte Joyner

Cedric Grant

Antonio Bigtenor

Peggy L. Elliott

Tyrone McCoy

ccv CHOP DOWN By Floyd J Williams

| | | |
|---|---|---|
| David Flowers Jr | Edith Jones | Fonsteina Burgess |
| Derick Siler | LaShaunta Samuel | Corey Miles |
| Brinda Stanley | Perita Price | Jennifer Bettridge |
| James Bryant | David Fernandez | Williams-Taylor Deven |
| Latoyree Hill | Bridget Spivey | Ben Fullwood |
| Pricilla Spellman | Chuckie Thompson | Thomas Green |
| Deautry Daniels | Walter Daniels | Brandon Hankins |
| Terrance Fullwood | Bobby Jackson | Malik McNeil(Hold Ya Head) |
| Edison Gore | Larissa Vargas | Kecia Graham |
| Fat Baby (Hold ya Head) | Angela Daniels | Marie Grissett |
| Isaac Galloway | Samuel Sesay | Erica Leblanc |
| Bobby Johnson | Micheal Darby | Jennifer Combest |
| Myra Byrant | Courtney Placker | Kaiwan Hankins |
| Clifford Vereen | Lisa Sowells | |
| Shanta Hemingway | Jr Bulla | |
| Jeremy Bryant (Hold ya Head) | Willie Hewett | |
| | Erick Smith | |



ISBN:1492979643
ISBN-13:9781492979647

Made in the USA
Charleston, SC
19 October 2013